ON THIN ICE

a Juniper Falls novel

Entangled Publishing, LLC
2614 South Timberline Road
Suite 105, PMB 159
Fort Collins, CO 80525
rights@entangledpublishing.com

Entangled Teen is an imprint of Entangled Publishing, LLC.

Visit our website at www.entangledpublishing.com.

Edited by Stacy Abrams
Cover design by Clarissa Yeo
Cover images by Shutterstock
583789774, 343286558, 347677361, 24139271
Interior image by GettyImages/yuran-78
Interior design by Heather Howland and Toni Kerr

ISBN: 978-1-64063-410-7
Ebook ISBN: 978-1-64063-409-1

Manufactured in the United States of America

First Edition February 2019

10 9 8 7 6 5 4 3 2 1

entangled teen
an imprint of Entangled Publishing LLC

JULIE CROSS

ON THIN ICE

Chapter One

–BROOKE–

I t's not that I can't speak. Or that I don't want to or don't have anything to say. I do. But I've recently become addicted to listening. And it's extremely difficult to talk and listen at the same time.

But try explaining that to a small-town high school guidance counselor and see where it gets you.

It got me regular—and mandatory—Friday appointments in Mr. Smuttley's office (yes, that's his real name, though I keep hearing other students call him a bunch of variations of it, most of them pretty nasty), where I continue to *not* talk about my feelings.

"How is your mother doing?" Smuttley asks.

I shrug. Not to be evasive, but because I have no idea. She doesn't talk to me. All the pills the psychiatrist prescribes have turned her into a zombie version of my mother… Except, this isn't completely true. A few days ago, she must have woken up from her drug-induced haze and decided to go to the store…in her pajamas. Then she got there, couldn't remember what she came for, and broke down crying. The shop owner called my grandmother, who promptly came to pick her up. And now everyone in town either gives me this look of pity or they avoid eye contact altogether. Or, in Smuttley's case, they try to get me to talk about the incident in a productive, helpful manner.

"How about we try something new today." Smuttley stands and walks around his desk, heading for the door to his office. I'm still seated in my designated student chair when he swings the door open, gesturing that I should follow him out.

I stare at the name placard on the door: JOSEPH SMUTTLEY.

If he just dropped one of the *T*s, he'd have way less nicknames from the student body.

"Come on, Brooklynn," he says, trying to look enthusiastic about his plan. "It's my duty as guidance counselor to make sure you've been shown all the best places around the high school. Which includes the coffee shop next door."

Brooke, not Brooklynn.

Only my grandmother calls me Brooklynn.

Sighing, I stand up and follow him out of his office and eventually outside. The October air in Minnesota is crisp, and even without us talking, the leaves crunching under our feet kill the awkward silence.

I zip up my pink hoodie and stuff my hands deep into the front pockets. We walk a whole block away from the high school before Smuttley says anything more. "Your grandmother said you've always been very active in—was it soccer? I can't remember…"

I *could* answer him. It would probably be his greatest monthly accomplishment if I did. God knows I must be his most cooperative student—not that I have much competition. But I give it ten more seconds, and he finally admits to already knowing the answer. "Wait…dance, right?"

Right. Dance. The thing that doesn't exist in Juniper Falls, Minnesota, not beyond the tiny recreational studio on Main Street that prides themselves on their toddler tap classes. I nod, and he seems satisfied with that response.

Smuttley opens the door to the Spark Plug, which is an insanely awesome name for a coffee shop, in my opinion. It's also a place I visit daily.

"Betty's hot chocolate is out of this world," Smuttley says.

I nod and flash him a smile, which he returns, though it fades quickly when Betty, the owner, spots me and says, "The usual, right?"

Betty might have memorized my order, but an hour from now, she'll be replaced by her granddaughter Melanie, who usually asks me to repeat my order more than once. Melanie may not be as committed to this shop as Betty obviously is, but she's still super sweet. Also very committed to great dental hygiene. She spends hours behind the counter with her Bluetooth on, confusing customers by holding a conversation with the dentist's office at the same time that she takes orders.

Smuttley requests a hot chocolate with extra whipped cream, and then when he sees my black coffee, he says, "Sure you don't want to try the hot cocoa?"

I'm one of those strange individuals who doesn't like anything sweet. Not desserts or candy, not pastries or muffins or soda. Not even chocolate. My mom always says it's because she fed me only pureed vegetables as a baby. No sugar for the first three years of my life.

"Coffee is fine," I say so quietly I'm not sure if the words came out of my mouth. "Thanks."

Smuttley's eyebrows lift, but he keeps his excitement in

check. "I thought we could take our drinks and walk over to the ice rink. Have you been inside?"

"I hear the team is getting ready for tryouts," Betty says. "I can't wait for game season. We'll have lines out the door."

I live across the street from the ice rink. I haven't been inside yet, though I've been meaning to check it out for a couple of weeks. I shake my head and follow my guidance counselor to the building next door. In Texas, for years, I took skating lessons once a week. Every Saturday morning, my dad drove me to downtown Austin, helped me lace up a pair of brown rental skates, and stood by the wall while I learned to skate forward, backward, turn on one foot, all the beginner stuff. When dance took over my life, I had to ditch the recreational lessons. Maybe if I take up skating again, my grandmother will get off my back about coming home right after school every day. Or maybe they need a Zamboni driver? Or someone to clean the bathrooms? Anything to avoid extra hours in that old farmhouse that is definitely not my home.

Except, it kind of is.

Back in Austin, I had been planning to try out for cheerleading at the beginning of freshman year. I wasn't a shoo-in for varsity or anything, especially considering the number of girls in Texas who were bred for the sport from walking age, but thanks to years of dance, I had a killer toe touch and some decent acrobatic tricks that would have gotten me at least a spot on JV.

That's what I should have done. But I didn't try out for cheerleading. And I stopped taking dance. Basically, I spent most of freshman year doing everything I shouldn't. All while my dad was on trial and my mom fell apart. It's impossible not to associate those things with the same cause...me and my bad choices.

This year needs to be different.

This year *will* be different. I promised my dad this right after two police officers handcuffed him in the middle of the courtroom, right before they took him away.

Smuttley opens the door to the ice rink. The smell hits me immediately—sweaty socks and frozen toilet water. Somehow, it's not a completely unpleasant odor.

"Are you a hockey fan?" he asks.

Am I a hockey fan? I could be, I guess, if I have the opportunity to see some games. Hockey is an Olympic sport, right? I've always loved watching the Olympics.

I shrug and turn my attention to the ice rink.

Smuttley goes on and on about the importance of making friends at a new school and exploring new options and new territories, not being afraid of change. Like how he got completely impulsive and decided today's hour-long appointment would take place outside his office. *Bad Boy Smuttley.* That's what I'm gonna start calling him in my head—it's way better than the nicknames the other kids use. Maybe he's not riding around town on a Harley, but dealing with angsty, cruel, and disrespectful teenagers daily definitely earns him a risk-taker badge, in my opinion.

I listen carefully to his usual motivational speech while keeping my eyes on the ice rink, hoping for some shiny tights and sparkly dresses to look at—I've always loved watching figure skating and even tried my hand at sewing a skating dress years ago. But instead of twirling figure skaters, a group of hockey players in mismatched practice jerseys are out on the ice. There doesn't seem to be any teacher or coach. Nor are any of them doing much besides horsing around.

"They haven't started the season yet," Smuttley explains, though we'd already established this over at the Spark Plug with Betty. "Preseason pickup games on Friday nights are an Otter hockey tradition.

"The games are a way for the seniors to show the freshmen who's in charge and put them in their place." Smuttley's gaze follows a skater with HAMMOND on the back of his jersey. He's moving so fast that when one of the smaller players gets in his path, instead of stopping, Hammond shoves the kid down with one hand until he's bent over, staring at his skates. And then leaps right over the kid's back. The landing is so light and graceful, I'm certain if this Hammond guy spent a little time in a ballet studio, he could pull off a mean grand jeté. The kid who just got shoved stands upright again and removes his helmet. His cheeks and neck are bright red.

Smuttley continues to give me a lecture covering thirty years of Otter hockey history while I watch this impromptu game come together. Smuttley's details and explanations are as interesting as any tourist attraction, and I'm starting to wonder why we haven't talked about hockey in any of our previous sessions. A town rich in history, with deep hockey roots, is way more interesting than a small town in the middle of nowhere. Maybe I've been looking at this place from the wrong angle. This is why shutting up and listening can show you a new perspective. But I guess guidance counselors are trained to reach for words like "depressed," "withdrawn," "removed." I don't feel removed. Right now I feel alive and alert. More so than ever.

Hammond, who is wearing number 42 below his name, does a lot of pointing, tugging on jerseys, and somehow everyone seems to understand which team they're on and what the objective is outside of getting the puck into the goal (because even I understand that's the main objective).

"...So you can see how important it is to create your own history, to have memories you can carry with you for years," Smuttley says.

Smuttley is obviously a lifelong townie. I wasn't positive of that until now. I wonder if he played on the team or if he just wished he'd played? Last year, when my life was falling apart, I'd wished that I had joined cheerleading. I'd wanted that mask to hide behind. I'd wanted something to look forward to. Now I want that again, but for different reasons. To keep a promise to my dad and hopefully drag my mom out of her zombie state. If she was proud of me... If she had something to look forward to herself, maybe it would help her get back to her old self?

"Outside of dance," Smuttley continues, "what are you passionate about, Brooklynn?"

Brooke.

And that's a very good question.

Maybe I'm passionate about passion. About caring. Whatever the opposite of numbing yourself with antipsychotics and sleeping all day is.

Smuttley doesn't press me further for an answer. He's smart like that. He knows the honest answer won't be the first thing to tumble out of my mouth. It will take time and thought.

I watch number 42 fly around the ice. The puck slides between his skates, then it's cradled in the curve of his stick, and then almost too fast for my untrained eyes to follow, the puck soars into the net. The guys on his team cheer, but he doesn't. He heads back to the center and waits for another player to drop the puck in front of him.

When he takes off again, I close my eyes and listen. Without even seeing, I can recognize the sharper, more purposeful sound of number 42's skates cutting through the ice. Clear, precise movements compared to the jagged choppy vocals of the others nearby. I open my eyes again and see Hammond making circles around a small area of the ice while he stays back, allowing other players to handle the puck. He glides forward, then backward, crossing one foot over the other, then changing sides, making sharp, abrupt turns but never pausing his movement. I imagine a true hockey fan would be watching the puck during a game, but I can't look away from number 42.

It's the closest thing to dancing I've seen in months.

Chapter Two

–JAKE–

One of the midget freshmen rips off his helmet and bends over, clutching his side. He glances at me and pants, "Water break?"

I roll my eyes but twist my body, stopping in front of him and spraying his legs with shaved ice. His eyes widen, giving me a clear view of his face. I know this kid.

Pratt.

Luke Pratt's little brother. Luke graduated three years ago. When I was a freshman, he used to wait for me to pull my helmet off at the end of practice, then he'd pound me in the head with his stick... *I wouldn't take that off if I were you, Hammond.*

Little Pratt is still standing there staring at me like I'm the fucking president of pickup hockey. "What are you waiting for?" I say, waving a hand toward the drinking fountain.

The game comes to a halt, and I catch another freshman

rushing over to the nearest garbage can to regurgitate his cafeteria tater tots.

"What just happened?" Red asks, crashing into the boards beside me. He's not the best at stopping, even though he's been playing his whole life. "Did that fucking rookie stop our game?"

I don't answer him. I reach over the wall into the penalty box and grab a roll of tape. "My stick's screwed up."

Paul Redmond has been my best friend since peewee hockey. Now that we're seniors and he's six-three and well over two hundred pounds, the freshmen already nicknamed him Big Red, and lately it's his head that's been growing bigger.

"Think Langston will make varsity?" Red asks.

"Don't know. Don't care. Coach picks the team, not me." I busy myself wrapping tape around my stick. I know Langston will make varsity. He's a sophomore this year and he's fucking Langston Juniper. As in *Juniper Falls*.

Red lowers his voice. Senior or not, he's not stupid enough to mess with the Juniper family. "That kid is a lost cause. Look at him…"

I lift my eyes just enough to see Langston Juniper IV take a shot at an empty goal from three feet away and hit the crossbar, sending the puck over the wall and toward Mr. Smuttley, the guidance counselor.

"Heads up, Mr. S!" I shout. He shifts himself and the girl beside him to the right just in time to avoid a puck to his forehead.

"Thanks for the warning, Jake." He flashes us a grin and waves like he's some fan waiting for an autograph. Sometimes I wish teachers would treat us like inferiors the way they do the rest of the students—special treatment makes me feel in debt. But then again, Smuttley is a guidance counselor, so he'd probably cause mental instability or something if he went around yelling at kids.

Red nudges my shoulder. "What's the new girl doing with Smuttley?"

It's kind of pathetic that we can use the phrase "new girl" and everyone will know exactly who we're talking about. "I don't know, guiding her? Does anyone know what Smuttley actually does all day?"

"That's a question someone should be exploring." Red nods toward the new girl again, not making any effort to be discreet. "What's the deal with her, anyway? I heard she's mute."

"She's not mute." I don't know anything about her except that she isn't mute. Three hours ago she stood in front of me in the hot lunch line, and when Larry held up an ice-cream scooper full of soggy wilted broccoli, she said, "No thanks." It wasn't loud or anything, but I think that strips her of any mute label.

"Whatever. She's weird, has a crazy-ass family from what I hear," Red says, still staring. "But she's cute."

I give her a quick glance. She's not cute. Cute is when girls stare at you and the second you look back, they look away. New Girl has been staring at me for at least twenty minutes, and every time I catch her, she doesn't even attempt to look elsewhere. Cute is flat and one-dimensional. This girl obviously isn't either of those things.

Little Pratt and the barfing freshman finally return. I shove Red toward center ice. "Are we playing or talking about girls and guidance counselors?"

"Hey, I can multitask."

The game resumes with Juniper and me facing off. Tanley, another senior, is goaltending today. He poises himself in front of the net when he sees me cross the blue line, allowing the flood of players into his territory. Tanley's good. And he knows most of my shots. But I'm on fire today and pull off an easy fake. The puck slips right around Tanley and sinks into the net.

Red pounds me on the back, attempting to celebrate, but I shake him off and head back to center ice. We've only got fifteen more minutes of ice time, and I'm not wasting it cheering for myself.

Juniper Falls, Minnesota, might be a small town, but we've produced eighteen NHL players, five NCAA All-Americans, and three Olympians, including a member of the 1980 Miracle on Ice team. Hockey is in almost everyone's blood, and NHL games are only on TV for people like us; the Olympics are only once every four years. Juniper Falls High School hockey is a town event. No, it's *the* town event. Which is why, outside of the team and our coach, we're all treated like royalty.

But there's a rarely-spoken-of rule us players must adopt from our very first pickup game as freshmen—never outplay a senior. *Never*. No matter what tricks we've got up our sleeves, no matter how much gas we have left at the end of a game to breakaway and head for the goal, we're all taught to hold back. Wait for our turn. Or as my dad likes to say, "Otter hockey is a highly productive, fine-tuned machine. Everyone has to play their part or the machine breaks down and nothing gets made or sold."

I've worked my ass off for the last three years on varsity trying to keep myself inside that box, setting up seniors for great shots. But I'm sick of slowing down, sick of passing the puck when I've got a clean shot. I'm sick of holding back. If I have to do it for even one more game, I'll explode.

"Dude, you're insane!" Red shouts after I've scored a seventh goal for us and we've been given the one-minute warning by Al, the rink manager.

I rip off my helmet, and I'm surprised by the sweat running into my eyes and by my racing heart and labored breathing. I skate past a sophomore I'd just plowed over and pull him up by the back of his jersey.

"Nice fake, Collins. You almost had me."

"Yeah right," he says, but I can tell he looks a little less humiliated about ending this game facedown on the ice.

I'm starting to feel the impact (and desperate need for a shower) that comes from an hour of playing full-out, but when I exit the ice, Mr. Smuttley stops me.

"Looking good out there, Jake!" He glances at the new girl and then back at me. "I was just telling Brooklynn how great it is to get involved in school activities. Especially for a new student."

He says "new student" like we get one a month or something. I don't want to jump on Smuttley's *be true to your school* wagon, but I try to kiss his ass occasionally because he's great for getting me out of tardies and getting retakes on Spanish quizzes that I've bombed. All in the name of Otter hockey, of course.

I point a finger at Smuttley. "Yep, listen to this guy; he knows what he's talking about." What the hell am *I* talking about? Red steps off the ice, standing beside me now, and I don't miss the snort from him. I look at the new girl to see her reaction. Her gaze is fixed on mine. She's fearless with eye contact, which freaks me out a little. But I don't look away.

After a more careful examination, I can see that there's nothing out of the ordinary about her. She's wearing jeans and a hoodie like almost everyone our age. She's kind of short and small but not the shortest girl at school, either. Brown eyes, dirty-blond hair in a messy bun. She's the type of girl who would normally blend into the background, but for some reason she seems way more interesting than her similar female counterparts. Probably because I haven't gone to school with her my entire life. I don't know her family. I don't know anything about her. But learning more would be an unnecessary distraction from both school and hockey.

"What year are you?" Red asks.

Her mouth opens like she's about to answer, but Smuttley does the job for her. "Sophomore."

"There you go," Red says, smacking me in the shoulder. I glare at him. What is he trying to say? That I'm into underclass girls? Not a chance. "Sheriff Hammond needs more players for the new girls' JV hockey team. That's a school activity, right?"

My forehead wrinkles. "I thought the school board shot it down?"

Sheriff Hammond (aka my uncle Oz) unfortunately missed out on the Hammond family hockey gene. But his daughter didn't. My cousin, Rosie, is a freshman this year and Uncle Oz has been trying to get the high school to start a girls' team since Rosie was in seventh grade. Every argument the school came back with, Oz rebutted with a solution. No money for equipment? The Spark Plug offered to sponsor the team. No coach? No problem: Oz's going to do it himself. No ice time? Well, he's the sheriff and I imagine it was easy to point out some building code violations or unpaid parking tickets to get Al to clear a space for another team on the schedule.

Red leans against the wall, his eyebrows lifting. "Jake, I can't believe you're not supporting your own uncle in his pursuit for gender equality. Haven't you heard of title nine?"

Great. Thanks, Red. Throw me under the bus so you

can impress the new girl and Smuttley. Knowing Red, he probably needs those quiz retakes even more than I do.

"I have no problem with girls playing hockey," I say through gritted teeth. "But I think Rosie could hold her own with the JV guys' team."

And that isn't a lie. My freshman year, we had a girl on varsity—Jenny Miller. She was a badass and nobody questioned her ability to keep up, but she was also twice the size of the new girl and an anomaly. There's no way, in a town of three thousand people, we'll have a whole team of high school girls who are actually serious about playing and aren't committed to other sports, school clubs, or whatever else people do who don't play hockey. Plus, who the hell are they going to play against? Not many girls' teams nearby. They'll have to drive hours to big cities for every game.

"What about all those other girls besides your cousin, like your little sister? She'll be in high school someday," Red says to me. "I expected more enthusiasm from you."

I flip him off behind Smuttley's back. "Sounds like they're all set to go. They can have my blessing, but I doubt they need it."

"A girls' hockey team, huh?" Smuttley mumbles, like he's just now catching up. "That's an interesting project for Sheriff Hammond."

I bet "interesting" is a favorite word of guidance counselors everywhere.

Red steers Smuttley over to an empty corner so he can discuss a private matter concerning "his emotional well-being during Spanish class," leaving me alone in complete silence with the new girl. Who apparently doesn't talk after all.

"Well, I better hit the showers before Al starts griping about the smell." I turn to walk in the direction of the locker room but glance over my shoulder one last time at her. "What about yearbook club? I know a girl in yearbook. She's cool. You look a little small for hockey, Brooklynn."

She folds her arms across her chest, staring so hard at me that I sputter, "Wh-What?"

"Brooke, not Brooklynn."

Her eyes lock with mine again, and I don't know why but this feels important. Warmth rushes from my stomach down to my toes. I glance around to see if anyone else heard her, but it seems to be just me.

"Brooke," I repeat, holding her gaze, memorizing not only her preferred name but the swirl of brown and gold in her pupils. "I'll remember that."

Before anyone can catch me staring at the new girl, I tear my gaze from hers and turn my back on the rink. After walking into the locker room, I get a full ten minutes of peace and quiet before Red pounces on me. "Dude, tonight's gonna be awesome! I've been waiting my entire life to do this."

I roll my eyes. "Really? This is the highlight of your life?" It's disturbing that he's so into tonight's plans. I've been dreading it since school started six weeks ago. But I'll take the bad with the good when it comes to senior hockey privileges.

"I can't fucking believe you're going to ruin this for me," Red jokes. "I don't even know you anymore."

I laugh and push past him, heading out of the locker room, lugging my fifty-pound bag of equipment. "See ya at midnight, asshole."

"Not until midnight?" Red calls after me. "Haley is having a party. Maybe if you drink enough, you two'll end up hooking up again—"

That would be a negative. Been there. Done that. Last

year. Besides… "Haley's got a boyfriend now, remember?"

Red narrows his eyes. Haley's boyfriend, Fletcher, is a bit of a sore subject for Red. He's our teammate and a fellow senior, but this is his first year on varsity. Over the summer, Fletch busted his ass, working harder than anyone on and off the ice, and he nearly stole Red's spot. Rumor is that Fletch got an offer from a junior hockey team and might only be here for half a season. I'm hoping it is just a rumor. Fletch is quiet and calm, doesn't talk smack in the locker room. With all the rowdy-as-hell guys on the team, Fletch being around helps keep the balance.

Because I like Fletch (and because only a douche goes after someone else's girlfriend), hooking up with Haley is out of the question. But really, hooking up with anyone tonight is not in the plans for me. Dating, or even just hooking up, when you're stuck in a town this small sucks. You go out with someone one night, and everyone knows by the next morning. And by everyone, I mean even the fucking mailman knows. It's just not worth it.

Which is why I've recently allowed Red to spread a rumor about me and a college girl, who I met this summer at hockey camp in Michigan. Rumor has it we met after I snuck out and got drunk one night. I never snuck out. The place was like Fort Knox. And even if I had, like I'd just wander upon a herd of hot college girls the second I escaped? *Yeah right.* The guys and I would've ended up eating beef jerky and drinking Mountain Dew in the parking lot of a gas station a quarter mile away. But no one thinks about these types of logistics when it comes to gossip.

Smuttley is gone from the rink lobby, but I spot the new girl—I mean Brooke (enough with this 'new girl' shit)—standing on her toes, reaching up to write something on a sheet of paper hanging from the tack board. I wait until she heads out the door, then I walk over to see what she was writing.

**Tryouts for Juniper Falls First-Ever
Women's Hockey Team
JV level—Any freshman or sophomore girl
is eligible to play.
No experience required!**

I scan the list and am surprised they've got five signups already. The first name is Rosie Hammond.

The second and third names are vaguely familiar, but I can't put faces to them. The fourth name says: *Red Redmond (just don't ask me to drop my pants).*

Oh God. Uncle Oz is going to beat his ass. But now I know how Red had the 4-1-1 on the girls' hockey situation before I did.

The fifth name, written in small, neat block letters is: *Brooke Parker.*

Guess she didn't like my advice about the yearbook club. Whatever. Uncle Oz is gonna need a lot more than five players to field a team. Actually, he only has four legit players so far. And tryouts are next week. Not holding out much hope for this girls' hockey endeavor, but it might be cool if it did work out.

I head to my truck just in time to catch Brooke Parker crossing the railroad tracks and heading toward the lone farmhouse seated in front of Juniper Falls Pond and the woods I spent my entire childhood exploring.

Maybe I should have tried harder to talk to her. Or said something nice. If the rumors about her mom are true, fitting in here might be tough.

Chapter Three

–JAKE–

Pointless town gossip is usually not my thing, but for some reason, I'm searching my memories the whole drive home, trying to remember Dad and Oz's conversation a couple of months ago about Judy Gleason's daughter coming back to town with her kid. I finally land on one detail when I pull into my driveway.

Austin. That's where they moved from.

I toss my hockey bag in the garage before heading inside. My mom flips out if any smelly gear comes within a few feet of her immaculate house. Yes, I mean *her* house. The other three residents, including myself, have long ago conceded any ownership over the property.

My stomach growls when I enter the foyer and inhale the scent of our regular Friday night supper—black bean and cheese enchiladas.

I'm still focused on getting the dirt on Brooke Parker's family, so I steer clear of the kitchen and head for Dad's office. Before I make it there, the hall closet door springs open and Maddy flies out, a hockey mask strapped around her head.

I clutch my chest and then snatch the mask right off my sister's head. "Are you trying to kill me?"

She flips her blond ponytail around and laughs at me. "I was just seeing if I could scare you. And don't go in Dad's office right now. Oz and Coach Bakowski are in there."

I shove past her. "I need to ask Oz something anyway."

But the presence of Coach Bakowski makes this idea much less appealing. It's hard not to be intimidated by my hockey coach after three years of being yelled at and humiliated by him. Especially when I've held back during a game to follow that unspoken rule of not outplaying a senior.

Maddy slides in front of me again, blocking my way. "They're talking about the girls' hockey team. Something about bus schedules and money. Can you believe we're going to have a girls' team? Isn't it awesome?"

"Since when do you need to play with all girls? And you won't be in high school for, like, ten years."

She holds her hand in front of her to count on her fingers. "Four years, Jake. I'll be in high school in four years."

That can't be right. She's only ten… Okay, that's probably right.

We probably do need a girls' team.

The office door opens, and Coach and Oz both exit. Coach gives me the usual stiff nod and a "son" in his low voice. Oz flicks my ear and tells me to stay out of trouble, and seconds later both are out the door and my dad is calling me into his office.

"Hey, Jake." He tosses his feet up on the desk and points to the door, indicating I should close it.

Before I can ask him about Brooke Parker, he levels me

with his District Attorney look, and my stomach immediately does flip-flops. Between Dad and Uncle Oz, I hear about every criminal activity that takes place in this town, even the slightest of infractions. I know things my friends would kill to know. But it's always been clear that anything I hear in this house (or Oz's) stays inside these walls.

"So…first pickup game as a senior," he says. "How did it feel? I know the season hasn't officially started, but it must be nice to be on top."

I lean my back against the door. "It's great, actually. I'm looking forward to this season."

"Coach is planning on making you captain this year; he says the scouts are going to love you and I think he's right. But that's not what I wanted to talk about. It's your first pickup game as a senior…" His eyebrows shoot up. "I'm not an idiot. I know where you'll be tonight. I know the drill."

He knows the drill. Of course, he knows the drill. I was told it's been an Otter hockey tradition for, like, a hundred years. And Dad was no average Otter. He managed to score a scholarship to Minnesota State. I know college is the reason we have a nice house and we don't struggle with money like so many people around here do—like Red and his family. Like a bunch of the guys I play hockey with.

But I'm a senior and this is the first time Dad has brought up this particular Otter tradition. He never said a word when I was a freshman. Which is why I've never been 100 percent convinced this tradition existed way back in my dad's hockey days. And there's no way in hell I'd ever ask. No one would dare do that.

I open my mouth to comment, but Dad holds up a hand to stop me. "Don't say a word. I just wanted to tell you to be careful and not to do anything stupid. Got it?"

"Got it."

He closes the open folders on his desk, stacking them neatly before my mom has a chance to do the same thing. "And don't get anyone pregnant."

"Right." I laugh it off, but my neck heats up. I tug at the collar of my T-shirt. It wouldn't be terrible to be able to talk about girls with Dad, but again, small town, small world. Talking about getting to third base with a girl who my mom used to babysit when we were little? A girl whose diapers Dad had been forced to change on at least a couple of occasions when my mom left him in charge to run to the store or something? It's just not worth the incestuous connections that come up in these situations.

"Hey, Dad?" I pause, waiting for him to look up again. "What do you know about Judy Gleason's daughter? Besides the thing at the store the other day."

"Not much." Dad stands up and leads me out of the office into the hallway. "But I went to school with her, and so did your mom."

"Went to school with whom?" my mom asks, appearing out of nowhere with a stack of plates to set on the dining room table.

"Lauren Gleason," Dad says. "Well, she's not Gleason anymore, she's…"

"Parker," I supply.

"Oh, right," Mom says, stopping in front of me to fix my shirt collar after I'd messed it up moments ago. "Lauren didn't really run with our crowd. She was into art and music."

Art and music. Something that isn't hockey. Not that my mom played hockey, but she dated a hockey player, so that put her inside our world.

"But why is she back here?" *With a teenage daughter*, I want to add, but that would most likely turn the inquisition on me.

Dad shrugs and steals a carrot from the veggie tray on the dining room table. "Her husband got into some trouble back in Texas. Maybe she doesn't work and needed a place for her and her kid to stay? God knows Judy's got more room than she needs in that farmhouse."

Trouble in Texas? What kind of trouble? I push Brooke Parker from my thoughts and focus on the food I'm about to devour in a few minutes.

And the Otter tradition I'll uphold later tonight.

Chapter Four

–BROOKE–

I slap a hand on my leg, calming my bouncing knee. I hate this part of the day. I hate it with every possible decibel of hate. I shift around, trying to get comfortable on Grandma's stiff old-lady couch, complete with polyester ruffles all around the bottom.

My peripheral vision catches Grandma's eyelids flapping at a much more rapid pace, just in time for the local weather forecast. I take a breath and stare at the TV then count to sixty, three times in my head.

Please be asleep. Please be asleep.

I finally look over at her and sigh with relief when I see her chin tucked into her chest and her eyes shut. I creep as quietly as possible out of the living room and into the hallway, pulling the stairs down and making the climb up to my attic bedroom. I'm back on the main level in less than a minute, sporting running shoes, a coat, and my iPhone and earbuds. But I'm not fast enough to miss Mom's nightly sobbing. The sound vibrates through her bedroom door, down the hallway, and pierces right into my chest. I freeze in place, squeezing my eyes shut, taking a moment to memorize the sound. Even if it's cold as hell outside, even if my legs get so tired I can't take another step, I need to remember that sound and not come back home until I don't have to hear it anymore.

At least until tomorrow night.

"Good night, Brooklynn," Grandma grumbles from her chair. She rustles around, and then the old wood floors creak beneath her feet. I tuck myself half behind the folding stairs, hiding my brightly colored shoes. She stares straight ahead when she passes me but stops briefly in front of Mom's door, sighing and shaking her head before disappearing behind her own bedroom door across from the kitchen.

I collapse against the wall, so relieved. If she caught me sneaking out, I'd never be allowed out for anything but school again. I can't imagine giving up my early mornings and weekends at the Spark Plug listening to Melanie make repeated calls to the dentist office with tooth-related complaints or griping to someone named Shelly about another failed blind date. Or Betty bringing me coffee refills, never asking me personal questions but making the interactions *feel* personal somehow.

After the light turns off under Grandma's door, I make my way out the back and across the yard, around the pond, and then into the woods. Exploring the area at night, running on the trail without getting lost, isn't a novice activity at all. It took me weeks of daily runs to brave it without shining a flashlight the whole way. I have a tiny light clipped to my waist pouch, but now I turn it on only when the ground feels different or if I step on something unfamiliar.

Tonight, I don't have the urge to blast my dad's music

like I normally do. The events of this afternoon have given me some new things to think about. Things I'm grateful to think about. Like how to get a hold of a pair of skates in my size. Hockey skates, I guess. And skating, period. I used to be able to skate forward, backwards, do that snowplow thing to stop, but I haven't skated in years. And none of the lessons I'd taken taught me how to move on the ice like Jake Hammond. I'll probably be laughed out of the tryouts.

But the sign-up sheet had said, *No experience required.* And is there a better way to fit in here in Juniper Falls than being a part of a sports team? Probably not. It'll make my dad proud, maybe my mom a little happier. And it will give me something to do besides worrying about both of them.

Then there's that cocky-ass expression on Jake Hammond's face when he said, "*You look a little small for hockey, Brooklynn.*" It made me glad I choose my words extra carefully now. Lashing out with some snide comeback is not nearly as satisfying as proving him wrong by *doing.*

Tonight, it's cold enough to see my breath and cause my lungs to burn. But I don't hate the temperature as much as I thought I would when I first found out we were moving from Austin, Texas, to Juniper Falls, Minnesota—a place that was more fantasy than reality to me, considering I hadn't been here to visit since I was a baby.

By the time I get through my regular jog in the woods and I'm approaching the pond again, I've got a plan in place to check out the consignment shop downtown in the morning and see if they have any cheap used skates.

I hear voices before I exit the woods. I shut off my iPhone and change my jog to a walk. Out of nowhere, headlights blind me, and my heart jumps up to my throat. My first thought is that these are lights from an emergency vehicle. Is something wrong?

I shake the thought away and focus on the source of the lights and the voices I'm now hearing. My mouth falls open in shock. I slide halfway behind a tree and look again, just to make sure I'm not imagining things.

Twelve or so boys are lined up in a row, the headlights from a blue pickup truck parked in the grass shining behind them. And they're all barefoot and shivering, standing there in only underwear.

My gaze drifts over them one by one, taking in the various styles of boxers, boxer briefs, and a few unfortunate pairs of tighty-whities.

A group of seven or eight fully clothed and much older guys are wandering around, some holding what look like cans of beer. I zoom in on one of those cans, wistfully admiring it, remembering the numb relaxed state of mind that a few beers or a couple of shots of liquor could bring on.

But no, not anymore. Feeling is better. No matter what. It's always better.

I recognize a big guy from the rink this afternoon. Mr. Smuttley had called him Red. And I spot number 42, Jake Hammond, and his sandy-colored hair and blue eyes. Okay, so I can't see his eyes from here, but I remember them from earlier. And I remember how beautiful his skating was and how I'd like to watch him glide around the ice for a few more minutes.

"Any of you freshman midgets ready to call it quits?" Red shouts to the shivering boys.

They all shake their heads even though I'm positive they'd rather be anywhere but here, like this. What had Smuttley said this afternoon about the pickup games? *It's a way for the younger players to learn their place…*

I guess *their place* doesn't allow for proper clothing or individual thought.

"This is no ordinary team you're joining," Red continues, pacing dramatically in front of the group. I blow on my hands through my thin knit gloves and slide around the tree to get a better view. "This isn't your little rec league or peewee squad where Mommy brings you cookies after the game. This is a chance to be part of our history. A history that includes Olympic champions, college scholarships, and maybe a shot at the pros. But more importantly, a chance to be part of the Otter legacy. Are you with me?"

"Yes, sir," they all grumble.

"We didn't hear you," one of the other fully clothed guys says.

"Yes, sir!"

God, this is weird. It must be some kind of freshman hazing. I thought only fraternities did that stuff. And more like fraternities twenty years ago. Don't they have zero tolerance on bullying here? I know this place is backwoods but I didn't think it was, like, *backwoods*...

"Good," Red says, "now it's time for the real initiation games to begin."

Another big guy steps forward, not as big as Red but still huge. "All right, you little scumbags, get down on your stomachs!"

"On our stomachs?" a pale, skinny boy who looks vaguely familiar asks.

The older guys erupt in laughter, and then Red walks behind the boy and shoves him facedown onto the branch-and leaf-filled ground. "What's your name, kid?"

"Pratt," he says, squeaking out the word.

Elliott Pratt. He sits in front of me in health class and he's nearly as quiet as I am. I'm surprised he spoke up here.

"Pratt," Red repeats. "Is that right?" He turns to his older teammates. "Check it out, guys, we've got a little Pratt."

I'm shivering now and I'm wearing running tights, a long-sleeve shirt, hat, jacket, and gloves. I can't imagine how cold these freshman boys must be.

If I stepped out into the open, could I end this little game, or would they just repeat it again the next night?

Red steps hard onto Elliott Pratt's back, and then the other big guy says, "Everybody on the ground, hands behind your backs."

I watch with disbelief as all the older guys, including Jake Hammond, move forward and produce several sets of handcuffs.

Oh my God, what is this, *Fifty Shades of Grey*?

Chapter Five

–JAKE–

I pick the biggest freshman to snap my pair of handcuffs on. I make sure they're loose enough to pull his wrists out of if he really needs to. The enchiladas from dinner sit like a brick in my stomach.

Tate Tanley moves beside me, handing me a flask he produced from inside his jacket. I think he's enjoying this about as much as I am based on the way he keeps downing alcohol and looking away from the freshmen. Red, on the other hand, is on fire.

I sort of get the excitement. *Sort of.* I felt that surge of power for a minute, when all eight of us seniors stood in front of the line of boys, knowing they were literally going to do whatever we told them. But the second we gave the command for them to strip down, I felt the first twinge of indigestion. It's too hard to do this without remembering what it felt like to stand outside in twenty-five degrees wearing only underwear while guys I'd looked up to for years humiliated me. And then the barefoot walk home. They took our clothes and shoes and didn't give them back. I remember Red had to wear a pair of gym shoes three sizes too small for months before his mom could afford to get him a new pair.

Jenkins, who is nearly as big as Red, stands at the end of the row of freshman boys. He drops a puck on the ground beside the kid at the end of our line. "Your first test is to take this puck and pass it all the way down to the last guy."

While lying on your bellies with your hands cuffed behind your backs, he doesn't add because it's obvious. All my classmates stand behind the younger guys, stepping on their backs when any of them tries to stand or push up onto their knees. I take a huge swig of Tanley's vodka, cough a little, then look away.

"A stick jabbed me in the stomach," Tanley says quietly enough for only me to hear. I watch him lift his jacket and shirt, then he shines his cell phone on his abdomen. There's a long scar across the middle. "Seventeen stitches."

I exhale and divert my eyes from the scar. I don't know what I would have told my parents if I'd come home with a cut big enough to require an emergency room visit.

The guys roar with laughter watching the freshman midgets squirm around on their bellies trying to push a puck down the line with their noses. Maybe the three years of steering clear of this Otter tradition was enough for the rest of the guys to forget how much it fucking sucked to be on that cold ground nearly naked. This event is exclusive to freshmen and seniors. Either you get to be pond scum or God. There is no in-between. In fact, the lock is so tight on this tradition that we even have one senior missing tonight— Fletcher Scott. He just moved up to varsity over the summer and he didn't play as a freshman, which means he doesn't even know about this most likely.

I hit the flask several more times over the next twenty or thirty minutes while Red and the other seniors force the guys to do stupid shit like spell Otters with their bodies or imitate the sounds of Juniper Falls native wildlife. Not only do the freshmen need some serious spelling lessons, the seniors really need to research Minnesota wildlife. Armadillos are not roaming these woods.

I almost head to my truck to wait out the rest of this nightmare when Red and Jenkins force two freshmen to kick the shit out of each other while their hands are cuffed behind them. Through my truck's headlights, I can see several sets of blue lips. It's too cold for this. Too cold to be out here this long with so little clothing.

"You've done well, boys," Red says after getting them back on their feet and in a straight line. "You've shown that you have what it takes to be a part of this legacy. Just remember your place."

"Finally," Tanley mutters beside me.

Red walks over to us and lowers his voice. "Jake, this one's yours. We all dished out something. You have to take a turn. It's tradition."

The indigestion returns. "Yeah, I don't think so."

Red blows out a frustrated breath. "Come on, Hammond, I left you the easiest part. Since you're such a pussy tonight."

I shove him but head toward the group. I know what he left for me and it's something I can handle. Probably the only part of this nightmare I can handle.

"We have one last test for you," Red continues, read-dressing the group. "This initiation has been part of our team for more than a hundred years, but the tests and games have changed through the years. All except for one." Red grabs my sleeve again and pulls me front and center. "Jake

Hammond is going to be our captain this season, and the assumed captain always conducts this last test. If you're an Otter, you're gonna learn right now that when your captain says jump, you jump. When he says pick your bloody ass up off the ice and help your team win, you do it. No hesitation. No question. That's because Otter captains are never crazy bastards like me and Jenkins. Never players who would do something dangerous or stupid. An Otter captain is the brains and the heart of our team."

I might have been touched by Red's speech if I hadn't heard Luke Pratt deliver those same words three years ago.

But I'm so happy for this to be over that I'm looking forward to the final event. I think it's probably the only part I'm gonna find entertaining.

"Okay," I say, addressing the shivering boys and trying to recall the speech I'd heard three years back. "Every freshman hockey player in our school's history has completed this famous walk across Juniper Falls Pond. A place named by our founder. When you risk your life and meet on the other side as a team, you'll have formed an unbreakable bond. Are you guys ready to take the long walk?"

A few of them sputter out a *yes*, but most of them, I can see, have connected the dots and realized that October equals a half-frozen pond at best despite the smooth sheet of ice covering the entire surface. I hold back a laugh and make my way over to a nearby tree. I want the perfect view for this one. It takes me a minute to climb up to a branch big enough to sit on. "All right, on the count of three!"

My classmates position themselves casually off to the side, but in a place where they can cut off the guys before they touch a foot to the pond. I remember, three years ago, thinking for a second that I'd give it all up before I stepped foot on that unstable ice. And then concluding that there was no way every player had done this in the history of our high school hockey team.

"One!" I shout, watching the boys squirm and whisper. "Two!"

"Three!" all the seniors shout together.

A few boys bolt forward toward the pond and are cut off by shouts from Red and Jenkins. A couple of them never move a muscle, and the remaining boys fall somewhere in between, not completely sure it's a joke. I throw my head back and laugh. Maybe the vodka relaxed me. Maybe I'm okay with a decent prank as opposed to physical torture and public humiliation.

"Stop, you idiots!" Red shouts, laughing harder than I am.

A small, pale figure continues to move quickly in the dark, out of the shine of the truck headlights. The laughter dies in my throat.

"Hey!" I shout at the kid. "Stop!"

He's fast as hell and is on the ice and out a couple of feet before my brain can process what's happening. All the seniors start yelling at the kid to come back, but he's still going.

"Pratt, you little shit!" Red shouts. "Get the hell off the ice!"

Little Pratt.

I swing a leg over the branch the same moment the ice cracks beneath Pratt's bare feet. Seconds later, he's swallowed up by the pond.

Holy shit.

"Fuck!" My body jolts into action, quickly moving down from the tree, but my foot catches on something, and I hit the ground shoulder-first. I barely feel the sting of the fall or register the way my left arm feels disconnected from my body.

All I can think as I run toward the half-frozen pond is the fact that *I* told him to jump and he jumped. *And the handcuffs.* He can't climb out. Shouts and cries emerge from all around me. I hear them, but I don't stop to contemplate what to do next.

"Jake, no! What the hell are you doing?"

"Somebody call for help!"

"He's cuffed; he can't swim!"

"We need to get out of here! We're all going to get caught!"

I run across several feet of ice, hoping speed will prevent all of it from cracking beneath me. It's not ready for foot traffic; it's gonna give no matter what method I use of getting across. I look for signs of Little Pratt and catch a glimpse of his red hair peeking through the frozen water, bobbing under a chunk of ice.

He's not moving.

Holy fuck, he's not moving.

I toss my jacket and shoes aside, grinding my teeth at the pain shooting down the left side of my body. I jump in the water without another second's hesitation.

Knives. A hundred thousand knives stabbing every inch of my skin. *Get the kid. Get the kid,* I recite in my head until my hands are feeling around, grasping a lock of hair and then the bound-up arms. I tug his head to the surface and use every ounce of strength I have left in my body to toss Little Pratt up onto the most stable part of the ice.

The water on my eyelashes freezes, ruining my vision, but through the haze, I see Tanley two or three feet away, carefully sliding across the ice. I give Pratt's foot one last shove until he's close enough for Tanley to grab his shoulder and tug him to shore.

"Get out, Jake! Get the hell out!" Tanley says. "You won't be able to swim for long!"

My clothes weigh me down. I fumble to bring my hands out of the water and reach for the nearest slab of ice, but my left arm gives the second I try to push up. *Something is wrong.* Something more than frozen water.

My arm is broken. Or maybe my shoulder. The tree. I fell out of the fucking tree.

My limbs begin to seize, my head bobbing under then emerging just in time to see Red shouting at someone or something coming from the other side. *Help? Did they get the fire department or paramedics here that fast?*

"Get off the ice! What the hell?" Red says. "I'm coming, Jake."

"No!" a higher female-sounding voice says.

I manage to turn myself around, and when I do, Brooke Parker is lying in her stomach on the ice, reaching both hands into the water.

The pain is too much. The cold is too much. I'm slowly losing consciousness.

But I feel Brooke's fingers hook around the belt loops on the back of my jeans. And when she starts to pull me out, instincts kick in, ordering me to climb, to move. And then I'm lying on my back, cold air hitting me from every direction. It's almost worse than the water.

A brown ponytail tickles my nose, and Brooke's face is hovering over mine, panic in her eyes.

"Don't move," Red says.

I'm shaking everywhere, vision blurring, sound fading. Red slides me across the ice until I reach the bank, and he lifts me up before tossing me onto the ground. Tanley starts to go after Brooke, to help her back to solid ground, but when I turn my head, she's crawling on hands and knees across the pond. She reaches the shore and then takes off running toward the Gleason farmhouse.

"Come back!" Tanley shouts. "Hey!"

I try to shout those same words at her, too. *Is she okay? What the hell was she doing out here tonight?* But sirens replace the questions in my head, and when Red leans over me and says they have to run, I nod.

We can't get caught. Not as a team.

He shouts to the other guys, yelling at the freshmen to get their clothes from my truck and run. I attempt to climb to my feet and follow them, but nothing will move, and the already black world turns completely dark.

The last thought in my head before I pass out is that I don't know if Pratt was conscious when I pulled him up. I don't know if he was breathing.

Chapter Six

–BROOKE–

I'm shaking so hard I can barely control my limbs well enough to creep quietly through the house. Water from the pond splashed all over me, soaking my clothes. I'm chilled completely to my bones.

The sirens grow louder as the emergency personnel draw closer to the pond. I chance a glance outside the kitchen window, eyeing the spot beneath the tree where I left my cell phone. Idiot. I'm such a freakin' idiot. Any minute now they're going to knock on this door, wake up Grandma, and tell her how I called 9-1-1 while hanging out near the pond with a group of upperclassmen and naked freshmen boys.

I shudder, remembering the bluish tinge of Elliott Pratt's lips when Jake pulled him out. And watching that ice crack under his feet. I've never been so scared in my entire life.

But this is what happens when you don't think. When you dive in and do something stupid and impulsive. Why would that ice be any more forgiving to me than it was to

Elliott? Except it *had* been more forgiving.

I stumble into the bathroom, locking the door behind me. I can't strip my frozen clothes off fast enough to calm my chattering teeth. I blast the shower on high heat and crawl into the tub, sitting on the bottom with my knees pulled to my chest. I bury my face and try to block out the sting of hot water mixing with my frozen skin.

Any minute now. Any minute now, someone will bang on the door and tell Grandma everything. Why couldn't I have just stayed inside listening to Mom cry? It would have been better than what I ended up witnessing. Why did I have to crawl across the ice and help Jake Hammond out?

But I already know the answer: Because no one else would have.

Chapter Seven

–JAKE–

I've been in a twelve-hour pain-medication haze and coming out of that, realizing that I'm back at home in my bed, it's impossible not to think that maybe last night wasn't real. Maybe I dreamed it. Maybe school hasn't even started and it's still summer.

But the shooting pain across my chest and down my left arm tells me otherwise. Not to mention the complicated sling I've been tied into. It's like a straitjacket. My bedroom door opens and Dad, Oz, and Coach Bakowski walk in. Dad closes the door behind them.

My heart races, causing more pain in my chest. I try to sit up but then quickly realize I've been propped against, like, fourteen pillows and I'm as upright as I can get.

Coach looks me over, his face revealing nothing to tell me what he's thinking. "Feeling better, Jake?"

No. "Uh…yeah, much better." I glance at Dad, and he immediately looks away. My stomach sinks. This is bad.

Really bad.

Uncle Oz is in full sheriff uniform, including his holster and gun. He snatches my desk chair and turns it around backward before straddling it. "Want to tell us what happened last night?"

My breaths come out in short, labored bursts, giving away my guilt. I clamp my jaw shut and say nothing.

"Right." Oz nods. "Figured you'd go this route. The hospital did blood work. Showed you'd been drinking."

Drinking? I hadn't been drunk, just took a couple of swigs of whatever Tate had in that flask. Okay, maybe it was more like four or five swigs, and it *was* strong stuff. But still, I definitely hadn't been drunk.

"Nothing happened," I protest. "I was just hanging out by the pond—"

"Nothing happened? Look at yourself, Jake!" Oz blows out a frustrated breath, shaking his head. He turns to Coach Bakowski. "See? This is the empire you're helping to keep afloat. He's more afraid of selling out his damn hockey teammates than he is of having criminal charges on his permanent record."

Criminal charges? Shit.

Coach folds his arms across his chest and stares me down. I hate that I'm sitting while he's standing. It makes this so much more intimidating. "Sheriff seems to think this was a team gathering. Was it, son?"

I hesitate then shake my head.

Oz groans. "Fine. So here's how the story looks from our angle. Emergency services gets a call around one thirty in the morning; they arrive at Juniper Falls Pond, and what do they find?"

What *did* they find? I was unconscious by that point, and the rest of the night is so hazy I can't even form a concrete image.

"They found my nephew fully clothed, drenched from having fallen in the frozen pond, with a broken collarbone," Oz continues. "And then a naked Elliott Pratt, blue in the face—"

"P-Pratt," I sputter, remembering that I hadn't seen him breathing after I pulled him out. "Is he okay? I mean…I never thought he'd—"

Dad makes eye contact for the first time since stepping into my room. He shakes his head ever so slightly, and I clamp my jaw shut again.

"He's alive," Coach says.

"Barely," Oz adds, narrowing his eyes at me. "He was flown to a hospital in St. Paul. He's still in critical condition."

Nausea sweeps over me. I'm seconds away from spewing my guts out. Lucky for me, my uncle has dealt with the drunk and disorderly enough to recognize the signs. He grabs the garbage can beside my desk and holds it out for me. The remains of the pond water I must have swallowed last night along with sour-tasting bile push their way out of my stomach and into the trash can. The effort of turning sideways to puke causes stabbing pain to shoot across my chest again, down my left arm.

I heave some more and then try to catch my breath while staring at the liquid vomit. Can it get any more fucked up than this?

Oz eventually takes the garbage can and sets it out in the hall. I wipe my mouth and watery eyes with the sleeve of my T-shirt and then rest against the pillows again. I squeeze my eyes shut, blocking out the searing pain.

"So you see the dilemma I'm in, Jake," Oz continues as if I hadn't just barfed in the middle of his interrogation. "The facts I've got? You with alcohol in your system, a naked Elliott Pratt, and articles of clothing found near the pond belonging to two other freshman boys. Hockey team hazing gone wrong if you ask me, and I can't be the only one to put it together. Imagine how that will look on the front page of the paper. Are you gonna tell the truth or let people make up their own version?"

So Red and the other guys got away without being seen.

"It wasn't a team thing. It was just an accident," I plead. "Just me and…and…"

Oh shit, I can't even remember the kid's name. *That idiot kid*, why the hell didn't he stop when I yelled at him?

One more piece of last night returns to my memories… Brooke Parker and her brown ponytail, her fingers curling around my belt loop. Was I delusional and imagined that? She had been on my mind. She looked so panicked, though; it had to be real. And the way she took off with Tanley shouting after her…

"Who else was with you, Jake?" Oz demands.

My gaze bounces between Dad and Coach, and I think I might puke again. Both say nothing but I can read their opposing arguments. Finally Dad speaks up. "Just tell us who was there and we'll make sure no one knows it was you who talked. Oz needs you to name someone before we can do anything else. We know you wouldn't do anything to hurt that boy, but the way it looks now…it isn't good."

"And what if I do?" I ask Oz. "What happens if I start naming names?"

"A couple of the freshman boys' families want answers; they're calling this a hazing attack." Oz shoots a glare at both Dad and Coach.

My uncle didn't play on the team. He doesn't understand.

"We can't get the other two freshmen to talk, and Pratt is obviously out of commission," Oz says. "But I'll warn you: Pratt's mom has put up a few big fights with the school board over in Longmeadow. She won't go quietly here. I don't think you want to take a chance of everything being pinned on you alone."

"What do you mean his mom has put up a fight?" I ask, thinking about Luke Pratt and his own efforts to give me permanent concussions three years ago. "And why Longmeadow? He's not from here?"

"This is the second wife," Dad explains. "Luke's stepmother. She's from Longmeadow."

"The kid's been bullied or something," Coach says, and it's obvious this is a weakness he'd never have tolerated in one of his players. "'Cause he's deaf."

Oz rolls his eyes. "He's hearing impaired, Bill."

"He can't hear?" I say, my voice going up one too many octaves as I play back last night… *Stop! Pratt, you little shit, get the hell off the ice!*

He didn't hear us.

Fucking hell.

More bile rises up to my throat, but I close my eyes again and force my stomach to calm down. "But he talked to me," I argue even though I never met the kid until yesterday. "At the pickup game, he asked for a water break."

"He speaks clearly, hears some with aids in, and he reads lips," Oz spits out as if warning me that we're getting off topic. "Final chance to sell out your teammates, Jake…"

Coach stares hard again like I'd better not open my mouth, and Dad looks like he's pleading with me to do the opposite, maybe? I'm not sure.

But it doesn't matter. I'm an Otter hockey player. There's only one choice.

I shake my head.

Oz sighs but doesn't look surprised. My dad's face pinches with worry, but he seems to be restraining himself from saying anything.

"What's the timeline for this injury?" Coach asks my dad. This is probably the other reason he's here right now.

"ER doc said six weeks is the average; some heal in three, but he'll still need to rehab it," Dad rattles off, looking distracted.

Six weeks? Plus rehab. The reality of missing the first several games of the season hits hard and fast. It would be nice to have a moment to myself to process this.

"I'll call Doctor Murphy, get him to see you later today," Coach says. "And we'll need to contact college coaches, tell 'em whatever they need to hear so they don't worry about him playin' again."

"I'll take care of the college coaches," Dad says firmly, exchanging a look with Coach that I can't quite read. Then he mumbles something about needing to make some phone calls and turns his back on me and walks out of the room. I don't know what he's thinking, but I wish he'd come back and say something more. Or tell me what to do.

I can't play hockey. I'm a senior, and I can't play. And people might blame me for what happened to Elliott. This is too much, too fucking much.

Coach leaves my room, and I'm alone with Oz, feeling this pain that I know he doesn't understand. And yet he gives me the smallest, teeniest look of sympathy before patting my right shoulder and saying, "Elliott Pratt will pull through; he's a strong kid. I'm willing to overlook the underage drinking if you agree to some community service hours."

I close my eyes and groan. I need more of whatever pain meds they gave me earlier. Or more vodka from Tanley's flask. Though that would be a really bad idea considering what I'm in trouble for. I can't exactly complain about the fact that I've done plenty of underage drinking and haven't ever been in trouble for it before. Why now? "Community service? Like ride-alongs with you?"

Oz laughs. "Have you heard about the girls' hockey team I'm coaching?"

"I doubt I'll pass for a girl if that's what you're going for."

"Agreed," he says, "but I'm gonna need an assistant coach."

I shoot upright just in time to get hit with more pain and Oz's abrupt exit.

Wait…what?

Chapter Eight

–BROOKE–

I walk into school Monday all too aware of the subject currently creating a buzz of whispered conversation. I walk with my head down, my body tense, waiting.

"Elliott Pratt almost died…"

"I heard they had to shock him with paddles."

"Jake Hammond was there, too. Both his arms are broken. A leg, too, I think."

"Is no one going to talk about the fact that Elliott was naked?"

This weekend has been one of the worst of my life. I couldn't get myself to do anything. I wanted to tell someone what happened—I still want to. But every time I think about it, I'm frozen, unable to make a move. My dad's trial keeps coming back to me… The testimonies, the lies, the truth that went unheard. You can make anyone believe just about anything. What if people don't believe me? So instead of making a move to do something, I just sat around in my grandmother's depressing old house waiting for someone to knock on the door and demand to question me, ask me why I made that 9-1-1 call Friday night.

Is this what my dad felt like when he—?

After a trip to my locker, on the way to my first-period class, I feel someone behind me, their steps deliberately matching mine. My heart quickens. A tall shadow looms over me in the base of the stairwell.

"We should talk," a voice says from behind.

I pick up the pace, taking the steps two at a time. But on the second-floor landing, he places a palm on the door handle, preventing me from walking through. I turn slowly and am face-to-face with Jake Hammond. His arm is in a sling, his face is pale with a bruise across one cheek, but other than that he looks okay. I close my eyes and try to erase the image of his head sinking beneath icy pond water. It was scarier than watching Elliott go under because I saw it up close.

"We need to talk," he says, glancing around, his voice low.

I press my back against the wall beside the door, wait for him to speak.

He rests his good hand right beside my head and leans close. "Look…I know you haven't talked to anyone yet, and since you waited, I was hoping it was to give me a chance to explain…"

I look him over, take in his perfectly snug jeans and button-down shirt someone must have helped him put on. I hate the way my stomach jolts at the sight of him.

"Friday night, things got really…" His head dips so he's even closer to me, and my heart picks up speed. "Out of hand. It was an accident and…" He bites his lower lip in this completely adorable way. "I just need you to pretend like you didn't see anything. Is that at all possible?"

Maybe it's the fact that I don't love the idea of telling this story to anyone even if it seems like I should. Or maybe it's the fact that he seems so defeated, like he's sure I'll say no. But I want to tell him that, okay, I was never there.

Come on, Brooke, you know better.

"Elliott's in bad shape," I whisper. I've picked up that much just walking to my locker.

Jake squeezes his eyes shut, releases a breath. "I know. But he's gonna pull through. I heard that from lots of people…"

His face, his body language…all of it contradicts his words. He looks like he's in worse shape than I am, is even more distraught than I am.

"How…" I start and then stop. I'm not used to conversing with people at school more than this. "How are you?"

His jaw tenses. "What do you want? Name it and it's yours. You want to hang out with me and my crowd? Done. Answers to tests…I can get just about any of them. A homecoming date, votes at cheerleading tryouts—whatever you want, Brooke."

I ask him if he's okay and he's offering to buy my silence with what…popularity? I'm sure my face must reflect the disgust I feel because Jake drops his hand from beside my head and takes a step back.

"I'm sorry; I'm not an asshole," he tells me, but again, his words contradict his actions—or his offers, actually. "But I mean it. Let me do something for you and you can do this for me. For the whole team. Okay?"

"Fine," I tell him, my voice still unable to rise above a whisper. "You can help me out."

I open my bag and tear a sheet of paper from my notebook. He stands there, looking curious, while I jot down a short list and hand the paper to him. His eyebrows lift as he reads.

"This is what you want?" Jake says. "Hockey equipment? That's it?"

I nod slowly.

"Consider it done." Jake tugs the paper into his pocket with his free hand. "And you'll keep your part of the deal?"

"Yes," I promise.

The door beside me flings open, and I instinctively tug the front of Jake's shirt, pulling him toward me and out of the way of the swinging door. It misses hitting his injured shoulder by not more than an inch.

He exhales and shakes his head. "I probably deserved that."

And then he steps through the door, leaving me alone.

After a few seconds, I head out of the stairwell and sink into my seat in first period, more than ten minutes early. My heart still beats wildly, but there's no doubting the fact that I feel a hundred times less nervous, less anxious. I don't know what story was told to authorities about Friday night but whatever it was, it likely wasn't the truth or he wouldn't have asked me to keep quiet.

I only get about three minutes of quiet before two girls and a guy enter the classroom, talking loudly, excited.

"Jake Hammond is too popular for his own good," one girl says. "That shit goes to your head."

"I don't know," the other girl says. "It doesn't sound like Jake."

The guy trailing behind them laughs. "Oh, like you know him so well."

"She wishes she did," the first girl says.

The girl defending Jake turns bright red while her friends laugh at her expense. Someone slides into the desk beside me, looking nearly as distraught as I feel. I glance sideways to check out the tall skinny guy wearing an Otter hockey sweatshirt. *Cole*. I think that's his name.

Mrs. Watterson, our oral communications teacher, enters the room with Haley, the senior girl who works as a classroom aide this period. Haley glances wearily at Cole, who now has his head ducked and is pretending to read from the textbook.

Haley stops her conversation with the teacher and heads over to Cole's desk. She squats down beside him and speaks in a low voice, though not low enough for me not to hear. I stuff my earbuds into my ears, giving them the illusion of privacy.

"Do you know anything more than the BS floating around the halls?" Haley asks. "Fletch says he doesn't know anything, either, but—"

"He's telling the truth. He wouldn't know anything."

Haley starts to argue, but Cole stops her, adding, "He wasn't there, Haley. Trust me."

It's obvious that last statement was more than he wanted to offer because he looks around nervously. I take a note from him and bury my face in my own textbook.

The classroom fills up quickly, and Haley returns to Mrs. Watterson's desk and begins stapling packets together for her. When the bell rings, Mrs. Watterson jumps right into today's lesson. I take detailed notes, needing to put my mind elsewhere, but soon the lecture is over and we're being handed packets for an upcoming project and assigned groups. I end up in a group with the girl who came to Jake's defense—Rebecca—and Cole.

Rebecca doesn't even try to hide her disappointment as she gathers her things and trudges toward the front of the room where Cole and I are seated.

"Great," she whispers to her friend. "Oral communications project with partners who have public-speaking phobia."

I glance at Cole, who turns beet red and diverts his gaze from this girl. And I quickly realize that Rebecca is kind of right. Cole doesn't seem to be the outgoing type, and I'm committed to being the opposite of outgoing.

Rebecca takes one look at Cole's red face and rolls her eyes. "This should be a blast."

Cole studies the assignment packet, ignoring Rebecca for the time being. "I'm pretty good with slides…"

"Fantastic," Rebecca says. "Cole's making slides. For a topic we have yet to decide on."

Haley must have mean-girl radar, because she grabs a chair and pulls it up right between Rebecca and Cole. "Sounds like you need some help brainstorming topics."

"What's a social justice topic anyway?" Rebecca asks, flipping the top page of her packet. "Like world peace or the Great Depression?"

"The Great Depression is a historical topic," Haley says. "Social justice means it has to do with human rights and equality and its relevance and problems right now."

"Okay, so world peace it is," Rebecca says.

"That's way too vague," Cole argues, surprising both Haley and me and possibly himself. "It's a ten-minute presentation. The more specific the better."

Rebecca waves a hand as if to say, *You got a better idea?*

I open my class folder and dig for a handout Mrs. Watterson gave us a couple of weeks ago with a list of socially relevant topics for an essay assignment. While I'm searching, Rebecca plucks the graded essay from the opposite pocket of my folder.

"*A Step Backward for Transgender Rights*," she reads aloud, then looks at Haley. "Can we do this topic?"

"Sure—" Haley starts, but Rebecca doesn't let her finish.

"Cool, it will give me an excuse to catch up on the new

season of *I Am Jazz*," Rebecca says, then she looks at Cole. "You good with this?"

He shrugs. "Sounds fine to me."

After a less painful twenty minutes of planning, the bell rings, and we're released from class. In the hall, right outside the door, a dark-haired guy appears to be waiting for someone. Haley exits in front of me, and the guy pushes off the wall when he sees her.

"Hey, Fletch," she says, surprised to see him. "What are you doing here? I thought you had class at JF Community—"

"I skipped." He tugs Haley's hand, bringing her closer. "I was worried about...everything."

"I'm sorry," she blurts out, looking guilty.

Fletch offers her a tiny smile and rests his forehead against hers. "Cole straightened you out, huh?"

"Yeah." Haley closes her eyes for a moment, seeming stressed, though she'd been relaxed helping our group brainstorm. "I need to talk to Jake. Maybe I should cut second period and go over—"

"He's here," Fletch says. "I saw him walking toward the office."

Cole steps around me and joins Haley and Fletch. I take a moment to assess the path to my next class. I definitely don't want to go anywhere near the office. Before I can escape, though, Haley tugs the back of my shirt, and I turn halfway to face her.

"Nice job with the topic," she says, sounding relaxed again. "I'm excited for your presentation."

I offer her a smile and a nod before booking it down the hall. Haley's boyfriend, Fletch, doesn't act like the other hockey players, but he must be on the team, too, if he's wrapped up in this drama. The real questions is, who *isn't* wrapped up in it?

And how am I going to look at Jake Hammond again without seeing his head bobbing in that frozen water, remembering the intense sting of cold when I plunged my hands in and searched blindly for some part of him to grab hold of?

It occurs to me right then that if I hadn't been there, if I hadn't crawled across that ice, the conversations buzzing in the hallway this morning would be very, very different.

Chapter Nine

–JAKE–

"As I'm sure you're aware of, Rhett," Principal Hogan says, addressing my dad, "because the incident happened off school property, outside of school hours, and wasn't affiliated with any school organized event, the school has no justification for suspension or expulsion."

"I'm aware," Dad says drily. He points a glare at me for the thousandth time this morning.

But I can't do or feel much outside of dealing with the throbbing pain shooting down my arm, across my shoulder. My father, the experienced lawyer, public defender, and state senator decided that the risk of Vicodin addiction was too great and "we can't take a chance with any of that," so he dumped the rest of my prescription and forced my mother to agree with him. But I know potential drug addiction is not his driving motivation. He's pissed at me for not telling the whole story, and this is his passive-aggressive way of punishing me.

In addition to all the real punishments he's given me: no truck (like I can drive anyway), no going out except to school and community service, no friends over, no computer games, no TV. I do get to keep my phone, but that's only because he downloaded that app that allows him to follow my every move.

"Should evidence surface that Friday's incident was a continuation of an altercation at school," the principal says, X-raying me with his gaze, "then suspension and even expulsion will be revisited."

"What about hockey?" I brave asking. "Coach Bakowski suspended me from the team. But after my shoulder heals—"

"Playing on an athletic team is a privilege, son," the principal says. "Coach Bakowski has every right to decide that a player hasn't earned that privilege and therefore shouldn't play. I don't get involved in those disciplinary decisions."

I draw in slow, deep breaths, fighting the pain in my shoulder and the pain in my gut hearing that even if I heal, I still might not be allowed to play again. I barely listen while the principal drones on about zero-tolerance policies, an apology letter to Elliott's family, and weekly sessions with the guidance counselor to discuss my behavioral issues.

Finally, Dad and I can leave the office. He barely looks at me when he says, "Your mother will pick you up after school."

Then he turns his back to me and strides out the school's main entrance. It's been like this all weekend. But I've overheard him on the phone several times this weekend, too, going to bat for me, working to get the charges dismissed. He can't look at me, but at least he's still fighting for me.

I head to my class without a pen or notebook or anything. It's too hard to carry shit with this sling and the throbbing pain. All eyes are on me when I enter the room late for class, but when I attempt to make eye contact with anyone individually, it's even worse than it is with my dad. None of them want to look at me. Not even my calc teacher, Mr. Clubous.

I try to sit at the desk, in my usual spot, but I can't fit this sling without crushing the hell out of my arm. I grimace in pain, turn a little, but no, it's not working. Eventually I stand and drag an empty chair—one without a desk attached— from the back of the room.

By lunchtime, the pariah part I'm being forced to play is too much, and I finally respond to one of my teammate's texts, something I've avoided doing since Friday night.

ME: meet me at O'Connor's
TATE: on my way

My eyes are closed, my head resting against the booth, when Tanley seats himself across from me.

"I can't do this, man," Tate says immediately. "It's not right."

Red delivered the news to everyone for me over the weekend, making sure they knew that I hadn't named any names, wasn't planning to, and that they should all do the same.

"What's the alternative?" I say, closing my eyes again. I've been over and over this in my head for at least forty-eight hours.

"The truth?" he says.

I lift my head and glance around. O'Connor's is the town hockey bar owned by Tate's girlfriend's family. They serve food and are open during the day, but being a bar, it's pretty empty on a Monday at eleven-thirty in the morning.

"What will that accomplish?"

Tate scrubs a hand over his face. He looks like hell. Like someone who hasn't slept in days. "I don't know…I don't fucking know."

With anxiety bubbling in my stomach, I ask the question most looming in my mind. "Have you heard any update on Little Pratt? Did your mom—?"

Tanley's mom is a nurse at our local hospital. I saw her there Friday night while I was being treated for my broken collarbone.

"She said he's doing better," Tate tells me. "He has signs of normal brain activity…"

"Shit," I mutter, swallowing the lump in my throat. "Shit."

Tanley runs a hand over his face again, drawing attention to the dark circles under his eyes. "I keep seeing his head floating there—Jesus Christ. How the hell did this happen?"

"Did you know that he couldn't hear?" I ask, and Tate shakes his head. "Do you think anyone knew? Did you know he's from Longmeadow?"

"Probably some of the guys with him knew. He's a freshman; he's never been on the team before. How were we supposed to know this shit?" Tate straightens up, seeming to remember something. "What about that girl?"

The pain in my arm intensifies. "You mean the girl who pulled me out of the water?"

"What the hell was she thinking?" Tate muses. "She's gonna talk. Assuming she hasn't already."

"She's not big on talking," I tell him, avoiding mention of my very shameful moment of blackmail or bribery—not sure which, but it was ugly either way—this morning.

We sit there in silence for a long moment, and then Tate says, "I don't know if I can just keep playing while you're…" He stops, waves a hand at my sling.

"Even if Elliott had heard us, if we'd stopped him, I still

fell out of that fucking tree. The story still ends with me in this sling, on the bench, no matter how you tell it."

"I didn't even want to be there," Tate says.

"That makes two of us."

He offers me a sympathetic look that I don't feel like I deserve. "So what are you going to do now?"

"Besides being the subject of some highly creative homoerotic rumors?" I retort.

"Makes you wonder about our hockey ancestors, doesn't it? Why the fascination with young boys stripping down in front of them?" Tate says, laughing darkly.

Despite my grim mood, I can't help but laugh with him. The more I think about a hundred years of what happened at the pond last Friday, the more messed up those early Otters seem. "Oz busted me for underage drinking. Guess the booze you gave me showed up in my blood work at the hospital. He's keeping my record clean but making me work for it."

"At the station?" Tate asks. "And why would he bust you for that now? Not like he hasn't caught us with beer by the pond before."

"My thoughts exactly." I slide the saltshaker around the table, unable to look him in the eye. "And not at the station. He wants my help coaching the new girls' hockey team."

"Hmm. Might be cool," Tate says.

I stare at him, half-pissed, half-surprised he could say that with a straight face. "No. Definitely not *cool*. I'm not a coach. I'm a player."

He seems to contemplate a number of arguments before finally saying, "Guess it doesn't matter. You're doing it, doubt he's messing with you about the record thing."

Can't argue with that. Oz is a man of his word, that's for sure.

Chapter Ten

–BROOKE–

'm waiting anxiously on the bleachers in the ice rink when a dirty duffel bag lands beside me. I look up, and that hockey player, Red, is hovering over me in his giant way.

"There it is," he says. "Your whole list."

Where is Jake? I want to ask but figure I'm not supposed to. Obviously Jake and all that popularity he flaunted at me earns him his very own henchman.

I grip the strap of the bag, avoiding the temptation to tear into it. I really wasn't sure that he'd come through.

"Are we cool now?" he asks.

Are we cool now? As in am I cool with the way he tortured those boys? No, definitely not. This is why it was easier to make this deal with Jake than Red. It wasn't lost on me, the fact that even though all the seniors joined the torture, Red seemed to enjoy it in a way that I can't shake off so easily.

I nod and even offer a quiet "yes" in response. He leaves

quickly, probably not wanting to be seen with the weird new girl. I unzip the bag, remove the very worn hockey skates, and grin. They're perfect.

"Samantha Mason," Sheriff Hammond reads from his clipboard then looks up at the seven of us girls before landing on one shorter than me, but stockier. "Hi, Sammy, good to see you. How's your granddad doing?"

"He's better," the girl says.

"Kendra Allen?" He scans the group until he spots a girl from my PE class with long dark braids, a helmet tucked under one arm. "Great, Kendra. Glad you made it today."

Thanks to my Google research this week, I recognize Kendra's gloves as goalie gloves. She's wearing extra padding, too, different from what Red brought me today.

"Sophie Jackson," Sheriff says, nodding at the tall blond girl beside me.

"Rosie Hammond... Here."

I know from Jake and Red's conversation last Friday at the rink that this is Sheriff Hammond's daughter, Jake's cousin, but without knowing, I would have never guessed that. Rosie has shiny black hair compared to her dad's dirty-blond shade. He's also a bit nerdy while Rosie is stunning.

"Brooke Parker," he says, looking up from the clipboard again, scrutinizing me. "They play a lot of ice hockey where you're from?"

In Texas? Um, no. I shake my head, and he laughs.

"No worries—we're happy to have you," he says. "If we can get you ready to play a game this season, then great. If not, I know you'll learn a lot and be ready for next season."

I catch Rosie's brows lift, her gaze shifting downward at the floor.

Sheriff Hammond turns to the ice, then over to a bench where I imagine the team sits during a game. Jake Hammond is on it, slumped against the wall, his head resting on a balled-up sweatshirt. His mouth hangs slack, and his eyes are closed.

Sheriff stalks over to him. His full uniform, holster and gun included, is suddenly more threatening than it had been moments ago when he called roll. He claps his hands in front of Jake's face, jolting him awake.

Jake jumps up, glares at his uncle, and then prepares to sit down again. But Sheriff Hammond grips the front of his nephew's shirt, drags him out of the little box and over to the rest of us.

"Girls," Sheriff says, releasing Jake. "Jake has volunteered—out of the goodness of his heart—to be our assistant coach. He's looking forward to helping all of you develop into better, stronger players."

With a great deal of effort, Jake attempts a neutral expression. He takes us in one by one until his gaze lands on me. And it's another moment like in the stairwell at school, where I'm forced to think about last Friday night... The sound of the ice cracking beneath his shoes, the sting of the frozen water, his fingers failing to grip the edge of the ice, his head going under.

My chest tightens, my breathing a bit erratic. He seems to go through something similar, but just as quickly the tension is gone from his face.

"They're ready for you," Sheriff says.

Jake's eyes widen. "For me?"

"To warm up or whatever."

A silent argument flows between uncle and nephew.

Rosie ends up being the one to settle it.

She steps past her dad and Jake and moves out onto the ice. "Come on, everyone follow me. Sprints. Blue line to blue line."

Kendra and Samantha both dart forward, wanting to follow right behind Rosie. But their sticks tangle, and they end up facedown on the ice. Rosie turns, pivots so sharply ice sprays the girls in the face.

"Jesus Christ," she mutters, then she scoops up the sticks, tosses them out of the way, and gestures for the rest of us to do the same. "Obviously skating with sticks is too advanced for us right now."

"Rosie," Sheriff Hammond warns.

"Sorry," she says, forcing the word out before turning and skating away so fast none of us will ever be able to catch her.

I move tentatively over the ice, afraid of losing my balance with everyone watching. I would have loved to have had these skates a day early, even an hour early just to avoid this moment being so public. The hundreds of lessons I had as a kid come back to me somewhat. Enough to keep me moving forward. But these other girls have been in skates since the day they learned to walk, and I'm afraid if I try and keep up with them, I'll end up facedown on the ice. I proceed cautiously and, as a result, I catch snippets of an argument between Jake and the sheriff.

"Hours only count if you're actually doin' a service," Sheriff tells Jake.

"I'll make you a deal," Jake retorts, his voice tense. "You go to the station, unlock your drawer of confiscated drugs, get me some damn Vicodin, and I'll be the best assistant coach you've ever met."

"Spoken like a true addict."

Wait...what?

"I only had one dose! How can I be an addict?" Jake snaps.

"You know, that's exactly what an addict would say," Sheriff says, a laugh in his voice.

Jake mutters a string of swear words that gets his uncle laughing even harder. I must be missing something. Since when is painkiller addiction something to laugh about? And does the sheriff really have a drawer full of confiscated drugs?

I reach the stopping point on the ice at the exact same time that I realize I don't know how to do that fast, turning-stop thingy. Luckily the half wall is there to stop me. I catch both Rosie and Jake shaking their heads at my method of stopping. The girls head back in the other direction, and soon I'm way, way behind them. We do this four times and end up with everyone watching me finish the entire final sprint.

Sheriff Hammond flips through papers on his clipboard, looking nearly as nervous as I feel. He tugs a page free and brings it closer to his face. "Okay, so I think what we're gonna do is get our sticks and then move the puck around some cones— Rosie, did we bring cones?"

He stops when he sees that she's already placing orange cones out on the ice. I grab the stick Red brought me and put all my energy into dragging a puck along the ice, weaving around the cones.

Two hours later, I'm the first one changed and heading out of the locker room. I'm not ready to go back to Grandma's house yet, so I climb the bleachers and take a seat. Several dozen very young hockey players take over the ice. Sheriff and Jake are still standing near the wall talking.

"Resisting this, being a stubborn ass, it won't make this any easier," Sheriff tells Jake. "Won't make the time go by faster."

"I'm not being stubborn," Jake argues. "I told you: I'm

not a coach. Just because I know how to play doesn't mean I know the first thing about teaching someone else. Plus, it seems like you're getting these girls' hopes up for nothing. You've got seven freakin' players; you can't even do a line change. And at least one of those players has barely skated, never held a stick—"

"I get it," Sheriff says. "We need more girls on the team. They don't have a long history of winning state championships, but we both know those wins and that history come with their own demons."

Sheriff nods at Jake's sling, and Jake releases a breath, looking out at the ice. "I don't know what you expect me to do here. I mean, it's not like we're ready to talk game strategy or defensive moves or trick shots."

"Are you telling me that Jake Hammond, Prince of Juniper Falls, best player this town has seen in well over a decade, can't teach a player how to stop or skate faster?" Sheriff challenges.

Jake is still for a long moment, and then he tugs at his sling, making a point. "I can't do much of anything right now."

My heart sinks to the pit of my stomach. He can't skate. He can't play. It must be killing him. If it were Red in the sling, the same Red who went to his happy place tormenting those boys last Friday night, I wouldn't feel bad at all. I may have stuck my arms into that frozen pond to pull Jake Hammond out, but he put his entire body into that freezing water to save Elliott Pratt. He fell out of the tree trying to stop him from going on the ice in the first place.

The sheriff stops Jake from leaving. "Six weeks and you'll be back out there—the doctor said so, right?"

Jake offers a reluctant nod. "If everything heals correctly. And now I don't know if the college scouts will be too nervous about the injury to make an offer…"

His voice trails off, like he can't even say any of this out loud or it might bring bad luck.

"I'm not an expert, but I've heard your dad yapping about recruiting so much I feel like I know it all," Sheriff says, "and falling and getting hurt outside somewhere probably isn't the same for college coaches as a stress injury or long-term issue. You'll be in it before the playoffs. You have your life to play hockey, Jake. It won't kill you to take a break."

"I'm not so sure about that." He averts his gaze from his uncle's. "What about Elliott? What if he isn't— I mean what if he doesn't—"

Sheriff Hammond rests a hand on Jake's shoulder. "It doesn't have to be cop and suspect between us. I'm here if you want to tell me what happened last Friday."

Jake steps out of his uncle's hold. "I already told you… it was an accident."

He turns and exits the rink, heading out the front doors toward a minivan pulled up in front.

Sheriff Hammond, looking completely defeated from the conversation, notices me and climbs the bleachers, taking the spot beside me. He's quiet for a long minute or two, and then he finally speaks. "You did well today, Brooke."

"Thanks," I mumble. "I'm not as good as the other girls—"

"Give yourself a break. You're new at this," he says. "I'm new at it, too. I've never done coaching before. But…I imagine if we work at it, we'll both have things figured out before long?"

I nod, both to appease him and as a promise to myself. Despite my inexperience, they do need me. Seven players are better than six. But it's obvious the team's practice times won't be enough to get me caught up. I grab my bag and head for the skate rental counter and grab an open skate schedule.

While I'm at the counter, Kendra and Samantha exit the locker room. I hear Kendra whisper, not quietly enough, to Samantha. "My grandma said her dad is in jail. What do you think he did?"

My cheeks flame. I turn away from them and pretend to read the brochure in my hands.

"They're idiots," someone says from beside me.

I look over, and Rosie is standing a foot away, her eyes trained on the door Kendra and Samantha are about to exit through.

"Seriously," she says. "Both have perfect stay-at-home moms. Sam's dad is an orthodontist and Kendra's dad is an optometrist. The only reason they're gossiping about you is because they can't even imagine something different than their boring, perfect homes. You know what I mean?"

I shrug, trying to make it seem like it isn't a big deal.

"They're okay once you get to know them," Rosie says. "That's what I'm tryin' to say."

Since I don't want to lose this hockey team fantasy before it even begins, I decide it's best to trust her. "Okay."

Rosie glances sideways at me, studies my face to see if I'm cool with this, I'm sure.

"We're going to get pizza if you want to come?" she says so fast I'm not sure if I heard correctly. "My dad's buying. I haven't asked, but I'm sure he will."

I stand there for a long moment, turning this invitation over in my head. If Mr. Smuttley were here right now, he'd tell me to "say yes to making new connections" or "what's the worst that can happen, Brooklynn?"

"I have to ask my grandma," I tell her.

"Don't worry about that." Rosie turns her back to me and yells across the rink lobby at her dad, who's talking to one of the girls from tryouts today and her mother. "Dad! Can you call Judy Gleason and tell her Brooke is going with us to get pizza?"

She doesn't even wait for him to answer, just tugs my arm and drags me toward the exit. "We can wait in the car. I need to charge my phone."

Outside, the cold air hits me hard, and I rush to zip my coat.

Rosie sees me freezing to death and laughs. "This is nothing—just wait until January."

"Not sure I'm gonna make it," I tell her.

"You're a sophomore, right?" she asks, then points to a police cruiser parked out front of the rink. I nod and follow behind her. "Fifteen or sixteen?"

"Sixteen," I say.

She opens the door to the back seat and hops in. I hesitate, not ready to jump in a cop car. Rosie leans over the front seat—the keys were left in the ignition—and starts the car.

I slide in and start to shut the door to the back seat, but Rosie stops me.

"Leave it open a crack; they lock from the inside," she says. "You can probably meet my uncle, Rhett, at the pizza place. They usually go on Mondays or Thursdays. He was an All-American at Minnesota State. Kicked some serious hockey ass…"

She goes on, quoting her uncle's hockey stats, while I wonder—silently—if she has more than one uncle. Because if not, that might mean that I'm about to have pizza with Jake Hammond.

I just wish I could figure out how to not be excited about this possibility. Or how to keep my stomach from bubbling whenever I see him at school. I went weeks without noticing him, and then last Friday happened and he's suddenly on my radar; he's everywhere. Having a crush on the older, popular guy is a recipe for disaster. I know that better than anyone because I made the same mistake last year.

Chapter Eleven

–JAKE–

"I'm just sayin' that you could use some work on stops, turns, puck handling," a familiar voice says from behind me.

I glance over my shoulder, and I'm not surprised to see Rosie walking through the doors of Pizza House. But instead of my uncle being the recipient of Rosie's bossiness, Brooke Parker is with her.

She catches me staring and looks away immediately. A feeling of unease sweeps over me. I wait until they've ordered and are heading over to the pinball machines before I approach Brooke.

She's playing the Simpsons pinball machine while Rosie is annihilating the plastic buttons on the side of her machine.

I lean my good arm against the metal side of Brooke's game. "So...excited that you made the team?"

She gives me this look like, *You're kidding, right?*

"Okay, so everyone made the team. Makes it easier, right? No guesswork..." Now I'm rambling. I'm not good at this kind of thing. When it comes to talking to girls, I'm usually the nice one. Although technically I'm being nice, just with selfish motives.

She ignores me and focuses on the game, only she keeps messing up. It might be the thick coat she refuses to take off restricting her maneuvering abilities. But it is sort of cute how she's still all bundled up despite being inside a warm place.

I trace my finger over the metal edge of the machine. "Texas is a little warmer, I guess."

Brooke bangs a hand on the side button, releases a frustrated breath, then glances around the restaurant. Before I can even react, she grips the front of my shirt and nudges me backward until I fall into a booth. I'm so focused on the shooting pain in my arm and shoulder from her abrupt move that I barely notice her slide in beside me.

"Ow," I mutter, rubbing the outside of my sling.

She doesn't look guilty or even a little bit sympathetic. She leans in close and whispers, "Did you hear about Elliott?"

My heart literally drops to my stomach. I have to clear my throat before saying, "What—I mean, what happened?"

Brooke doesn't say anything for a long moment, just seems to be studying my face. "Good."

"Good? What the hell does that mean?"

If something happened to him, my dad or Oz would have told me right away, definitely before Brooke. Right?

"Good that you care what happens to him," Brooke whispers. "I promised *you* I wouldn't tell anyone, not that psychopath."

Psychopath. She must mean Red. "So Elliott...he's the same?"

The same as in not dead. I swallow the lump in my throat.

She nods and leans in closer. My heart picks up speed; I have a strong desire to unzip that thick jacket of hers and give us room to get even closer.

She catches me checking her out, leans back a few inches.

"Don't…" she says so quietly it echoes in my brain like a slap to the face.

No need to explain. I get the message. She doesn't need anything else from me. She really was doing me a favor but not for this asshole version of me.

"I'm sorry," I say.

Her shoulders visibly relax. She nods.

And for just a second, the fear of getting in trouble, getting my team in trouble, all of that…it just disappears, and I see last Friday night from her perspective. What made her run out on that ice to get me? She must have thought I was going to drown. She must have imagined me dying and felt compelled to stop me. And here I was acting like a shallow asshole tonight.

Her hand rests against the vinyl booth right near my knee. I shift my hand until my fingers brush hers.

"Are you okay?" I ask. "You aren't hurt or…?" *Traumatized?*

My fingers wrap around hers, and I detect a pull between us, her chest moving closer to mine. The world disappearing around us. But then she seems to jolt to life, her hand jerking away. She jumps to her feet and turns her back on me.

"There you are!" I hear Rosie say. "You gotta try the *Blade Runner* game. It's impossible to win."

I'm still watching Brooke walk away, the shock of her abrupt departure fresh, when Dad slides into the booth across from me.

His eyebrows are up. "Do I even want to know what that was about?"

Probably. I shake my head. "Just hockey stuff. Coaching."

"Coaching," Dad repeats, but I hear, *Bullshit.* "Dr.

Reynolds called, said your MRI looks good."

I perk up. "Really? What does that mean?"

"Probably six weeks, including some rehab if all goes as well as possible," he tells me. "Before the New Year you'll be off the bench."

Before the New Year. Before playoffs and all the important games of the season. I can do this. I can.

But then my mind wanders back to Elliott Pratt. Will he be okay by New Year's? Obviously he wanted to try out for the freshman team if he showed up at the pond and the pickup game last Friday.

It was easier to accept what happened to Elliott while feeling sorry for myself about being injured. But if I'm okay and he's not…

I stare at my dad. He's a lawyer; he could handle this if I just told him the truth. Which he has to know already. From his own experience.

"Jake?" Dad prompts. "What is it?"

"Nothing…" I glance down at my sling. "I just—I feel bad about Elliott. Here I am worrying about hockey—"

"It was an accident," Dad says sternly. "And of course we can worry about him, but *you're* my priority. It's my job to make sure things are okay for you. Try to move past this, okay?"

I hear what he's saying between the words: Don't stir up anything when it's calm like this. My dad has always avoided the serious talks with me. He keeps things polite, gets out of a situation when there's too much drama. And he keeps me out of it. We aren't ever the source of town gossip. We're probably the most transparent family in town.

But he's right. The best thing to do is try to move on. As long as Elliott Pratt is okay, I'll be able to do that. I think.

Chapter Twelve

–JAKE–

"Five-hour practice on a Sunday?" I say to Oz. "That's a lot even for my team."

Oz shrugs. He's off duty today—the deputy sheriff covers Sundays—and his lack of uniform startles the girls as they arrive at the rink.

"I reserved the aerobics room for two hours," he says. "Thought the team might benefit from some general fitness training. Maybe we can show 'em some things to do on off days."

He stops Samantha and Kendra from putting on their pads and skates. "Workout clothes and running shoes, remember?"

Soon all seven girls are spread out on the mats in the aerobics room, stretching. This community service isn't exactly something I look forward to, but today I'm relieved to be here. Eight days of this—not playing hockey, being trapped in this sling—and I'm going crazy. Before, I studied so that I was allowed to keep playing hockey, I played video games because my friends loved it, same with parties and all that shit. I messed around on my laptop because the rink had to close at some point and I could only stay outside in the winter for so long before frostbite became a thing.

Everything about my life revolved around hockey.

Past tense.

What if my dad and Dr. Reynolds are wrong? What if I can't play this season? Will that mean I won't be recruited or have any chance of getting on that top-player train again?

I set those nasty thoughts aside, distracted by something outside of my head. Most of the girls have stopped their stretches and are staring at Brooke just like I am. She's sitting on the floor with her legs completely out to either side of her body. Her stomach is flat on the mat and she's just chillin' like that, relaxed.

"Okay, that's just messed up," Kendra says. "How are you doing that?"

"How are you not screaming in pain?" Rosie adds.

Brooke finally notices them, tugs her earbuds out. "Sorry, what?"

"Nothing," Samantha says. "We were just watching you turn into Elastigirl or whatever."

Brooke seems embarrassed by this and shifts into a less conspicuous stretch. Uncle Oz moves beside me and says in a low voice, "Think we should be training her as a goalie? Aren't goalies flexible?"

I force myself to look away from her legs, hugged by those skin-tight leggings. I replay what she said at the pizza place the other night, that one word—don't. *I'm not an asshole*, I repeat inside my head, trying to believe it. *She's a player; you're a coach. Be a fucking professional.*

There. That should do the trick.

"Flexible or over six feet tall," I say in response to Oz, though I can't believe he doesn't know this shit. "I think you need an experienced goalie. It's pretty important."

Even though what I just said is completely true, I can't help watching Brooke with a new eye while Oz sets up all the girls on their own treadmills. Yes, she's inexperienced in hockey but she's learning fast, probably faster than she realizes.

"You girls don't have the advantage of three sets of players to rotate through. You're gonna have to skate nearly the entire game, and that takes endurance," Oz tells them.

He hops on a treadmill himself, and I stand there, itching to join them and run off some of this frustration and boredom. I've never been the guy on the bench. Never. And it sucks.

But it's too soon to run. I'd do some serious damage to my collarbone and undo any healing that may have happened already.

I stretch out on the mats and prepare to take a nap. Sleeping with this broken bone isn't easy and, as a result, I'm always tired. But Oz yells for the girls to increase their speed, and I hear one or two beeps from each girl's treadmill except for Brooke's. She hits that up arrow at least five times. Her legs are pumping twice as fast as everyone else's, even Oz, and he's done marathons. Can't control a hockey stick to save his life but the guy can run.

I climb to my feet and wander behind the treadmills, checking out everyone's speed.

Samantha—6.2

Rosie—6.5

Kendra—5.6

I reach my good arm over Kendra and knock her speed up to 6.0. She opens her mouth to protest, but I give her a look that hopefully says, *Laziness will get you nowhere.* It feels wrong to say that out loud, but I can think it.

Brooke—7.7

"Not bad, but can you keep it up?" I mumble more to myself than her. She'll probably crash any minute.

But thirty minutes later and she's still going strong, even faster. Oz ends the cardio workout at forty minutes, and several of the girls are bright red, drenched in sweat, and panting.

Despite his lack of hockey knowledge, he's right to get them running. At this rate they aren't gonna make it through three periods of a hockey game. Not without more players or lots of cardio.

Except for Brooke. She could make it through. Except she's only been playing hockey for a week. That will likely be problematic.

Oz takes the team through some box drills, basic plyometrics to test how quickly their muscles work. Rosie shines here—no surprise, she's a Hammond. But again, Brooke Parker does surprise me. She's quick, on and off the box. So fast, her neon tennis shoes are just a blur.

Later, when the team is padded up and back on the ice, I mentally retreat to that place where I hate everything about coaching, especially when I can't just pick up a stick and show them what I'm trying to explain in words.

My vision hazes over, my brain tuning out the sounds around me. Until I notice a worn-out blue and white jersey flying past my spot in the center of the rink. I follow the skater, sharpen my focus.

Oz approaches me, his gaze following the team going around and around the rink. "Are you seeing this?"

Yeah, Oz, I'm definitely seeing this.

Brooke glides past two other girls, and soon she's right

behind Rosie. Rosie glances over her shoulder, does a double take, and then speeds up.

"That's impossible," I say, shaking my head. "It's only been five days—"

Brooke attempts to stop but ends up crashing into the wall, taking Rosie down with her.

"She's gotta learn to stop," Oz muses.

"No kidding," I say, shaking my head. I knew it was too good to be true. But damn, if she can get that much better in five days, what else can this girl do?

Chapter Thirteen

–BROOKE–

My legs are heavy as lead right now. I work hard to put one foot in front of the other. Today's workout was tough—the kind that will take several days to recover from.

"Parker!" Sheriff Hammond shouts, stopping me from leaving the ice rink. He jogs over and hands me a giant bottle of orange Gatorade. "Electrolytes. Get them in. Today and tomorrow."

"Thanks," I say, looking like I've surprised him a little. I take a big swig of the drink and watch the Otter varsity team pour out of the guys' locker room. Cole, from my Oral Communications group, spots me and waves, but he doesn't come over to talk. Not that I expected him to, but it might be nice to have someone besides the town sheriff and high school guidance counselor strike up a conversation. And Rosie, though she hasn't talked to me much since the pizza place the other night.

Jake is still here, and the sight of his teammates in full gear heading out onto the ice without him is clearly difficult for him to witness. He turns his attention to the rental counter, where an old woman is handing Red what looks like an Otter hockey jersey. The woman spreads the jersey out on the counter and points to a large C sewn on the shoulder. Jake's jaw tenses, his body rigid. Red catches him watching and quickly balls up the jersey and tucks it under his arm. The coach glares at Jake, and then turns his back on us.

Sheriff Hammond places a hand on Jake's shoulder, squeezes it. "Come get some dinner with Rosie and me?"

"I'm not hungry." Jake jerks away from his uncle, shoves the door open, and then calls over his shoulder, "Tell my mom I'm walking home."

Rosie appears at the glass doors, watches Jake stalk off across the parking lot. "Want me to follow him?"

Sheriff studies his nephew's retreating form and then shakes his head. "Nah, give him space. Can't be easy."

"Can't be easy for Elliott Pratt, either," Rosie says under her breath.

Wow. So even his own cousin blames him for what happened to Elliott.

"Enough of that," Sheriff says. "We don't know the whole story."

I glance between the sheriff and Jake, and then I push through the doors, heading after him.

He crosses the railroad tracks just like I do every day and then goes the long way around Grandma's house, over to the edge of the pond. I'm beat, so it takes everything in me to follow him farther, into the woods.

Eventually, when we're deep in the trees, the old farmhouse no longer in sight, he stops walking, turns sharply to face me. "What are you doing?"

I make him wait forever—not intentionally, but I'm stuck here taking in his handsome yet surprisingly vulnerable face, his nose red from the cold, the way he wears that sling like a thick unwanted sweater on a hot day.

"Are you—" I start, but the sound of my own voice in the silent woods startles me. I clear my throat, try again. "Are you okay?"

His look is one of disbelief and exasperation. "Am I okay? Seriously? No, I'm not fucking okay!"

He shouts that last part, and I fight the instinct to back away. Because I think that's really the problem right now. Everyone else in his life is backing away.

"He made Red captain? Seriously?" He lifts a hand, gesturing in the direction of the ice rink. "I'm supposed to be there right now. Practicing, getting ready for the first game. In a month, I was gonna sign my letter of intent. Pick a college like my dad…"

His voice breaks and he stops, takes a gulp of air. "My dad is doing everything he can to fix this, but he doesn't want to talk about it, won't let me talk about it. I don't think he trusts me. And Coach Bakowski treats injured players like they have leprosy. He hates weakness—makes him nauseous, or at least that's what it looks like. Is that what it looked like to you? Did you see him glare at me like I shouldn't be wearing a sling or whatever?"

I take a step closer. Leaves crunch beneath my running shoes.

"Here I am feeling sorry for myself that I can't have every little thing I want." He leans against a nearby tree, rests his head back. His eyes close. "And Elliott Pratt is… Well, he's in bad shape. I keep seeing him lying there, his eyes closed, blue in the face—"

Jake raises his head suddenly, looks right at me. "You saw it, right? You saw him fall through the ice?"

This is what I think he was trying to ask me the other night at the pizza place. Right before things got a little... Well, I don't know what was happening, but it wasn't something I was willing to let play out on its own. Not with this guy. Not with Mr. Popular Hockey Star.

After a long beat, I nod.

"What were you thinking, going out on the ice like that after you saw two people fall through?"

I shake my head, look down at my hands. "I don't know. I just... I don't know."

A long, awkward silence follows, and then Jake exhales. "Well, thanks. Should have said it the other night, but I was too busy trying to see if you were going to tell anyone."

A laugh escapes before I can stop it, and when I look up again, Jake is laughing, too.

"Sorry," he says, still laughing. "It's not funny."

I pull myself together, and I'm about to head home but Jake says, "Want to see something cool?"

And for reasons I can't quite figure out, I follow him.

Chapter Fourteen

–JAKE–

I lead Brooke through the thickest part of the woods, being careful not to trip on any fallen branches or tree roots. After about a ten-minute walk, the woods open a little, and the tree house my dad and I built nearly a decade ago enters our view. I tug the rope ladder with my good arm until it hangs down in front of me.

Wordlessly, I invite Brooke into my ten-year-old self's sacred space by climbing the rope ladder—one-handed—and holding it steady for her to follow. Her brown ponytail reaches the opening, and then she easily lifts herself up and onto the tree-house floor. I watch her look around, take in the carefully placed window with a telescope and binoculars. The pillows and blankets strewn all over one half of the tree house.

I spot the plastic green army men at the same time she does, and I quickly scoop them up, toss them into a metal trunk. "Those have been here forever. Probably should throw them out or donate them."

She smiles but at least doesn't laugh. I make a shift move to the window, grab the binoculars, and offer them to her.

When she's got them up to her face, I point out the window. "Look right there…"

I move to the other side, not able to sit still at the moment. I haven't hung out here in a long time, haven't brought a girl here since middle school. I turn on the police scanner that Red and I used to obsess over. The buzz of the device helps alleviate some of the awkward silence.

"That's my house out there in the clearing," I tell her while adjusting the dial on the scanner. "From the rink it's a three-and-a-half-mile drive, but through the woods…a mile, maybe a mile and a quarter tops. Weird how that works, huh?"

Brooke lowers the binoculars and assesses the scanner I'm toying with.

"Police scanner," I tell her. "Stupid yet common small-town hobby. Hearing the gossip the next day isn't soon enough for some people."

The voice of Jimmy Valdez, the deputy sheriff, booms from the scanner. "We've got a possible three-eight-seven, southwest corner of Birchwood and Alpine. Suspect female, white, eighty-four…"

"Do you know what a three-eight-seven is?" I ask Brooke, who shakes her head, her eyes wide with concern. I grin. "It means someone dropped a grocery sack."

Brooke laughs, looking relieved.

"In this case an eighty-four-year-old woman who lives on Birchwood. That would be Mrs. Shoe. She teaches biology at JFH; do you know her?"

She nods, laughing some more. It's a nice sound.

"I'm not that into town gossip, I swear," I say, though I

don't know why it feels important to get this across. "But my friends and I used to come up here and listen to the scanner just to pretend we were my uncle Oz, wearing a holster and gun, pulling people over or saving the day."

My face warms at that. It sounds stupid now, looking back. But a few years back, this scanner was about the coolest thing my friends and I owned combined.

The grocery sack left behind spurs way too much back-and-forth chatter. I turn the volume down on the scanner until it's a low hum. "Deputy Sheriff Valdez loves to hear himself talk. It gets old real fast."

She leans against my pillows on the other side of the tree house and stares at me in the intrusive way she'd done that day at the rink, during the pickup game. I twist my hands, nervous.

"I bet scanners in Austin would be way more interesting. Probably real fights and weapons…" I stop rambling because she looks stricken all of a sudden, like I hit a nerve or opened an old wound. I sink back against the tree-house wall and debate silently until I finally decide to ask her a real question.

"My uncle said you had a tough time back in Austin…? He didn't tell me anything specific, just that it was tough and…" Jesus, this is going well. "Anyway, I'm sorry."

Her unwavering stare does nothing to help the awkward silence, but she eventually does say, quietly, "Thanks."

I pick at a loose bit of rubber on the sole of my shoe. "I get it—you don't want to talk about it. There's a lot of shit that I don't want to talk about…but I did talk about it a few minutes ago and, well, it kinda helped. You know?"

Okay, what the hell am I doing? Trying to be a therapist? I'm the last person who should be doing anything like that.

She chews on one of her thumbnails. "I fell for the most

popular guy in school—a hockey player—and he broke my heart."

For several seconds I panic, words failing to exit my mouth. Then Brooke cracks a smile.

I sink back against the wall. "Not funny." But maybe I deserved it for the other night at the pizza place.

"The look on your face made it worth it," she says, then her smile fades. "But I was only partly kidding. He was a basketball player."

I wait for more, and when it doesn't come, I say, "I'm not sure what you mean. Or what that has to do with me?"

She rolls her eyes. "You manipulated me. Used your popularity to try to get what you wanted."

But it wasn't my popularity that convinced her to keep quiet. She's trying to toss me into a box that both of us know I don't fit in, not completely.

"Then what are you doing here?" I prompt.

Brooke just shakes her head as if to say, *I have no idea.*

Normally I'm a bit slow to pick up on these signals but tonight, I'm pretty sure she just opened a door. Only a crack, but still. Those feelings from the other night at the pizza place return, and I'm fighting the urge to move closer, to let our fingers touch again. But the floor beneath my feet lifts and I jolt back. The door to the tree house swings open, revealing first a blond ponytail and then a familiar face, one I've been avoiding for more than a week now.

"Halcy, what are you doing here?"

She continues her climb and then pulls herself up the rest of the way. "Your dad told me where you were. I wanted to check on you; we haven't talked since…"

I point a finger at the sling my arm is trapped in, and Haley nods.

"Wow, I haven't been up here in forever—" Haley's gaze

finally lands on Brooke, and it's clear this girl is possibly the last person she expected to see with me. "Oh, hi… Sorry, I didn't mean to—"

Brooke is all wide-eyed, probably imagining her name popping up on the police scanner with Deputy Jimmy's voice telling the town where she's been hanging out for the last thirty minutes. Can't really blame her—I mean, that *is* basically how things work around here.

"I was just showing Brooke how police scanners work. Apparently, people in Austin don't like to get into one another's business." Brooke looks terrified, so I shift the attention to Haley instead. "Brooke, have you met Haley Stevenson? Head cheerleader, role model for little sisters like mine, dating the smartest guy in our class, princess of Juniper Falls—"

Haley flinches at the mention of princess for some reason, but then she rolls her eyes at me. "Thanks for the oral résumé, Jake. But we've met. I'm teacher's aid for her communications class."

"Oh, forgot to mention habitual volunteer and do-gooder and aspiring teacher," I add, hoping to resolve some of the panic on Brooke's face.

No such luck. She moves quickly toward the opening and the rope ladder, and I'm already reeling at how much worse this will look if she actually takes off running without an excuse.

"I have to go," she says quickly. "My grandma's probably worried."

Haley definitely has those wheels inside her head spinning in all directions, but like the pro she is, she smiles like this isn't weird. "See you in first period. Brooke, not Brooklyn?"

Brooke pauses for half a second to glance at Haley and

nod. Then she panics all over again and climbs quickly down the ladder. While Haley shuts the door to the tree house, I watch Brooke run, faster than she'd run on the treadmill earlier today, through the woods and out of sight. Guilt fills the pit of my stomach. I should have just told her thanks and left her alone.

"Well, that was interesting," Haley says in the most leading way.

I study Haley carefully, wanting to trust her but also reminding myself that she and I haven't been as close since that party almost a year ago. The party where both of us had way too little to eat and way too much to drink. She was trying too hard to get over her breakup with Tate, and I made the mistake of making it my responsibility to make sure she was having fun that night. Stir all of that together and you get a big pot of almost-sex and awkward after-the-fact conversations.

But we've been better since she finally got over Tate and then she and Fletcher Scott got together over the summer. I don't know all the details of their relationship, but if Brooke and I seem like an unlikely pair, it's nothing compared to Haley and Fletch. Not that Brooke and I are anything. She's not into asshole hockey players. But am I into quiet sophomore girls who risk their lives to rescue me from frozen water and have amazing legs and lips that I can't seem to stop eyeing—?

Oh shit. I *am* into her.

"Don't make a big thing of this. There's nothing between us," I tell Haley, trying to mean it. My eyes narrow at the grin that twitches her mouth. "I'm serious. You mention this to anyone and you're gonna give that poor girl an anxiety attack or something. You saw her just now, right? She completely freaked. Probably imagining the rumors that our town can spin."

The grin drops from Haley's face. "Hey, I'm not in the market of hurting people. You should know that about me."

I study her again. She's right. I do know that about Haley. I glance out the window; it's almost dark. Hopefully Brooke can find her way home. "I'm helping Oz with the girls' hockey team."

Haley gets comfortable in Brooke's spot near the big fluffy pillows. "I heard something about that. And...?"

"And Brooke is on the team." I exhale, forcing myself to tell her some of the truth. "After practice today, the guys were coming out of the locker room, onto the ice, and I..."

"Had a moment?" Haley offers when I don't finish the sentence.

"Yeah, you could say that." I brave looking at her.

"A girl ice hockey player from Texas," Haley muses. "Definitely a surprising twist to her story."

"Well." I laugh. "'Ice hockey player' might be a bit of a stretch. It's only been a week."

"Don't be a snob," Haley warns. "Not everyone grows up wearing skates."

"It's not an opinion; it's a fact," I argue. "She's never played, has barely skated before."

"Okay, I see your point," Haley says. "But enough about the sophomore who is clearly not on your radar."

I sink back against the wall again and secretly hope that my dad or mom shows up to interrupt. I've been avoiding Haley for a reason.

"What happened with Elliott Pratt, Jake?" she demands. "You have to tell me something..."

"You want to know if I hurt that kid on purpose? Or maybe you heard the rumor where I sexually violated him? He was naked, after all."

Haley's face flushes, but she holds my gaze steady. "If I believed any of that, do you think I would be here right now?"

"It was an accident," I tell her, but it feels so fake that I add, "but I'm not completely innocent."

"What are you, then, Jake?"

"Human. A product of more than a hundred years of hockey rituals." I laugh drily, hating the version of me who believes that shit. "I'm the guy who said jump."

The truth of that statement hits me hard after it's tumbled from my lips. I'm the guy who said jump. There is no changing that. And I said it knowing the clout I have in my town, in my school, like Brooke said, using my popularity to manipulate. I was in a position of power, and that command holds a lot more weight than a request among equals. As captain of the team, it was my responsibility to understand that.

"If you were me, what would you do?" I ask Haley.

"I don't know." She shakes her head. "I wasn't there; I don't know what—"

"No, I mean now," I interrupt.

She sits straighter, draws in a breath. "Well…the way I see it, you have two options. Let all the rumors and negativity get to you so much that you decide it's best to quit hockey and maybe even drop out of school."

I open my mouth to argue, but she lifts a hand to stop me.

"Worked for Mike Steller," she points out. "Or you can grow that tough skin you've only needed for Coach Bakowski until now and pray for Elliott if that's your thing, serve your time, offer your apologies, keep your grades up, and rehab the injury. The second you're allowed and healthy enough, you get back on the ice. It's who you are, Jake. And I can't—no, I *won't* believe that there is no end to this nightmare you're in right now."

I tug at the rubber on my shoe again, processing each bit of Haley's advice slowly. "Guess I don't need to ask which of those two options you recommend."

Haley laughs. "Sorry, I'm opinionated. If you want impartial, ask someone else."

"Mike Steller was about to become a father when he bailed on hockey and school," I say, referring to the guy who started out as captain and our number one goalie last season. His girlfriend was pregnant, he had to work three jobs, his parents kicked him out... Hard to keep showing up at practice while dealing with all of that.

"I know, but I still think he didn't have to give up everything," Haley says. "Deep down, I think he regrets it. It was a big eff-you moment that he needed in the short term, but now...?"

I sit on that for a bit, not sure if I can agree with her.

"So basically, I should accept Red as captain, do my homework, let people gossip about me doing something—God knows what—with a naked freshman, and follow the doctor's orders," I repeat, just to make sure I've got the plan down.

"And take this coaching job seriously. Our town needs a girls' team at the high school," she says. "I would be all over that if I were a freshman or sophomore."

"If we had you on the team," I tell her, thinking out loud, "we'd be something to talk about."

At least Haley used to be an amazing hockey player. We grew up playing peewee hockey together, playing on the pond. My guess is that she's still got those skills.

"It sounds like those girls have nowhere to go but up, and maybe you can be the one to get them there." Haley lifts the door open again and swings a leg down. "I'm on your side, Jake. Keep that in mind when you're dealing with everything else."

"What about Fletcher?" I ask tentatively, because he's been avoiding me as much as I tried to avoid Haley.

She sighs. "Fletch is putting all this through his own filter. He doesn't know you like I do. And he's got big issues with any kind of bullying."

I release a breath. "Okay, that's good to know, I guess."

Not that we were ever very close, but all summer we'd been practicing together, and he seemed cool with me.

"Tough skin," Haley reminds me. "And leave the poor sophomore girl alone. You're a little too easy to fall in love with, you know?"

"Speaking from experience?" I challenge, knowing the answer already. Haley and I have had more than enough time together to fall in love. It would have happened already.

"You've always been in a serious, monogamous relationship with hockey," Haley says cryptically.

And then she leaves me alone.

I stay there until my toes are numb, wondering if Haley is right. Maybe my reluctance to get involved with anyone isn't only about the pitfalls of dating in a small town. Not that my concerns regarding said small-town dating aren't valid—they absolutely are—but if I really wanted someone, I probably wouldn't care about any of that.

When I finally head home, my parents are sitting at the kitchen table. I can't keep holding all of this in, pretending I'm okay with just moving forward as my dad said to do. So I take this opportunity to speak my mind while I've got both of them together.

"I want to go see Elliott Pratt," I tell them. "Maybe one of you can take me there? Or go with me…?"

My dad glances at Mom, taps his fingers against the table.

"Not sure that's such a good idea."

My hand stills on the refrigerator door handle. "Why not?"

"We met with the Pratts' lawyer this afternoon," Mom says, eyeing me warily.

The Pratts' lawyer. My stomach turns. "Lawyer? Why?"

"Elliott didn't grow up here, and neither did his mother," Dad reminds me.

I forgot that Elliott and Luke Pratt—my least favorite senior when I was a freshman—are stepbrothers, not actual brothers.

"But Elliott has the same last name as Luke?" I say.

"Ronnie adopted him, since his father's never been in the picture." Dad takes a long swig of his coffee.

"Your dad handled the paperwork," Mom chimes in, and I hear a hint of bitterness in her voice. "Didn't charge Ronnie a penny for it, either."

I sink into the chair between my parents.

"They want to sue the school district for not preventing what they're calling a 'hazing incident,'" Dad explains, then after a deep breath says, "and they plan to make you testify as a negative by-product of the school's hockey program."

Mom flinches at hearing this, though I'm sure it's not the first time. "We don't know that's what they want from Jake…"

Dad gives her a look. "Yes, we do."

"It isn't only the Pratts," Mom says. "It's the two other freshman boys… They admitted to being at the pond last Friday after Oz found their clothes—"

I squeeze my eyes shut, waiting for the nightmare to end. "So they want money?"

"No." Dad drums his fingers on the table. "All three families agreed to let the school hold a hearing and investigate the matter. If they take appropriate action, then the lawsuit will be dropped."

"A hearing," I repeat. "Guessing that involves me?"

"And your uncle," Mom answers with a solemn nod.

Dad almost looks afraid when he says, "You and Uncle Oz are expected to give a statement."

"A statement?" I ask. "Like an apology?"

Mom eyes me wearily. "They want the story. They need you to tell them what happened last Friday night."

"It's really about the hockey team," Dad tells me. "They want to know if this was a team effort or just one bad guy."

I look from my dad to my mom. I don't know what Mom knows about Friday. Which means I don't know what to say it was, a team effort or…just me? Both options sound horrible. Equally horrible.

"Jake, listen to me," Dad says. "You don't have to sell out the whole team. But we can't just leave you as the monster in the story. It will ruin your life, son. If we just throw a few more names into the mix, suddenly you're one of several. You tell the board that someone dared the Pratt boy to go out onto the ice as a joke, you tried to stop him, but he still fell through. And then we get character witnesses on the stand—"

"The stand?" Mom says. "It's not a trial. Don't make it into something it isn't, Rhett."

"You're right." Dad nods. "We'll ask individuals who know you to tell the board what a good person you are, a team player… And soon you're just the guy who was along for the ride. We can smooth it over with colleges recruiting you; I can work with that plan. But the way it is now…"

I glance over at my mother again. Color has drained from her face, but her voice is steady when she speaks. "We aren't asking you to lie, honey. We know you weren't there alone."

My sister yells for Mom from upstairs, and my mother stands, pats my hand. "Just think about it, promise? We know what's best for you."

"Okay," I promise her, hoping it will bring back some color to her face. When she's upstairs, though, I turn to my dad. "Who exactly am I supposed to name?"

"Coach put together a list." Dad glances over my shoulder, then he slides a piece of paper across the table. "These are guys who, unlike you, don't have offers yet from colleges, probably won't have any. This will be a slap on the wrist for them."

My stomach is sick when I look down at the names Bakowski and my dad conjured out of thin air.

Paul Redman
Casey Overstreet
Lance Ellis
Fletcher Scott

"Fletcher Scott?" I stare at Dad, trying to figure out if he knows that Fletcher wasn't even there Friday night. "You know he hasn't been on the team very long, right?"

"Exactly," Dad says. "He's not a contender for college hockey. Bakowski only put him on the team as a favor to Coach Ty."

"He's really good," I argue. "A junior team signed him already, asked him to start right away, but he wants to play out this season—"

"Bakowski said that's just a rumor floating around the high school," Dad says dismissively. "Has *he* told you about the junior team? Have you seen any evidence of this?"

"No, he hasn't, but…" Fletcher isn't the type to talk about himself.

"When the police questioned him, he admitted that he wasn't home Friday night, and he refused to say where he was."

The police questioned him? No wonder Fletch isn't talking to me anymore.

"He wasn't there," I say firmly. "I'm not naming him."

My dad releases a frustrated groan. "Work with me a little here, Jake. I'm trying to dig you out of a very deep hole, and I swear to you, my goal is to have the most gain with the least amount of impact. Leave the Scott kid out of it if you want; the others will be enough."

And the others were actually there last Friday night.

I stare down at the paper until my dad finally stands, preparing to go to his office. He gives me one last look as if to say, *Do the right thing.* "Have your mother help you press a shirt and tie for the hearing. It's tomorrow night."

"Tomorrow?" I say, but he's already walking away. Why is it so soon?

I climb the steps to my bedroom and close the door behind me. The piece of paper burns in my hand. I stare at it, trying to justify this plan. Trying to justify Coach Bakowski and my dad sitting in a room conjuring up Fletcher Scott's name, deciding he was a hopeless cause and might as well sink with this ship I'm on. I knew my dad wasn't above bending some rules here and there, but this is surprising. Then again, the second I told him point-blank that Fletch wasn't there, I could see that flicker of panic on his face. And he was quick to concede and leave him out of it. He's willing to have me name some of the guys who were there but not someone who wasn't, not if I've officially confirmed his absence.

Even if I don't consider the fact that they're asking me to sell out my best friend and two other guys who have been my teammates for three years, no matter what angle I look at this from, I can't get past the fact that Coach is willing to sacrifice Fletcher's reputation, his record, to get an overall better outcome for the team in this bad situation. So now if you become an Otter hockey player, you're fair game for *whatever* the team might need you for? Even off the ice?

Maybe Coach was just getting desperate? Or maybe he thought Fletch was there that night?

Either way, I can't mention Fletcher tomorrow. But the other guys… Maybe Dad's right. Maybe that's the best possible solution.

Chapter Fifteen

–BROOKE–

"Stay on your outside edges when you turn," Jake shouts from the center of the ice.

I assume it's directed at me because I'm usually the one doing things incorrectly, but I'm too sore from yesterday's five-hour practice to convince my body to do something different. Too sore and too deep inside my head.

When I got up this morning, my mother was awake, standing in the kitchen, looking sort of happy. By "happy" I mean that she wasn't crying or wearing the drug-induced zombie face I've become so familiar with. Grandma and I both tried our best to not make a big deal of it, but it was hard to hide the surprise and fake calm from my voice.

Mom had put a bowl of cereal and the jar of milk on the table in front of me even though I've grown accustomed to skipping breakfast. Then she sat down across from me, her hand wrapped around a mug of coffee, and it was like we were back in Austin. I half expected my dad to emerge in his worn-out jeans and untucked button-down shirt.

"So…" Mom had said, smiling at me. "We need to celebrate your birthday."

Grandma joined us at the table, nudging the cereal box closer to me, directing me silently with her eyes. I could only nod and pour. I was too afraid to pop this bubble by pointing out that my birthday came and went. A month ago.

"Sixteen," she said. "That's a big birthday. What would you like to do to celebrate?"

I stared, frozen, until Grandma tossed me a look, urging me to answer. "Pizza," I said, dumbly. "And cake."

That's basically the most generic clichéd party ever. But somehow my mom accepted this answer and stood, preparing to get more coffee. "Pizza and cake. That's what we'll do, then."

Even though this hockey stuff has been a great escape, mentally I'm not in it today. I just want to run home and see if she's still there, like that. Like this morning.

"You're offsides!" Jake shouts. "Brooke!"

I jerk my head to look over at him, realizing that he likely said my name a few times before this. Also, I forgot what offsides means.

"Are you in this or not?" Jake demands. "You were offsides *and* Sam was wide open for a pass. You missed it."

"Sorry," I mutter, and then refocus, vowing to do better. Luckily I have a helmet and mask on, making it difficult for anyone to see my face, which is probably tomato red. "I'm ready now."

Rosie skates up behind me. "Don't take it personally. He's got that school board hearing thing tonight; I'm sure he's all uptight about that."

School board hearing. That doesn't sound good. I glance at Jake. He's tugging at the sling strap around his neck with more force than is needed to adjust the thing.

"And offsides…" Rosie continues. "You went up too far, past the blue line before the puck left the scoring area. That's all it means, and honestly, it happens all the time. Even in pro hockey."

I tell her thanks and stare in surprise. Normally it's Rosie yelling these things and having little patience for explaining. She's the most competitive girl I have ever met.

Sheriff Hammond steps onto the ice and speaks to Jake quietly. Then he addresses all of us. "We're gonna do some shooting drills. Line up in front of the goal and Jake will talk you through it."

"That's right, I'll talk you through it," Jake says drily. Then he waves a hand at someone who is just exiting the locker room.

Cole Clooney.

Cole isn't fully suited up like us, but he's wearing skates and carrying a stick.

"Start with slap shots," Jake instructs. "Then on one foot. After that, add passing before the shots."

He walks away from the group, nods for me to follow. "You get your own goal today."

Cole has already set up a row of pucks along the ice in front of the goal. He slides the puck back and forth, waiting for instructions from Jake.

"Slap shot," Jake starts. "It's the easy one to remember… The puck is stationary; you wind up, swing, and hopefully connect."

Cole demonstrates by swinging and connecting with the first puck in the row he laid out, and it hits the net with such force the goal slides backward. He repeats this, moving from one puck to the next so quickly I can hardly keep up.

"Wow," I mutter.

Jake laughs at my reaction. "He's just showing off. Don't worry about where the puck goes as first. Focus on the technique."

While Cole resets everything for me to do the practice drill, Jake explains how to hold my stick and how to aim. Feeling both sets of eyes on me, I take my place in front of the first puck and focus on it and not the goal. I lift my stick, swinging as hard as I can.

The puck soars through the air, hits the crossbar with a *clank* so loud my ears ring. It rebounds off the metal bar and spins as it heads back my way. Before I can decide how to react, warm hands wrap around my arm, tugging me out of the way. Jake and I end up in a heap on the ice. The puck lands about three inches from my head.

I sit up quickly and turn to Jake. His sling is still on, but it's shifted, his elbow now hanging out of it.

"Oh my God," I say under my breath. "It hit you, didn't it?"

Worry takes over, and soon I'm raising Jake's shirt, staring at a large red welt forming on his side.

Cole skates over, pulls Jake to his feet. "You okay, man?"

"Fine," Jake says, dismissing the huge red mark.

I leave my helmet on the ice and scramble to my feet. "I'm sorry... Maybe I shouldn't do this again—"

"You are definitely doing that again," Jake says, grinning now. "You might have a killer slap shot."

The "killer" part definitely seems likely. I look from Jake to Cole. "Are you sure?"

"Yes," both of them say together.

To my surprise, Jake doesn't move to a safer location. I'm even more nervous this time, facing the next puck. But the nerves help me concentrate, and instead of coming back at me, the puck hits the net and stops.

Jake's eyebrows lift slightly, but he says nothing. I move to the next one, put even more force into it. The puck bounces off the sidebar and heads straight for Cole. He easily dodges it, looking unfazed.

I practice thirty slap shots total, and only make eight of them, but Jake and Cole both seem thrilled by this number. When we take a five-minute break, Cole arranges himself nearby the other girls but doesn't make an effort to talk to them. He does glance at Rosie several times, glancing away when she looks over at him.

"So that's why he agreed to help me today," Jake muses, watching the same painful scene I'm watching. "Rosie will eat him alive and then arrange his bones into an abstract art piece."

I look at him questioningly. Rosie can be intense, but she's not *that* intense. "I didn't know that she's an artist."

Jake laughs. "Yeah, 'cause that was the point I wanted to make."

I turn around to face him, see him raising his shirt again. The red welt is now turning a dark purple. "Jesus... Are you okay?" I ask, reaching out on instinct to touch it.

Slowly, he slides his hand down, forcing his shirt back down but also bumping into my hand in the process. His eyes meet mine, and the warm fingers touching mine turn hot. I move back, taking my hand with me before I even can process the electric buzz that shot through me.

Jake clears his throat. "You're definitely gonna play forward. I'll let Oz know."

He walks away, and I don't follow this time. My heart is racing, and it's not from the workout. And I think Jake felt something, too. This wasn't him trying to get me to like him; it was something else entirely.

After Jake talks to Sheriff Hammond, he leaves. Coach

gathers us up and calls an end to practice. I hurry into the locker room, showering and changing as fast as I can.

When I get home, the house is warm with the scent of dinner cooking. I drop my hockey bag in the mudroom and enter the kitchen, unsure what I'll see. My heart sinks. It's just Grandma lifting a pan out of the oven.

"She's in bed," Grandma says before I can even ask. "Just got her to sleep, so keep your voice down."

Right. 'Cause I'm such a big talker these days.

Grandma places a plate of roast and potatoes onto the table and points for me to sit down. Before moving to Minnesota, I had been a proud vegetarian for four years. But not eating meat is something Grandma doesn't understand at all. We tried it at first, but she just kept serving me vegetables and eggs cooked in bacon grease. I gave it up quickly for fear of starving to death.

Now the roast smells amazing to me. But I'm too scared to pick up my fork and take a bite. Grandma sits across from me, in the same spot my mother had occupied this morning, and releases a weighted breath.

"Your father's lawyer called today," she says. "Nothing new to report on that end, but it set your mom back quite a bit, talking about everything. After her episode, I called the lawyer back myself to find out what he had said to upset her."

She pauses, urging me with her eyes to eat. I can't, but I hold the fork and knife, make a show of cutting the meat.

"The lawyer thinks we need an expert opinion," she tells me. "He did some research, says we should take her to a specialist in Minneapolis. Maybe someone not so focused on pills."

"Okay…?" I say slowly because she had mentioned it like a question, like she isn't sure if it's good advice. I'm so on board with this plan. This is exactly what my mom needs.

"But it's real possible," Grandma adds, "that doctors will want to keep her somewhere, like hospitalized. How do you feel about that?"

I stare down at my hands. How do I feel about that? It would mean both of my parents being trapped somewhere they aren't allowed to leave. But in Mom's case, it could make her better.

"What does she think?" I ask quietly, remembering Grandma's earlier directions.

"Haven't asked her yet," she says. "I wanted to talk to you first."

"Can we…?" I start. "Can we pay for that?"

Grandma looks down at her own plate. "Your folks only have the basic insurance—musician and an artist, not exactly the best job security—so it would mean using some of your college money. Your daddy gave me access to that account so we don't have to tell your mother, won't let that be a factor in her decision."

College feels like a million years away. I don't often agree with Grandma—her world is so much different than the one I grew up in—but tonight I'm with her 100 percent. We can be a team on this.

I offer her a sharp nod, yes to all of it, and she returns the nod, looking satisfied with how this went. I abandon my plate and walk down the hall toward my mother's room. I stand outside the open door, watching her sleep, counting the many prescription bottles at her bedside table. I wonder which one holds the magic pill that got her to sleep tonight.

From the kitchen, I hear Grandma's voice, probably on the phone to one of her many old-lady friends. I didn't know anyone in Austin who had a landline in their house, but Grandma does. Complete with a corded phone confining her to a two-foot radius while talking to someone.

"She hardly said a word... Her college fund at stake and she's quiet as a mouse," Grandma tells whoever she's talking to. I tense, hating eavesdropping. "You know that child used to be such a chatterbox, couldn't get her to ever shut her mouth."

Is that true? Or is that just how Grandma saw me on her twice-yearly visits to Texas?

"No...I don't think it's anything to worry about. I got the feeling she understood most of what I was sayin' to her."

I close the door to Mom's room and head upstairs to get my running shoes. I can't listen to any more of Grandma simplifying my feelings, my identity, to nothing more than too quiet or too talkative, not to mention how she and whoever was on the other end of the phone seem to think "quiet" and "dumb" are synonymous. I know she loves me; she's changed her whole life to take care of Mom and me, but it's hard to love her back knowing that she'll never get me and likely has no idea what's best for me. That's why I don't give a crap about my college fund. I need my mom back. I need someone who gets me and knows what's best for me.

I scribble a quick note for Grandma, saying I went to a program at school, didn't want to disturb her phone call. She'll drill me with questions later, tell me not to do that again, but right now I don't care. I need out.

Outside, across the railroad tracks, cars are pulling into the high school lot. Several men and a couple of women dressed up as if for a business meeting enter the building through the auditorium. I watch for a few minutes and eventually see Jake and his parents heading inside the same entrance.

The school board hearing.

Chapter Sixteen

–JAKE–

The tie squeezes my neck. The sling immobilizing my shoulder weighs more tonight. I debate pulling it off, but I know my arm isn't ready to hang loose. Behind me, I feel my dad's eyes focused on me, sending me answers to questions that haven't even been asked yet. Beside me, Oz taps his foot in a part-soothing, part-annoying rhythm. One by one, the seats placed behind a long table on the stage are filled. Ten seats. Seven men, three women. Three microphones on their table. One on the table Oz and I are sitting at. It's all so official. I didn't know it would be like this. Like a fucking murder trial.

I regret those words the second I think them. Elliott Pratt is still in serious condition. But his parents managed to get here tonight. They're huddled in a pair of seats to my left, far as they can get from my family and me. Releasing a breath, I count the empty seats on the stage—four. I silently repeat the names from Bakowski's list:

Casey Overstreet
Lance Ellis
Paul Redman

That last one will no doubt be the most difficult to say. Couldn't bring myself to warn him in advance. But maybe that's because I'm not completely sure I can say *anyone's* name.

"Hey," Oz says, leaning in closer to me. He glances at the door where Coach Bakowski has just entered and then turns to me again. "I know they've cooked up something for you to say, but trust me on this, Jake, it isn't worth lying—"

"We're ready to begin," one of the male board members says. "We'll start with Sheriff Hammond."

"Yes, sir," my uncle says into the microphone. Then he gives me a look, long and hard, a look that is supposed to convince me to tell the truth. But that has never been one of my options.

"You were the first to arrive at the scene on the evening in question, correct?"

"Yes, sir," Oz says. "Along with Officer Jennings."

"We have the police report, but for the sake of our audience, can you tell us what you saw when you arrived?"

"First thing I noticed was my nephew's truck, running with the headlights on," Oz says slowly, his voice calm and even. "Then I saw a pile of clothing on the ground near the truck. Three pairs of shoes."

I refused eating the dinner my mom made tonight, but the weight in my stomach, it feels like I ate enough for three people.

"Then I saw Elliott Pratt lying about ten feet from the pond, no clothes or shoes, just underpants," Oz tells them. "His skin and lips were blue. He was unresponsive, minimal breath sounds. Couldn't find a pulse…"

My skin prickles, my insides twist, and a chill passes over me as if someone propped open the large auditorium doors. I knew it was bad with Elliott, but I hadn't realized what Oz went through that night.

"I started CPR on the Pratt boy," Oz continues, looking nearly as haunted by this as I feel. "And then Officer Jennings found Jake. He was barely out of the pond, but Jennings said he was breathing, moving around."

"So you stayed with Elliott?" the board member asks.

"Yes, sir," Oz says. "We arrived quite a few minutes before the ambulance. Once they took over with Elliott, Officer Jennings and I got Jake into the squad car and drove him to the hospital. He was waking up by then, talking. I stayed with him in the ER, and Jennings went back to the pond and collected evidence."

That's the first thing I remember after blacking out…the sirens in the sheriff car, the bright lights as we approached the emergency room. I don't remember any paramedics or my uncle doing CPR on Elliott Pratt.

"In your expert opinion," the board member says, "what do you believe may have happened with your nephew and Elliott Pratt at the pond that night?"

"Excuse me, Jeffery," my dad says, standing and drawing attention to the people seated behind me. "The sheriff's idea of what *may have* happened is simply one man's guess against another's. How is that helpful in this situation?"

The board member lifts an eyebrow at Dad. "The sheriff happens to be an expert in crime scene and accident investigation. What he believes may have happened is substantial."

Oz looks from me to my dad, then back to me before leaning into the microphone again. "Here is what I'm sure to be true… Obviously both boys went into the pond. The Pratt boy was farther from the pond edge than Jake, removed his clothing and shoes, unlike Jake, indicating that one possibly planned to go on the ice while the other hadn't."

"Thank you, Sheriff Hammond," a woman on the board says, taking over for the other guy. "The big unanswered question, then, is what—or who—might convince the Pratt boy to put himself on that half-frozen ice and risk falling through?"

Oz stares right at me when he says, "That I can't say for sure."

And all I can see are those freshmen, lined up, looking at me. And me ordering them to run across the pond. The pressure coming at me from all sides, squeezing and pushing, increases, and I need relief. A way out of this fucking guilt.

I reach for the microphone, pull it toward me. "It was me. I dared Elliott to run across the ice."

My dad stands again, begins to protest; my mom gasps out loud. But the woman at the front table lifts a hand, shushing all of them. "Did you intend for Elliott Pratt to fall in that pond?"

I shake my head. "No. It was a joke. I didn't think he would do it. I told him to stop, but he couldn't…" I swallow the lump in my throat. "He couldn't hear me."

"Three pairs of shoes were found near your truck that night," the woman says. "And two other freshmen boys were reported as arriving home without shoes or clothing, freezing." She glances down at a sheet of paper in front of her.

My stomach sinks. Witnesses my father never named to me. What have they already told these people?

"Gunner Helming and Cody Garrett," the woman reads from her paper. "Did you dare them to walk across the pond as well?"

I take a gulp of the water in front of me. My hand shakes. "Yes."

"And did they step onto the ice that night?"

"No."

Behind me, I can feel my dad's anger thickening. He's going to kill me. Or just give up on me. Not sure which is worse.

Another man takes over a nearby microphone and shoots me this serious look. "We're going to ask you this once and only once. And I would advise you to tell the truth. The situation will be far less complicated."

I shift in my seat, avoid looking at my uncle.

"Besides those three freshman boys," the board member continues, "was anyone else with you that night?"

The silence in the room hums loud and clear. My heart beats wildly on top of it, from my chest up to my ears. *Yes* forms on my lips, but I can't spit it out. Are Lance, Casey, or Red any more to blame than I am? Considering I gave the command, arguably I'm the most to blame.

Still, I try to say *yes*, try to force out their names, but instead, with my face up against that microphone, I say, "No. No one else was there."

And this time, no one jumps to their feet to protest; no one gasps in surprise. I'm sure my answer will live as the final word.

I brave turning enough in my seat to see my dad. The look on his face, the deep, deep sadness and disappointment, it hits me right in the gut. If I thought everything was different before, I was wrong.

Everything is different now.

Chapter Seventeen

–BROOKE–

I'm nearly done with my run when I hear movement coming from the trees in front of me. I slow down to a walk, approach the noise carefully—there's a good chance it's a deer, and I'd feel bad scaring it away. But when I peek through the trees, getting a glimpse of the pond, there is no deer. It's Jake.

He's not wearing a coat, just dress pants and a dress shirt and that sling that seems to have become a part of him. He takes a step forward, closer to the pond. Then he presses a black dress shoe onto the ice. I inhale a sharp breath. What is he doing?

"Jake!" I say, not wanting this to go a step—literally—further.

He jumps, his foot jerking back to solid ground, his body snapping around, following the direction of my voice. I step out into the open, and he swears under his breath.

"Sorry," I say quickly.

Jake scrubs a hand over his face. "*Jesus Christ*, Brooke."

"Sorry," I repeat.

He inhales a slow, careful breath and then turns back to face the pond. The air is sharp with frost tonight, but the sky is clear, the moon nearly full. The layer of ice covering the pond shines in the moonlight.

"Of course you're out here tonight," he says. "Ready to witness my worst moments. Again."

"What are you doing?" I demand.

He levels me with a look. "What are *you* doing?"

I shrug. "Running."

"Is that what you were doing that night?" He nods toward where Elliott Pratt fell in. The spot has a new layer of ice covering it, but like Jake, I still remember its precise location.

Instead of answering his question, I watch his right foot lift and move toward the ice again. He touches it with his toe, and already it's too much for me. I grip his shirt, tug him back.

"It's more solid now," he explains. "Not ready for skating, but if it had been tonight, he may have had a chance."

Jake swoops down, picks up a long stick that fell from the tree branch above our heads. He taps the surface of the ice, gently at first, then more forcefully, more aggressively.

"I told them it was my fault, that I dared Elliott and that I acted alone." With his good hand, he reels back and thrusts the stick harder into the ice, finally earning the crack he'd been working for. "I also told them it was accident. I hadn't ever meant for anyone to go on the ice. So really there's nothing anyone can do, and yet Elliott's family isn't satisfied enough to drop the lawsuit. And regardless of my lack of punishment, I'm still the guy who nearly got a fourteen-year-old boy killed. There's no hiding that from anyone in town, no hiding it from college recruiters or junior hockey coaches. I'm screwed. But then again, so is Elliott." He laughs this sort of dark and sad laugh. "My family might be screwed, too. The Juniper Falls Women's League, a group my mother is actively involved with, thought it would be best if she stepped down from her position on several committees to spend more time at home. And they also thought it would be best if I gave up my remaining responsibilities as Prince."

He glances at me, probably wanting some kind of reaction, and all I give him is a look of confusion. "Prince?"

"Juniper Falls Prince?" he prompts, and I shake my head. "Right, you haven't been force-fed that crap since birth. A committee of old, important townspeople get together and they nominate four guys and four girls from the junior class. New Year's Eve, the town puts on this fancy ball—pretty much everyone goes. They crown a prince and princess and you volunteer and stuff throughout the year, take a photo that hangs in town hall forever."

He looks at my face, laughs. "Yeah, it does sound stupid." His expression darkens. "But still, it's gonna be weird as hell having people know that I've been kicked out or asked to spend more time at home. Kinda wish they'd kicked me out of school, too. Then I wouldn't have to face everyone whispering about me."

I don't know what to say, so I leave everything hanging in the air.

"My dad," Jake says. "He wanted me to do something—I couldn't do it. I lied. To the school board. Elliott's family was there, trying to decide if they wanted to sue the school or the hockey program. Not sure what they're gonna do, but I couldn't let everyone go down for this."

God, Elliott's parents were at that hearing? That must have been miserable for Jake. For everyone.

Jake tosses the stick back into the woods and turns to me, some amount of resolve on his face. "Do you want to do something fun?"

I hesitate, glance across the pond at Grandma's house. "I don't know…" I start.

"Don't worry—it's just a friendly activity. I remember how you feel about popular guys." He rolls his eyes at me and then pauses. "But I'm no longer Prince, not currently playing hockey or captain of the team, so maybe I'm not even in that category anymore."

Now it's my turn to roll my eyes. "Right. You've just been washed of that mindset completely in a matter of hours. Doubtful."

"Fine," he concedes. "Tomorrow we'll pretend we don't know each other."

I glance back at the house again, still unsure what to do.

"I promise not to use my popularity to manipulate you," he says, sounding so sincere, his blue eyes wide and striking in the dark.

"You're literally using it right now," I point out.

His energy deflates. He kicks a rock with his dress shoe, and it rolls in my direction. "So that's a no?"

I suppress a frustrated sigh and point in the direction of the woods where he had been about to enter. "Come on, let's go."

And yes, I hate that I can't bring myself to say no to him. He's too vulnerable, too alone…too *beautiful* when he turns on the charm—and especially when he doesn't.

He heads into the woods. "It's about time someone showed you the best town sights."

Okay, it's not like I haven't been given a tour of Juniper Falls, but I haven't been given one from Jake Hammond, *Prince* of Juniper Falls.

Ex-Prince now, apparently.

We walk a long way, through the woods, past Jake's childhood tree house, until we finally reach what looks like a giant garage. Jake's house is visible now without binoculars, but still a good distance away.

Jake lifts the top from a tiny box on the side of the big garage and punches in a code. The electric door opens and, late at night, in the dark, the sound seems loud enough to travel all the way to the house nearby. A light shines into the large space, revealing a small covered car, a riding lawn mower, something that I think is a snowmobile, and then another small vehicle-looking thing. It's like a golf cart without the top and with giant tires.

"My dad took the keys to my truck, but he forgot about the four-wheeler."

In the bright light, Jake's devious grin is unmistakable. The four-wheeler keys appear to be stored in the ignition. He approaches it, preparing to sit down, and then his grin fades. He tugs at the sling around his neck. "Clearly I didn't think this through."

Before I can offer any kind of protest against this plan—it sounds like Jake's already in trouble, and I'm well past the time frame of any school event Grandma thinks I'm attending—he lifts the sling over his head, removing it and tossing it on the ground.

He walks over to the far wall where a slew of various winter gear hangs neatly. He grabs a navy jacket and puts it on, being extra-careful with the one arm. I know from all the hallway gossip at school that Jake broke his collarbone the night he and Elliott fell through the ice. But I have no idea how painful that is and how much putting his arm in a sling helps alleviate it. Still, I flinch at the sight of him stuffing that arm into a coat. He grabs a pair of gloves, too, thicker than mine and waterproof. Then he brings us each a helmet.

"My little sister has a big head. This should fit you." He places the helmet on me and then tugs the straps free so I can buckle them. His fingers brush the side of my face, and my stomach flips. Over and over. I thought he said this would be friendly…

After our helmets are secure, Jake points to the four-wheeler, urging me to sit down. I glance warily at the thing and then back at Jake.

"It's perfectly safe, I promise." He gives me a look that shows his feelings all too well—trapped, cooped up, on the verge of explosion.

It's pretty much how I feel every night when I escape to run through the woods. I get it, I do. And how nice would it be to have some company? I swing a leg over the four-wheeler, sit down. This seat definitely isn't made for two. Without even a moment to be nervous, Jake slides in behind me. Close. Warm. Smelling like snow and the woods.

"I still have to be careful," he says, his breath warm against the back of my neck. "You're gonna have to help steer."

Wait…what?

He slips his feet beneath mine, reaches around me to hold the handles, and instructs me to do the same. "Sorry, there's no other way to do this without…you know, invading personal space."

He clears his throat, sounding a bit nervous himself. This makes me at least 20 percent calmer.

"Next time, when it's light out, I'll show you how to drive this on your own," he promises, back to business. "You can borrow my little sister's."

In the corner of the garage, I notice a smaller purple four-wheeler.

The engine revs. I tighten my grip on the handlebars and squeeze my eyes shut. Jake slowly turns us around, and then he accelerates so fast I slide back against him even more.

And soon the garage is long behind us and we're flying through woods. Already, I can tell this will be my favorite tour of Juniper Falls.

Chapter Eighteen

–JAKE–

I pretty much never get in trouble. Not that I've never done anything I shouldn't; I definitely have. But always shit that I know my dad did when he was my age. Stuff that won't get me more than a lecture, like drinking beer by the pond or setting off illegal fireworks.

Tonight that's all changed. Now I'm the troublemaker in the family. The kid my mom should stay home and supervise. I'm the one people tell their kids not to hang out with. I had no idea how suffocating it would be to cause all that disappointment. The only thing I want to do is run. And keep on running.

Which is why I'm probably going way too fast for Brooke's first time on a four-wheeler. Especially through the woods, in the dark, but I know this path so well that I don't need light to find my way.

She's holding the handlebars with a death grip, and her shoes press harder against mine the faster I accelerate.

Hopefully she won't hate me after this. But honestly, I wasn't only doing this for me. I don't think it's a coincidence that I've seen her in the woods late at night twice now. She must be escaping her own version of suffocation.

"In a couple of weeks," I yell into her ear, "this path will be covered in snow. You won't see the ground again until at least March."

We speed farther and farther from home, staying off the main roads and following a path mostly through the woods. A couple of miles into our trip, Brooke begins to relax. The tense stone she was moments ago softens, and soon her body is molded against mine. And it feels good. Maybe too good. I wasn't trying to do anything like this.

I shake off the new vibe I'm getting and focus on what I promised her: a tour of town free of manipulation.

I stuff my feelings away to deal with later, and we ride all the way outside of town, to Lake Estella, a place where my friends and I like to hang out. Tanley's stepdad, Roger, has an ice fishing cabin, and when the lake freezes over, he has the cabin moved out here and lets us guys use it whenever we want. Tate and his girlfriend, Claire, came out here quite a bit last winter, though I doubt they did any fishing.

I slow down near a part of the lake that flows into a waterfall. "That fall freezes over in the winter," I tell Brooke. "And it makes the biggest icicles you'll ever see."

My phone buzzes from under my jacket. I stop the four-wheeler near the falls and tell Brooke to take a look. The moon is bright tonight, allowing us to see. I tug my phone free, take in the half dozen texts from my parents, demanding that I come home. Ignoring them, I turn off the location-sharing feature on that tracking app Dad made me install. He'll be pissed as hell about this, but considering he's already likely pissed as hell, the threat loses some of its power.

We step off the four-wheeler and stand near the falls. The sound of water trickling over the mass of rock is calming. And for a long while the two of us just stay. Brooke is easy to read tonight, even without talking much. I feel her patience, feel her calmness wafting in the two feet of space between us. I'm not sure, but it seems like she doesn't need me to keep talking, keep doing, keep up any kind of act. I can just be.

After a few minutes, I sense her eyes on me, on the side of my face. I turn toward her.

Even though I talked myself out of those feelings earlier, I have the strong urge to take her hand, hold onto it. But unlike all the hands I've held before, this one feels important. Maybe too important. She's not someone I can jump into something with on a whim or impulse.

"Jake?" she says, so quietly that I barely hear her over the falls. "Do you want me to tell?"

"Tell what?" I say, though I have an idea. My stomach knots at the thought, and yet it would be out there. I wouldn't have to hold on to everything all on my own.

"Tell someone what I saw that night," she explains. "If it came from me, it wouldn't be your fault, and then—"

"It's still my fault," I interrupt. "No matter how the story is told. And would it change anything? Elliott is still in the hospital, I'm still hurt."

She's quiet again, staring out at the falls.

"Why haven't you told anyone?" I ask before I can stop myself. "Why don't you look at me like you do Red? You don't even know me all that well. How did you just decide that he's bad and I'm...not?"

"I don't know." Her eyes burn into mine. "But I think it has something to do with the reason my dad is in prison—"

Blue and red flashing lights interrupt what was likely about to be a revealing conversation. I heard a rumor that her dad was in jail, but I didn't think it was true. And what the hell does that have to do with me? And was she really going to confide in me? The last time we got to this point, she was so quick to shut things down.

Brooke and I both turn toward the lights at the same time, and disappointment hits me; she's definitely done talking for the night, possibly for longer. Brooke looks petrified, but I'm just pissed off. The sheriff car pulls right up to the shoulder of the road about twenty feet from us.

"It's just my uncle," I tell Brooke.

Oz rolls down his window. "Better head on home, Jake. Let me give Brooke a ride."

She looks at me, a question in her eyes, but then moves toward the squad car. Her hand lands on the back-door handle, but Oz tells her to get in the front.

"You're not under arrest," he says, then calls to me. "I'll meet you back at the house."

Great. Just great. Now I get to endure a lecture from Oz, probably followed by one from my parents. And I have to figure how to steer this thing one-armed. Should be a blast.

I swing a leg over the four-wheeler, start it up, and hit the gas hard.

Twenty minutes later, I've barely got the four-wheeler into the garage when I hear Oz's boots crunching leaves, heading toward me. He steps into the light and leans against my dad's old Porsche.

"Your dad was worried about you." He scoops up my sling from the garage floor and tosses it. It hits me right in the face. "Says you turned off your tracker or something? He thought maybe you were upset, not out having fun."

"Out having fun?" I say, even though that was the intention. "Right. After the hearing, that's exactly what I wanted to do."

"Yes, fun," Oz repeats with a nod. "With Brooke Parker."

I'm sure he catches the guilt that crosses my face. "It wasn't like that."

But what *was* it like? What are we? Friends? Neighbors? Coach and athlete? None of those seems like the right definition.

My uncle looks like he's deliberating something. Thinking. It reminds me how different he and my dad are.

"You know that girl's been through a lot," he says carefully.

I shift from one foot to the other, uncomfortable with where this is headed. I'm not sure I want to know. Definitely not from my uncle.

"So?" And yeah, I know I sound like a defensive shit-head. "What does that have to do with me? I was just being neighborly."

He looks like he wants to say more, to open this topic a bit wider, but then he shakes his head. "Go on inside. Your dad's waitin'."

My insides ice over. I take a deep breath and head out of the garage and toward the house to face my parents, who likely have a lot to say after that hearing.

Chapter Nineteen

–BROOKE–

A firm hand grips my shoulder, shaking it gently, and I jolt awake. The whiteboard blurs and then comes into focus.

"Focus on streamlining your presentation slides. Less is more, same goes for word usage," Mrs. Watterson says. "Look for symbols and icons to replace some of the words; it changes things up, creates more interesting visuals."

Beside me, Cole offers a sympathetic look. At least she didn't call me out in front of the class. I yawn and pick up my pen. Last night I only slept a few hours. Grandma was not happy. Not at all. I'm surprised she hasn't banned me from going to hockey practice later.

But honestly, it was worth it. Maybe it's just too much work to fight this crush on Jake—and a crush is the only way to explain why I'm willing to keep quiet for him and not for someone like Red. If I admit it, at least to myself, I can just enjoy things like being pressed up against him while riding on the four-wheeler. Even if it doesn't mean anything to him. Last night I felt like I could say anything to him and he would listen, wouldn't judge me. But now it seems like that bubble has popped. I don't know what Jake knows about my family, but it would be nice if he could hear the truth from me instead of getting a version of the real story from the town gossip mill. Would he look at me differently, like my old friends in Austin have? Maybe I don't want to find out.

"Go ahead and get together with your presentation groups; try to have a working outline and a theme for your slides before the bell."

I turn my desk to face Cole's, and our third, reluctant group member comes over to join. Before she can start rambling about how we're not getting anything done, I tug two copies of the outline I wrote over the weekend from my binder and offer them up.

Cole reads his carefully, nodding a few times. "This is really good. I like the balance of policy and personal stories."

"Yeah," Rebecca agrees, surprising both Cole and me. "The policy stuff gets super boring, especially if we can't show it in real life, you know?"

Cole points to a statistic I incorporated into the outline. "Do you think we need a citation for this fact?"

Rebecca stands and takes the paper with her. "I'll ask."

"She probably wants to pass this outline off as her own work," Cole whispers.

I laugh but shrug. I don't care.

"Nice slap shots the other day," he says carefully, as if prompting me. Or maybe he's about to make a joke. "You were skating pretty fast, too…"

"But?" I prompt because it's clear that's where he's headed.

"But stopping…" He smiles, and it's friendly, but still I

hear the judgment there. "I could probably help you, you know, if you want?"

His gaze drops back to the paper, and his cheeks turn slightly pink. I'm not sure if he's just being nice or he's expecting more to come out of this act of kindness. Jake's comment about Cole being into Rosie comes back to me. But maybe it doesn't matter why he wants to help me, just that he does, and I can use all the extra practice I can get.

"Yeah, sure," I say quickly. "That would be great."

"Today at three thirty?" he suggests, and I nod.

"What's at three thirty?" Haley asks, coming up behind us. She had been running copies in the office for Mrs. Watterson. "Anything exciting I should know about?"

Cole scratches his forehead, embarrassed. "Nothing, just helping Brooke with her skating. You know, for the girls' hockey team."

"Wow," Haley says, eyeing him curiously. "Such a do-gooder, Cole."

His face turns a deeper shade of red. He opens his laptop, hiding behind the screen. "Should I start building our slides?"

My stomach bubbles with nerves. Hopefully I didn't give him the wrong idea, saying yes to this meet-up. Maybe Rosie hates him and he's going to end up hurt.

But I already said yes. Too late to change my mind.

Chapter Twenty

–JAKE–

Tate stares at the piece of paper I've just set on the ground in front of him, and the look on his face... It's safe to say that I know exactly how he feels.

"Fletcher Scott," Tate says. "I can't believe Bakowski would do this. It's low, even for him."

Tate tears the crust off one side of his sandwich, tosses it out onto the blacktop behind the school gym. A crow immediately swoops down and clamps it in its beak.

"Maybe he thought Fletch was there," I offer, because it would be easier to think that, to believe it.

"He knew he wasn't." Tate shakes his head. "And if he can fucking do that, what else is he doing that we don't know about?"

My own sandwich pauses on its way to my mouth. "What do you mean?"

Tate releases a breath. "I don't know what I mean, not exactly. But Claire said something the other day that is making a whole lot of sense right now."

Claire, his anti-hockey girlfriend. "What did she say?"

He takes one look at my face and laughs. "Come on, don't go there. Claire isn't the antagonist in this story."

"Okay." I lift my hands up. "I won't go there. Now tell me what she said."

"She said that Bakowski isn't teaching us to think for ourselves. When it comes to hockey, we get all our information from him. He's controlling the narrative."

I sink back against the brick wall of the gym. It's true that he was definitely trying to control my narrative. But then again, so was my dad.

"Maybe," I say, still doubtful. "But I don't know what we're supposed to do about it. I'm not even on the team right now. Actually, I'm on the girls' team. A glorified water boy."

"We both know that Sheriff Hammond is the glorified water boy," Tate says.

Both of us laugh at that.

But with only a few minutes of lunch left, Tate turns serious again. "I don't know if I can do it…get through the season…play without you there. It's so fucking unfair. You didn't even want to be at the pond that night. Every senior guy knows that, and we're just supposed to keep our mouths shut?"

I've never seen Tanley like this before. Like he's going stir-crazy or something. Whatever it is, he needs to shut it down. "There's a good chance I'll be cleared in January. That means I can play in sectionals and state. College coaches won't care about rumors about misbehavior if I play well enough. And by the end of March, we'll be free of Bakowski for good. What else is there to do?"

Tate is quiet for a long moment, staring out past the

blacktop. "What if Elliott pulls through this and tells everyone what really happened?"

My insides ice over. "You think he won't pull through?"

"I hope he does," Tate says quickly. "But do you think he'll confirm your story or tell everyone what really happened?"

"Well, the other two guys who got caught haven't told the real story," I say, thinking this through more thoroughly. "Those are his friends, so probably—"

The bell rings, signaling the end of lunch. I pull myself off the ground. "Did you hear that I've been de-crowned or whatever?"

Tate nods, a weary look on his face. "They asked if I wanted to take over your responsibilities. Guess I was next runner-up or whatever."

"Well, at least something good came out of that," I tell him. "You probably deserved to win, putting up with your dad's shit and still playing like you do."

Tate's dad was one of the town's greatest players, but he got injured during his first year of college. He's also an abusive asshole who almost tricked both Tate and me into violating some NCAA rules last winter and ruining our eligibility.

"I turned the offer down," Tate tells me. "Told them I had too much going on right now."

"Then who—"

"Who do you think?" He holds the gym door open, allowing me and my slinged arm to walk through first. "It's always a hockey player."

Only two other guys were nominated last year—Red and this douche Kennedy Locust. "So Red, then?" I conclude. A weird feeling sits in the pit of my stomach along with that turkey sandwich my mom made me. Why didn't Red tell me? Why hasn't he talked to me at all since the hearing last night? He didn't tell me he was getting my spot as captain, either.

"I'll catch up with you later," Tate says, meaning it.

Unlike a lot of the guys on the team.

Chapter Twenty-One

–BROOKE–

"You are so close!" Cole shouts from the middle of the rink. "Try again, but don't think so much."

Somehow, he managed to pick a time when the ice was completely free. It helps not having to try and fail at this in front of six-year-olds who learned how to stop years ago. And I can stop, just not when I'm skating my fastest.

I skate toward Cole, build a bit of speed, then attempt to twist my hips and stop. But my outside blade just sticks to the ice, doesn't glide across the surface, shaving a layer of ice in the process like I want it to. My body pitches forward, and I end up falling on my side. Again. My hip is gonna be bruised from this lesson. Cole had said I wouldn't need full pads, but maybe I shouldn't have listened to him.

"She's using that inside foot too much, Cole."

I look up and see Haley's boyfriend, Fletcher, leaning against the half wall, watching us. My face flushes and I scramble to my feet.

"What do you mean?" Cole asks.

"Try this…" Fletcher, who is dressed in full pads along with his skates, steps out onto the ice. He skates at us then twists to a stop, only he lifts his back foot, performing most of the turn on one leg. "Make sure you aren't putting all the pressure on the ball of your foot. It's got to be even."

I glance at Cole, since he's the one who is supposed to be teaching me. He just shrugs like, *Sounds good to me.* I turn my back to them, preparing to skate away and try Fletcher's idea.

"Front leg only," he reminds me.

Working hard to stuff down any insecurities, I attack this at full speed. I twist to a stop, lifting my back leg at the same time. I concentrate hard on bending my knees more, and instead of my body being thrown forward, this time my left skate slides out, away from me. Snow sprays up onto my black skate, and I stop moving. Like actually stop. After skating at my fastest speed.

I turn slowly to face Fletcher and Cole.

"Nice!" Fletcher says. "Try it again."

Even though I want to celebrate, I also don't want to jinx it. So I try again.

Ten minutes and at least thirty successful stops later, I notice Jake staring and looking very serious. Quite a contrast to my mood.

"Next time," Fletcher says, having taken over Cole's job, "you should work on stopping on the other side. With that speed, if you can harness it, it'll be awesome. Cole also mentioned something about a killer slap shot…?"

"Yeah, I nearly killed Jake," I admit.

"In that case, I definitely need to see this," Fletch says, and there's a cryptic undertone that I don't understand and don't know him well enough to ask about.

After I thank Cole and Fletcher, I head off the ice so I can put on the rest of my gear. Jake touches my sleeve, stopping me.

"From now on," he says, his voice low, "I'll work with you on this stuff. Right after school, before practice. Okay?"

I look up at him, hesitating to answer. I don't want to seem excited about this, but I totally am. "Okay."

I wait a moment for him to explain his serious mood, but when he doesn't, I'm left to head into the locker room, confused. Was he jealous that Cole and Fletcher were helping me? Didn't seem that way, but if not that, then what else?

Or maybe I just *wish* that he were jealous?

Chapter Twenty-Two

–JAKE–

Okay, so I was jealous of Fletcher and Cole teaching Brooke to stop. I kind of like my free half hour right after school, but not if I have to spend it imagining Cole and Brooke spending time together. He's her age, and yeah, he's sort of a hockey star but also quiet and more inconspicuous. It bugs me that they might fit well together. And it bugs me that it bugs me. But I am the assistant coach; it's my job to get all the players ready even if that means sacrificing my own free time. So yeah, that's my excuse for keeping Brooke and Cole apart.

While I'm waiting for the team to get out onto the ice, I spend several minutes jotting down a plan for practice. We need to do more shooting drills and put our goalie under a bit more stress. I don't want her panicking during the first game because I haven't done enough to simulate game stress.

But before the team is even on the ice, I spot my uncle, my dad, and the principal standing near the entrance of the rink. The principal glances my way and then turns his attention back to Dad and Oz. My stomach turns. What now? Did Elliott Pratt get worse…or did he—

Oz heads toward me while Dad and the principal stay put, but they're watching him. Several of the girls exit the locker room. Rosie picks up on the tension she's just walked right into the middle of, grabs Samantha's practice jersey and holds her in place near the locker room entrance. My palms are sweaty, my heart racing.

"What?" I demand the second Oz is close enough for me to speak without shouting. The anticipation is painful.

"Elliott Pratt took a turn today," Oz says quietly.

Panic rushes over me, ice-cold panic. "What— I mean—"

"A good turn," Oz clarifies, realizing his mistake.

I reach out and grip the wall. My legs are literally shaking. If Elliott Pratt had… Well, if he were worse—God, I don't even want to think about it.

"He was up, moving around a bit," Oz explains. "His parents and doctors decided it was okay for me to go and get his statement."

I knew this was coming eventually, but last I heard, Elliott hadn't been fully awake, hadn't recalled anything about how he ended up in the hospital. My dad and Oz had both told me that short-term memory loss was common in accidents.

From the corner of my eye, I see Rosie whisper something to Brooke, who has just exited the locker room.

"His statement," I repeat, trying to switch gears. I'm still stuck on the image of Elliott's blue face and lifeless body.

"He confirmed your story, that it was just you and his two friends," Oz begins, his tone oddly careful, concealing some feelings of his own. "He said you didn't do anything wrong, that he doesn't blame you at all."

I stare at my uncle, confused. This feels like a trick. A trap I'm walking myself right into.

"His family might reconsider the lawsuit after hearing this," Oz adds.

I don't know what to say. It feels dirty, this whole thing. I mean, I guess I'd been holding out hope that he spent enough time in the Otter hockey realm to understand our law of secrecy and would simply confirm my version, keep the team out of it. But hearing it play out this way, I'm not getting the closure I need. Something feels off. And I hadn't anticipated how much relief I would feel, hearing that he's okay. In fact, I need a minute to process without twenty people staring at me.

I take a step past Oz, but he sets a hand on my arm to stop me. I tug free of him. "Just…just give me a minute. Okay?"

The side door of the ice rink is closest. I push it open, fill my lungs with cold air. It's already dark, and I can stand unnoticed against the side of the building. I close my eyes and take deep breaths. I should be celebrating. He's okay, and maybe his parents won't sue the school and bring my name into it. This is all good news.

But I can't celebrate, can't shake the weird feeling. Like I now know what it means to sell your soul to the devil. But whose soul was sold? Mine or Elliott's? And who is the devil? It doesn't help that Oz obviously knows the story isn't true. No proof of that, but I imagine he has a hunch about a lot of things regarding Otter hockey.

The door opens and shuts, and I keep my eyes squeezed shut. I'm not ready to talk to my dad or Oz.

Someone moves beside me, brushes against my arm. Soon warm fingers wrap around mine. Soft, warm fingers. I turn my head, look over at Brooke, who came out here with skates on.

"Elliott...he's okay," I tell her, and for some reason my eyes burn, my throat constricts. "He's gonna be fine."

"I heard," she says. "What about you? Are you gonna be okay?"

I pull my shit together, carefully wipe my face with my shirtsleeve, hoping she won't notice. I glance down at our linked hands, try to ignore the heat building inside me. "It's weird...I don't know what to think or feel."

"Maybe you should go and see him," Brooke says.

I nod, too afraid to test my voice. "Maybe I should."

She doesn't say anything else, just stands there, her fingers tangled in mine, until I tell her we should go back inside. When we return, our hands now in our own space, it's obvious the other girls are whispering about this. However, Brooke seems okay with it, takes it in stride, unlike that day with Haley in the tree house.

I head straight over to Oz, offer a nod to my dad, hoping he sees that I got the message but I'm not talking about it now, not here. He and the principal head out the doors, and the team begins their skating drills. Oz sticks beside me, both of us leaning against the wall.

I watch the team touch the blue line, stop—even Brooke—turn, skate again. They're actually getting better at this, even starting to gel as a team.

"At the hearing, you said you had to do CPR or whatever on Elliott," I say to Oz quietly. "What was that...I mean what was that like?"

"It was fucking hell," Oz says, a haunted look on his face. "He's fourteen, like Rosie. And then Officer Jennings said you were unconscious, and I nearly left the kid..."

"I'm sorry." I glance down at the wall. That constricted feeling happens again in my throat. "It really was an accident."

"I know," he says, and relief hits me deep inside, where I'd buried that fear that my uncle thinks I'm a monster, that maybe I am one. "But how long before another *accident* happens, Jake?"

He leaves me, walks out onto the ice. And now it's clear where the weird feeling is coming from. It isn't just about the past, about what happened to Elliott. It's about the future.

I turn my attention back to the team, now going through the passing drills I taught them last week, and like a magnetic force, my focus is immediately pulled to one player. One who I'm trying and failing to convince myself is just a friend of sorts, someone I'd like to help.

Brooke makes a solid pass to Rosie and glances up at me, a small smile on her face. And I'm hit with a swarm of feelings that I don't know what to do with. But why her? Why this girl? Why now?

I can debate this all I want, but I'm not sure the answer matters much.

Chapter Twenty-Three

–JAKE–

Elliott's mom greets me and then looks right at Tate, a question in her eyes. Internally, I start to panic. Maybe I shouldn't have brought him here. He's not even supposed to know Elliott. And really, he doesn't know him, but he did help drag Elliott's limp frozen body to safety.

"Tate offered to drive me," I tell her, pointing to my sling.

Tate reaches out to shake her hand. "Always looking for an excuse to miss class."

The woman looks exhausted and like she has no idea what to say to me. She finally nods toward the room to our right. "Elliott's in here; he's excited to have visitors."

On the drive, Tate and I debated what we might see — everything from respirators to urine bags. Neither of us had expected to see Elliott Pratt, sitting up in a hospital bed wearing sweats and looking completely okay.

Textbooks are spread out over the bed, and the TV is tuned to ESPN. Elliott looks up when we enter, and his eyes widen, his cheeks flush.

"Oh, hey." He scrambles to pack up the books, maybe embarrassed to be seen studying. "You just missed Coach Bakowski...or did you come together?"

Coach Bakowski was here? That's surprising. Tate and I exchange a look, and I can tell he's wondering about this, too.

"We came on our own," I say, standing awkwardly in the middle of the small hospital room. "So...you look good. How are you?"

It's clear he's intimidated by our presence; how could he not be when our torture led to him nearly dying? But he looks right at us while he talks. Probably doesn't have a choice, if he reads lips like my uncle said.

"I'm good." He glances over at two empty armchairs. "You can, like, you know...sit down if you want."

I realize I'm holding a package of treats that are meant for Elliott. I hand it to him, and then Tate and I sit down.

"Thanks." He pulls out a few of the bags of cookies and candy and then sticks them back into the bag. "I can't eat these yet, but they look good."

"The hospital doesn't allow outside food?" Tate asks. "That sucks."

"No, they do." Elliott tucks the bag under the bed. "But I can't eat solid food yet because I had that tube down my throat for several weeks..."

His voice trails off, probably after getting a look at the horror on our faces. He had a tube down his throat for weeks? My heart picks up and my chest tightens. A vision of Oz pressing on Elliott's bluish-white chest swims around inside my head.

"Are you okay, man?" Tate asks me. "You look like you're about to puke."

I draw in a deep breath through my nose and fake calm. "Fine."

"My mom told me you got hurt when you…" Elliott starts, and then forces out the rest. "Pulled me out."

"It's nothing," I say. "And I fell out of a tree. I'm done with the sling in a few days."

"But you can't play hockey?" Elliott asks, like this is a death sentence.

I shake my head. "It's healing. I'll be fine."

"What about you?" Tate asks, redirecting the conversation. "When do you get to go back to school and maybe join the freshman team?"

"School…next week," he says. "And I have to wait to play hockey, but Coach offered me a varsity spot for the season: honorary, he calls it, since I can't play yet."

I have to work real hard not to look at Tate. That doesn't sound like Coach Bakowski at all. He's up to something.

Elliott's mom hovers in the doorway, and her presence seems to remind Elliott of something. He clears his throat. "I just wanted to tell you thanks. For saving my life. I should have never gone out on the ice. It was stupid." He stares down at his hands. "I was just trying to be cool, you know?"

I'm feeling way too many things to respond, but luckily Tate jumps in again. "I get that. I broke my ankle in fifth grade because my sister dared me to jump off the garage roof."

I look from Elliott to Tate. How are we all just sitting here agreeing on a false version of that night without any deliberating first? How can this just be expected of anyone who wants to be on our team? Is that why Bakowski came to see Elliott? To remind him of what secrecy means to hockey players in Juniper Falls?

I feel sick to my stomach by the time we're walking

out of that room. Elliott's mom follows us into the hall. Her eyes are red-rimmed. "I'm sorry, Jake. For putting you through all that stuff with the school. We're dropping the lawsuit, and I just want to say…" Her voice cracks, and I shift uncomfortably from one foot to the other. She leans in and wraps her arms around me. "Thank you for saving my son."

I can't even bring myself to say, *You're welcome*. Instead I nod, and then Tate and I bolt out of that hospital.

In the safety of Tate's mom's minivan, I release a frustrated breath. "Is it me or do they all seem brainwashed?"

"It's not you," Tate says. "Definitely not you."

Chapter Twenty-Four

–BROOKE–

I enter the ice rink for practice early and take my time circling around the building. The door to the training room is open, and inside, Jake is seated at one of the trainer tables, his sling gone. I'd nearly forgotten what he looked like without it. The trainer lifts his arm, rotates it in a circle, and I'm watching for pain on his face but he appears calm, relaxed.

"You're lucky," the trainer says to Jake. "Healing time for a broken collarbone is three to ten weeks... You ended up on the lower end of that."

"When can I play again?" he demands.

Just a week of being back to Jake Hammond, popular nice guy, and already I hear the hockey captain in his voice, hear him sound like the player I watched dominating the first time I came to this rink. And yet, I know somewhere under that version of Jake is the guy who broke down last week, whose hand perfectly covered mine, and who likely isn't over what happened at the pond that night.

"Skating drills this week," the trainer says. "Physical therapy every day, but you don't pick up a stick until I say so, understood?"

"Yeah, okay," Jake concedes.

"I already broke all his sticks," a voice says from the other side of the training room. Tate Tanley. I lean into the doorway a little farther and see him at a different table, icing his knee. "He's not gonna do a single trick shot until you clear him."

"Hey, Brooke."

I jump at the sound of Rosie's voice. I turn around, offer her a smile and a nod.

"Getting iced, too?" she asks, stepping past me and walking right inside the training room.

"Um, yeah." I trail behind her and, remembering the ice on Tate's knee, decide I'll just ice my knee, too, even though it's perfectly fine.

While Rosie and I fill bags of ice, I feel Jake's eyes on me, feel him watching. He's helped me before practice every day for the last week but has been all business. No mention of our little moment outside. But maybe it was just that, a moment, nothing more. Doubt and disappointment circle in the pit of my stomach, and I try to will it away. Since Elliott's parents dropped their lawsuit and decided that Jake was a hero, the vibe around him has changed. People aren't whispering about him. With his sling gone, it's almost like things are back to normal. And the "normal Jake" is the one I'm not as excited about liking. Though that doesn't seem to change the fact that I do still like him. A lot.

Rosie and I head to the locker room and work on getting our gear on for practice. After a few minutes of not saying anything, Rosie slides next to me on the bench, holds my forgotten ice bag in the air.

"What's going on with you and Jake?" she asks.

The way she says it doesn't feel like a person who just wants some juicy gossip; she almost sounds worried. I shake my head, as if not understanding her question.

"Come on," she presses. "I saw you disappear after him the other day; I've seen you looking at him. It's kind of freakin' me out because he's helping coach us, not to mention he's my cousin but he's also Jake Hammond, you know? You get that, right?"

I release a breath, stuff my clothes into my hockey bag. "Yeah, I get that."

"Good." She sounds relieved. "But it's obvious he's helping you a lot, and now you're actually good enough to—"

She stops, shuts her eyes. "Sorry. I'm working on that filter thing. But you're getting good. It's insane that you've never even played before. Anyway... My dad is making his most edible dinner, and I thought maybe you'd want to hang out tonight. I can show you all kinds of game tapes. I think it'll help a lot."

I work hard to hide how pleased I am with this invite and focus on lacing my skates instead. "Yeah, sure."

I'm feeling pretty good at the start of practice, but then the sheriff arrives and drops a bomb on us.

"I have good news, ladies," he says. "I've arranged a scrimmage for us tomorrow afternoon."

"A scrimmage?" Sam says. "With who?"

"Longmeadow's girls' team," Sheriff Hammond says, and his grin grows bigger.

This doesn't mean a whole lot to me but seems to set everyone else off. All the girls start talking at once.

"We are so dead," someone says.

"Anyone but Longmeadow," Sam says.

"We're not ready for this," Rosie protests. "What happened to not playing until January? What happened to recruiting a few more players?"

"You can't get game experience without actually playing a game," Sheriff argues. "I hear your concerns, but it took a lot of work to arrange this, and if we're really going to play, we've got to start playing."

"You act like we haven't played a hockey game before," Sam says. "Most of us have been on a team since kindergarten."

"Yes," Sheriff agrees, "but not everyone."

Six pairs of eyes turn to face me, and my face warms all over again. Great. So I'm the reason we need this unwelcome scrimmage. Now I'm really on my way to fitting in.

Chapter Twenty-Five

–JAKE–

I wasn't at the girls' team practice yesterday because I had to do some extra rehab, so I missed seeing their reaction when Oz told them about the scrimmage today. However, all the girls are here, on time and ready to go in their new jerseys. Maybe the uniforms motivated them. Oz went all out, got their names on the back and everything.

"Hey, Coach, looking good without the sling," Rosie says when she sees me. "Does this mean you're ready to teach us some trick shots?"

I shake my head. "No trick shots. Just stick to the basics today."

The team is about to head onto the ice to start warm-ups when Longmeadow's team arrives. One by one they enter the rink, head toward the guest locker room, and I know the girls are doing the same thing I'm doing—counting their players.

Eight…nine…ten…eleven…twelve.

"Oh my God, we're screwed," Sam mutters.

Oz appears and watches the girls watching Longmeadow, and his excitement deflates. He fakes enthusiasm. "All right, let's get out there, get warmed up. Then we'll talk positions."

Brooke is seated on the bench, lacing her skates, while the other girls start their drills. I watch her carefully. She laces one skate several times, knotting and double knotting. She looks like she's about to barf.

"I think your skates are fine," I tell her, nodding toward the ice.

She stands, grabs her stick, but hesitates at the wall.

"When the game starts, you'll be fine, I promise," I tell her, moving closer, keeping my voice low. "You've got nothing to lose here. No one expects anything, Oz isn't going to kick you off the team if you suck today or forget how to stop…"

She cracks a smile, and I'm disturbed by how much it hits me right in the gut. She's not a girl who smiles often. Needing some space between us, I give her a gentle shove out on the ice. I study their passing, shooting, the goalie's moves all during warm-ups, and soon I start to get nervous myself even though I don't get nervous for my *own* games. Longmeadow's team heads to the other end of the ice and begins their own warm-ups, and I'm too busy studying them to notice Tate standing beside me, at least not at first.

"What are you doing here?" I ask him, not looking away from the girl Longmeadow is obviously counting on to score some goals for them. She's fast, with a decent slap shot, too.

"Figured the girls' team could use some support," he says.

Both of us turn to look at the stands behind us. A handful of parents are scattered around the bleachers, Betty from the Spark Plug, a couple of teachers, some younger siblings, but that's pretty much it. When the guys have their first home game next week, this place will be so packed some spectators will stand and watch from the walls.

The game is about to begin, so I head to the bench, grab the clipboard where Oz and I have planned out positions. Tate follows me, leans over to read the lineup.

"Rosie at center, just like her cousin," Tate says, nodding. "Brooke is your extra player? Where are you putting her when she goes in?"

"Wherever we need an extra player," I say, already hating this scenario. If the guys' team had to play with only one extra person… I can't even imagine. We'd never survive a game. We've got nearly three players for each position.

"Elliott went home yesterday, right?" Tate prompts.

"Yeah, I went to see him again, played video games for a little while," I tell Tate, and then, when I'm sure no one is listening to us, I add, "I heard something from Elliott even weirder than the honorary-varsity-player thing."

"What?"

"Apparently Bakowski is moving Gunner Helming and Cody Garrett from the freshman team to varsity, too."

"Gunner Helm—" Tate's eyes widen. "Wait, those are the two freshmen the school board named—"

"Yep." I shake my head, still trying to process this, to figure out Bakowski's angle. "And they aren't honorary mascots like Pratt; they're being put on the varsity player roster."

"No way those guys are ready," Tate says. "Gunner was set to be backup goalie for the freshman team, not even starting. I worked with him during their tryouts; he's completely green."

As a freshman, I had been on varsity, and last year we had Cole Clooney join varsity after the first few games. But Cole and I are more the exception than the norm. Tate's an amazing goalie, and he still played two years of JV before moving up to the varsity bench. He only went in last year, as a junior, because our main goalie, Mike Steller, quit the team after the first home game.

"What do you think Bakowski is up to?" I ask, glad I at least have Tate to talk to about this. "If you could have heard Elliott talking, it was insane. It was all, *Bakowski is the best; I'm proud to be part of the team even if I have to sit on the bench…*"

"This is getting really messed up," Tate mutters. "First the Fletcher thing and then this…"

"Yeah, I know." I draw in a breath, focus on the ice. "I've got a bad feeling about all of it."

We're both quiet for a few minutes, watching the team finish the warm-ups. Then Tate says, out of the blue, "Is it me or does Brooke Parker have a thing for you?"

I avoid his gaze, try not to look interested in this topic. "What makes you think that?"

"She keeps looking over here," he says quietly. "And yesterday she hovered outside the training room, then randomly needed a bag of ice. Seems like something to me."

I glance around, checking for listening ears. "We've sort of been hanging out lately."

"Hanging out? Like dating?"

"No, definitely not," I say, though now I'm distracted by the word "date" and Brooke so close together. "Just like we run into each other…in the woods, usually at night, and then we…"

"Hang out?" Tate prompts, one eyebrow raised. "Sorry, I'm just having trouble picturing this 'hanging out,' considering Brooke isn't much of a talker."

"She talks," I protest. "Some."

"Are you into her?" he asks carefully, not like Red or any of the other guys would, teasing or harassing me about it.

I watch Brooke skate toward the goal, practice her stop one more time. "Maybe."

"I don't know much about her," Tate says, "but you're fucking picky when it comes to girls, so she must be cool."

I replay Brooke in my tree house, panicked, trying to escape Haley. "Not sure 'cool' is the right word."

"Different, maybe?"

"Yeah." I nod slowly, seeing Brooke in that word, "different." "Definitely."

"You want my advice?" Tate asks, and unlike most people, he actually waits for me to answer. I offer a single nod. He's got a hot girlfriend who he seems to really love, so yeah, his advice isn't unwelcome, that's for sure. "If it feels right to you, go for it. Don't worry about what anyone else thinks."

"That's it?" I laugh. "Just go for it?"

He shrugs. "Whatever doubts you have, like the fact that she's a sophomore or new or whatever… If it feels right and it works out, people will get used to it. Give 'em enough time and all that other stuff won't be weird anymore."

"Okay." I release a breath, look out at the ice again. "That actually helps."

And I'm being honest with Tate. It does help. But still, I'm not sure I'll know if it's right. I mean, it felt right last week when we were outside alone, her hand touching mine. I wanted more. But I didn't do anything about it.

Maybe that means it *wasn't* right?

Chapter Twenty-Six

–BROOKE–

"Pass the puck, Allen!" Jake shouts at Kendra. "Keep your head up!"

I'm standing right beside him, the only extra player on the bench, so all his coaching during the first five minutes of the game has been shouted right at me, driving me to an even deeper level of anxiety. My helmet and stick rest right at my feet, but I'm hoping for a few more minutes before I need to grab them. I'm not ready. Not even a little.

"Ready to go in?" Jake prompts.

Out of instinct, I shake my head. That's probably not the answer I'm supposed to give. Lucky for me, Jake is too focused on the game to have noticed.

"Mason, dig it out of the middle!" he yells to Sam.

Her response is too slow. A Longmeadow player gets the puck from Sam, takes a shot at the goal. And she scores.

I can hear Rosie's string of swear words from all the way across the ice. Jake exhales then claps his hands together.

"All right, get back in it."

"Brooke," Sheriff Hammond says. "Go in for Rosie."

Jake and I both say, "No!" at the same time.

The sheriff shakes his head. "Right. That doesn't make sense."

Even I know that a team shouldn't replace their best player with their least-experienced player even for a few minutes.

"Go in for Allen," Jake orders.

When I don't move right away, he reaches down, picks up my helmet, places it on my head, and then shoves a stick in my gloved hand. "Go! Now!"

I toss a shaky leg over the wall and skate to Kendra. She sees me and immediately heads off the ice just in time for our unofficial referee—Coach Ty, the boys' JV team coach—to blow the whistle and send everyone in motion again.

Rosie manages to get the puck from the Longmeadow center and maneuvers right around her, heading straight for the goal. I try to remember all the situations Rosie walked me through last night via old game tape. I need to stay outside if she's in the middle. A Longmeadow player who looks like she could crush me with one gentle shove is right on me, won't let up. I try to get away from her while Rosie takes a shot at goal. She misses, it rebounds off the cross bar, and heads right to me.

I panic for a second, like the puck is a bomb nestled at the end of my stick. I attempt to pass back to Rosie, but it's intercepted by Longmeadow, and soon all of us are skating toward the other end.

"It was wide open in front of you, Parker!" Jake shouts. "Take the shot!"

I give him a bewildered look. Did he actually expect me to try and score a goal in the first minute of the first game I've ever played? He *is* Jake Hammond, so maybe he did expect that. I don't have time to think through answers to those questions. The game continues; the puck keeps moving. I follow the group back and forth on the ice, trying my hardest to not get the puck and getting rid of it the second I have possession of it. Finally, six minutes later, I hear Sheriff Hammond tell the girl on the bench to swap out with me.

Jake opens the door for me, and after I pull my helmet off, Sheriff Hammond hands me a water bottle with my name on it.

"You're doing great," Sheriff says, patting me on the back.

Jake shakes his head. "No, she's not."

My face is already hot and likely red from skating around, so I don't have to worry about showing any embarrassment from this comment.

"You're playing too careful," Jake says, his tone shifting from critical to more gentle. "You gotta get angry, aggressive, you know?"

No, not really. Hard to move all the gallons of fear out of the way to muster up some anger or aggression. Seconds after Jake's anger lecture, Rosie shoves a Longmeadow player, knocks her down, and ends up in the penalty box. Jake gives me a look as if to say, *See? Like that.*

"Brooke, go in for Sam," Sheriff says after only a couple of minutes of rest.

I secure my helmet and return to the ice. I keep up my running-scared tactics for the first two periods. I haven't screwed up in a major way yet, but I also haven't helped the team at all, and we're still behind two goals going into the third and final period.

And then something changes in me. I think maybe I'm more comfortable or maybe just completely fed up with this huge Longmeadow player who's constantly right on top of me. The puck stops about ten feet in front of the two of us, no one else nearby, and a fire ignites inside me. I cut her off, skate as fast as I can toward the puck, scoop it up with my stick. I hear Jake inside my head, from more than a dozen practice sessions, yelling to *keep your head up!* And I look up to see Rosie wide open in the center, about five feet in front of the goal. I pass to her then skate toward the player tailing Rosie and cut her off, keeping the space wide open.

Rosie doesn't hesitate; she takes her shot right away. It hits the sidebar and then flies right under the goalie's left leg.

Sheriff Hammond yells the loudest of anyone when Rosie scores, but Jake is a close second.

"Nice pass, Parker!" he says, "Great shot, Rosie!"

Rosie skates over, plows into me, nearly knocking me over. "That was awesome!"

We reset quickly, and I head into the next play feeling lighter, more excited. What a rush that was, seeing something I wanted and just going after it.

"That was so awesome," Sam says for, like, the tenth time since the game ended.

"I don't even care that we lost." Rosie holds the locker room door open for the girls who are finished showering and changing and are ready to leave. "Next game, we'll win. Especially with our secret weapon, Brooke Parker."

I roll my eyes at her. "Secret weapon" is definitely a bit of an exaggeration.

In the rink lobby, Jake and Sheriff Hammond are still here, both standing around looking tired and bored. Probably not used to how much longer it takes girls to get ready after a game. We only have two shower stalls in our locker room and need to take turns. I lug my bag on my shoulder and glance out the glass doors. My hair is wet from the shower, not a great combination with the cold night air, but I'm too happy to care.

Sheriff Hammond claps for us—again—and he's still grinning from earlier. "First-ever Juniper Falls High girls' hockey game! It's a historical moment, ladies. Take a minute to think about that."

It is pretty cool. Being a part of anything first in this town. Not an easy feat in a place that thrives on hundred-year-old traditions.

Sheriff Hammond gathers us together for a team meeting. All of us are so exhausted, having played nearly the entire game, that we drop our bags on the floor and sit right on top of them.

"I know all of you weren't exactly thrilled about this scrimmage," Sheriff says. "But I think tonight you proved to everyone, with only seven players, that you're the real deal. A high school hockey team—"

His speech is interrupted by the wail of an ambulance passing by. Seconds later, a fire truck speeds past. Several of the girls cover their ears; the sound is so loud. Sheriff Hammond, being the sheriff and all, has a walkie-talkie attached to his jeans. He turns it on, slowly raising the volume until voices can be heard over the sirens.

Through the static, I latch onto five words strung to-gether…*thirty-eight-year-old female*…and I'm on my feet, heading toward the doors. The red lights blur together but hold still in my line of sight.

They're coming from across the street.

My heart thuds so loudly that it drowns out the sirens.

This is my nightmare. Coming to life right here, right now.

"Brooke…" I hear Sheriff Hammond say, and I know he knows, too.

Without my coat or bag, with my hair wet, I push through the doors, run as fast as I can across the railroad tracks. My heart and lungs are near explosion when I reach the sidewalk in front of Grandma's house. I can't breath or speak, can't do anything but push through the people on the sidewalk watching…watching my family fall apart.

A firefighter stops me from charging through the front door. I hear Grandma crying hysterically. I try to duck under the giant arm blocking me, but then I see her. My mom. Sprawled out in the hallway, lifeless, and blood…so much blood.

I stumble backward, away from the door. "No…no… She has an appointment on Monday; she was supposed to—"

And it all becomes too much. I can't watch this play out, can't face what is the inevitable truth. I'm not sure if the firefighter blocking my way chases after me when I take off, running behind the house, around the pond, and into the woods. I can't hear it, can't hear any of it. She was better. She was going to that program in Rochester.

She was better.

I run and run until the sirens stop. Until the nightmare stops.

Chapter Twenty-Seven

–JAKE–

I push through the small crowd gathering on the sidewalk and watch in horror as the paramedics lift a gurney into the ambulance. Her arm is heavily wrapped in bandages, but still, blood seeps through it. A frantic Judy Gleason gets into the back of the ambulance with the woman. Mrs. Parker. Brooke's mother.

The ambulance speeds away, avoiding the traffic coming out of the ice rink. Oz is in the yard, urging people on the sidewalk to head home. I run over to him. "Where's Brooke?"

"Did she go with her mother in the ambulance?"

I shake my head. "She must be here; she was ahead of both of us."

"I'll check the house," Oz says.

Since I haven't been in the Gleason house since Brooke and her mom moved here, it feels wrong to follow Oz inside. I wait impatiently while he's likely checking every room and closet. He comes out minutes later, shaking his head.

My heart races. The way she looked at the rink when Oz turned on his radio—she was haunted, like she knew before he did. "I might know where she is…"

"You want to go or you want me to?" he asks.

"Is her mom— I mean— Is she okay?" If I find Brooke, she would want to know.

Oz glances around at the people nearby then lowers his voice. "She tried to hurt herself. I think she'll be okay, physically. But the hospital is gonna keep her there, I'm sure of it. Probably won't let Brooke see her right away."

"I'll find her," I promise, not allowing myself to process what my uncle just told me. He said things were bad for Brooke, but I didn't think they were *that* bad.

I take off running, behind the house, into the thick trees, and toward home. I reach the tree house quickly, but I have to bend over, catch my breath. I'm out of shape.

I climb the ladder, look inside. I nearly miss Brooke, curled up in the corner, her face hidden. After shutting the door to keep the cold air out, I approach her slowly. Silent sobs shake her body. My gut lurches. I fumble for my phone and send Oz a two-word text.

ME: found her

Images of her mom in the ambulance, bleeding and looking like a fucking zombie flash in my head. If Brooke saw any of that, she must be— I shake my head, focus on the here and now. I scoot closer, rest a hand on her back, try to think of something to say but come up empty. She turns over, sees that it's me, and then sits up slowly. Her eyes are red, cheeks wet, hair wet and tangled.

"Is she—" she starts, and then closes her eyes, fresh tears tumbling down. "Is she—"

"She's okay." A lump rises in my throat. I shift closer, slide the hair off her face. "Oz thinks they'll keep her awhile. At the hospital."

"I thought she was dead," Brooke whispers after a long, silent beat. "I really thought that and—"

She covers her face with both hands, breaking down again. I don't know what to do for several long seconds, and then instincts take over. I wrap my arms around her, pull her close against my shirt.

"I saw her in the ambulance; she was awake, talking." I keep my voice calm, even. I can't imagine what Brooke felt moments ago, thinking her mom was gone.

She's shaking like crazy. Not just because of the crying. All she has on is a thin shirt and jeans, her hair is wet, and it's no more than twenty degrees outside tonight. I grab a blanket from the storage trunk, wrap it around her shoulders. Then I hug her tight against me, running my hands over the outside of the blanket, creating friction.

"I knew this was going to happen," Brooke whispers.

"No," I argue. "You didn't know. It was an accident."

Those feel like the words I'm supposed to say, but I know it's not true. Oz said her mom tried to hurt herself, succeeded in it so it seems, but maybe not in the way she intended.

"It wasn't an accident." She sniffles, leans in to me. "She's been in a bad place for a while. My grandma was supposed to take her to a clinic in Rochester on Monday. She should have just begged to bring her sooner. I should have done it for her."

I move a leg to the side of her and draw her even closer. I tell myself the cold is the only reason for this movement. It has nothing to do with the conversation Tate and I had earlier. "How long has she been like this?"

"It started during my dad's trial," she tells me. "But after the trial, when he went away, it got really bad. She couldn't take care of herself, let alone anyone else."

Trial? What trial? Oh right…she had mentioned the prison thing before.

Brooke releases a short laugh. "I can literally hear the questions you're thinking." She scoots back a few inches, freeing herself from my hold. "You really didn't know?"

"About your dad?" I ask, and she nods. "I don't know anything about him."

She shudders, tightens the blanket around her shoulders, and angles herself to face me. "My dad's in prison for five years, though his lawyer says it will be much shorter than that."

Already this is the most I've ever heard her say about herself, but I can hear more bubbling on the surface, can see it in her eyes. She's done keeping it to herself.

"What happened?" I lift the corner of the blanket, use it to dry her wet cheek.

"He turned a gun on a guy in a dark alley at night," she says all in one breath.

My stomach drops. "Wait…seriously?"

"That's what he got in trouble for, but it's not exactly how it sounds," she says. "The guy threatened my dad, pointed a gun at him. My dad wrestled it from him and basically beat the crap out of the guy to keep him from getting the weapon back."

I'm having a hard time following. "So it wasn't your dad's gun?"

She shakes her head slowly. "I mean, I know it wasn't his, my mom knows, and he knows. But it wasn't registered. The guy turned out to be a rich kid with powerful parents. They hired a fancy lawyer, dug up some old assault charges against my dad, showed photos of their kid's bloody face and bruised body."

"So your dad had priors?" Between my lawyer father and sheriff uncle, I have a good idea how much priors can influence a judge.

"He's a musician," Brooke says, like this is supposed to explain assault charges. "He plays gigs in bars and at festivals where everyone is drinking. Those assault charges were bar fights with no serious injuries, ones he probably didn't even start. Plus he was in his early twenties. He's not like that anymore."

"Jesus," I mutter. "Five years?"

She tears up again, nods. "That kid's lawyers…they completely changed the narrative. I didn't know people could do that. None of us knew. And when that trial was over, even while it was happening, people in our lives started pulling away. As soon as the verdict was out, everyone just said, *well, it must be true.* You know, I'm not even a hundred percent positive that my own grandma believes his story."

"I'm sorry," I say lamely. God, that must suck. And yeah, even I have a shred of doubt, knowing that a trial took place and a judge made a ruling. Hard to argue with that.

"My friends all got weird around me," she says, staring over my shoulder, looking far away from here. "Eventually, they steered clear of me completely. I didn't know what to do with myself. My parents were pretty much absorbed in the trial night and day for six months. So when I started high school, I found some new friends…but they weren't the best kids to hang out with."

Yeah, so that doesn't sound like Brooke at all.

"I did some stuff last year that I wish I could take back," Brooke admits. "I should have been home more, spent more time with my dad… I didn't really think it would turn out like it did; I thought they would sort it all out. Maybe if I had been home more, my mom wouldn't have gotten so depressed. She was trying to help my dad and probably worrying about me on top of everything, and I just wanted to be selfish. I didn't want to listen to anyone. She needed me, and look where she is now."

Her voice breaks again. She starts to cover her face with the blanket, but I stop her. My heart is racing, my insides jumbling around. I tuck her loose tangled hair behind her ears, and my fingers linger on her face, roam over the smooth skin on her cheeks. Her eyes widen, but she doesn't protest—quite the opposite.

I know where this is headed, and I should stop it right now, but I don't think I can.

Chapter Twenty-Eight

–BROOKE–

The butterflies in my stomach flap wildly. It's bizarre to think about this after everything that's happened today. Like two very mismatched socks and yet, it feels like the moment is inevitable.

Jake's fingers brush across my cheeks. I close my eyes, enjoy it without the pressure of looking right at him, right into those very intimidating blue eyes.

"When I was younger…" Now that I've started talking, I can't seem to stop. "My dad used to take me to skating lessons every Saturday."

"You miss him?" Jake asks.

"So much." I open my eyes again, hold his gaze. "I miss my mom, too. Even though she's here, she's not really *here*, you know?"

He cups my chin with one hand, shakes his head. "I guess I don't really know."

God, he's gorgeous. I think if I could just look at him

all day, I wouldn't ever feel bad. I lean forward, rest my forehead against his. His breath catches in a way that makes me think this isn't a one-sided thing. I press my palm against his heart, feel it speed up.

"Jake?"

He slides closer, our legs bumping into each other, overlapping a bit. "Yeah?"

"Do you— I mean—" I exhale. "Do you want to kiss me?"

"Yes," he says, breathing out the word, and then the heat of his mouth is on mine.

He's warm and solid and oh so very beautiful. My mother, the artist, could spend weeks sculpting his hands, his jawline, the curved back of his neck... My hands follow this pattern, taking note of the shape and feel of him, piece by piece.

Soon, our mouths part. Both of us slide back a bit, needing space, air. Jake's hand stays resting on my knee as if wanting us to stay connected. I watch him watching me, assessing if I'm okay.

"I'm okay," I tell him.

His chest rises and falls rapidly. "Yeah? Maybe that was a bad idea considering—"

"No, it wasn't." I lean forward, kiss him again on the mouth but quicker this time. I'm scared that if we leave the safety of this space, this moment, kissing him won't be something I can just do whenever.

He slides his hands along my arms and then frowns. "You're freezing."

"I'm fine." But of course my teeth start chattering. And then I realize even if I wanted to go home, to be in the warm house, no one is there. The high from our kiss fades, and I'm back to worrying about Mom.

"Come on," Jake says, standing and holding out a hand to me. "Let's go to my house. It's closer."

Chapter Twenty-Nine

–JAKE–

Brooke and I enter the house through the front door instead of the kitchen like I usually do. My parents are both in the living room, the TV muted but brightly lit. My mom takes one look at Brooke, the dusty blanket draped around her shoulders, and rushes over. She politely extracts the dirty outdoor blanket from Brooke's body and disappears, probably to toss it in the washer, and returns with a thick, soft hand-knitted blanket.

She steers Brooke toward the kitchen. "Hot tea or cocoa?"

My dad stands and joins me in the foyer. He waits until my mom and Brooke are out of sight before speaking. "How is she doing?"

I scratch the back of my head, not sure what to say. *She seemed fine while we were making out* doesn't seem like a good answer. "She was pretty upset when I found her, didn't know her mom was okay."

"Jesus," my dad says under his breath.

"She seems better now," I tell him.

My mom returns, alone, the phone to her ear. She grabs my dad's arm, tugs him into the living room, and makes a shooing motion, ushering me out of the "grown-up" conversation. I move into the dining room, heading toward the kitchen, but stop when I catch bits of my mom's conversation.

"Oz says we can't take her home," my mom whispers to my dad. "Apparently there is quite a mess there — might be traumatic for her to see…"

A mess?

Oh. The blood. Her mom's arm had been heavily bandaged.

"He says we can't leave the girl alone," my mom says.

Dad makes a noise of disapproval. "Well, we weren't planning to drop her at a motel."

"No, he says not even here in the house," Mom tells him, sounding worried. "She has a history of…cutting."

My stomach drops, a sick feeling washing over me. I'm not sure if it's the actual information I've just heard or the fact that I learned it without Brooke's permission. I push it out of my head for the time being and rush into the kitchen.

Brooke is at the table; a cup of cocoa stuffed with marshmallows sits beside her, untouched. Her phone is to her ear, and I can hear Judy Gleason's voice on the other end but can't make out what she's saying.

"Do you think she can still get into that place in Rochester?" Brooke asks. "Will they move her?"

It sounds like Judy says she doesn't know yet, then asks how Brooke is doing.

"I'm fine…" Brooke sniffles, seeming to force around any unwanted emotions. "I'm gonna stay with a friend tonight.

Don't worry..."

She hangs up, and I cross the kitchen, sit down beside her, then I tug her chair closer so we're facing each other, our feet touching.

"Everything okay?"

She wipes her eyes with her shirtsleeve. "I think so. My mom didn't need surgery... Apparently that's good. Lots of stitches, though."

"And she's safe," I point out, sensing her slipping deeper into worried mode. I take one of her hands, tangle our fingers together. "So are you."

I watch her slowly process those words, feel her way through them. After a few seconds, she inhales sharply and nods. "You're right."

"And you can stay here tonight." I avoid telling her about the reason she can't go home, though she may have guessed already, but it feels like a big deal to sit on the other information I overheard. Like maybe if I don't put it out there, we'll lose this honesty we have going on and I like it too much to give it up. "Oz told my parents not to leave you alone...for reasons we don't have to talk about..." I hang on that for a beat. Brooke's gaze shifts to her lap. "It's possible my parents will be a bit flustered by this, so let's just tell them you're not tired and we'll watch movies in the basement and I'll hang out with you. Avoid any awkward alone time with my mother or you having to sleep in my little's sister's room—she farts in her sleep."

Brooke laughs a short laugh. A wave of relief hits me. "Yeah, okay. I'm good with avoiding both those scenarios you mentioned."

"Great, because..." I glance over her shoulder, see the approaching adults. "Here they come."

Chapter Thirty

–BROOKE–

The basement in Jake's house is mostly dark. I stare at the side of his face as he stares at Cary Grant on the TV screen, dodging a crop duster for the fourth or fifth time.

"Why have I never seen this movie before?" Jake asks. "I mean, it's kind of corny but also cool, you know, 'cause it's so old."

"And because it's Hitchcock," I point out. "Considering there is one theater in town and it shows only hockey-related films for six months out of the year, I'm not surprised that you haven't seen this one."

I snuggle deeper under the thick comforter that Jake's mom gave me and fit myself perfectly in the middle of this soft sectional coach. Jake gave up the best spot on the couch without any protest. One point for him. He's got about five hundred already tonight.

Jake tears his gaze from the TV and scoots closer to me. My heart picks up, my hands twisting under the blanket. He kisses my cheek lightly. I reach out, cup his chin, and kiss him on the mouth. He responds quickly, angling his body toward me, resting a hand on my face, in my hair. But it's over much too quickly.

"My parents…" he says, a bit breathless. "They're gonna take turns checking on us. My mom is probably setting hourly alarms."

I laugh, and then the humor deflates in an instant. "They're not gonna like this. Too much drama, too much heavy stuff… Kinda don't blame them."

He holds my gaze, lifts my palm to his lips. "I'm kind of over needing them to like everything I like."

"What's that revelation like?" I'm honestly curious. My parents have always allowed me room to be myself, to have my own opinions.

He laughs. "You are so different than basically everyone else in my life."

"I'm an outsider, remember?" I kiss him one more time, quickly, my gaze bouncing toward the basement steps and the lit hallway at the top. Then I turn back to the movie, and Jake does the same. A minute or so later, I feel his fingers beneath my blanket, searching for my hand, tangling us together in at least a small way. It feels safe, right, a relief. Not unlike the night I plunged my hands into the freezing lake water, searching for some part of him to grab on to.

What a relief it was when I finally found him.

Chapter Thirty-One

–BROOKE–

Grandma's house is quiet when I walk in, Jake trailing behind me even though I told him he didn't have to come in. Everything looks in order, except it's unnaturally cold. I think Grandma talked the sheriff into turning down her thermostat to save money while she's gone at the hospital. I point to the living room where Jake can hang out, and then I tug the rope in the hallway, releasing the attic steps. I'm still wearing yesterday's clothes and feeling pretty grungy at the moment.

While I'm upstairs changing, I hear the back door open and close several times. When I come downstairs again, in fresh clothes, my hair now brushed and shiny, there's a fire blazing in the fireplace, a stack of wood nearby, drying.

"You were out of dry wood," Jake says, looking slightly embarrassed.

I smile at him. "You don't care if your parents like me but you're trying to win points with my grandma."

"Not her," he clarifies. "You."

My face heats up; I don't know what to say. I turn my back to him, head to the bathroom to brush my teeth.

"Plus it was cold in here," he calls after me.

I stop in front of my mom's bedroom, spot the pill bottles still there on the nightstand, and then I quickly close the door, hoping Jake didn't go past this room. After I come out of the bathroom, Jake is standing at the bottom of the steps, looking up into the attic.

"This is your bedroom?"

"Yeah." I edge past him, put a foot on the bottom step. This room is by far my favorite part of Juniper Falls. The first week or so we were here, my mom was actually doing better than she had been in a while. Good enough to help me fix this room up, make it my own. She went downhill after that. "You want to see?"

He hesitates for a beat but ends up following mc to the steps. And the second he's fully in my room, in my space, for the first time I get an idea of what it might feel like to meet Jake somewhere else, outside of Juniper Falls.

The ceiling slants in the attic. Mom and I painted the back wall a bright yellow to warm and expand the space. The rest of the walls are a soft gray. The bookshelves wrap around three walls and my clothes are stored in fabric bins on several of the shelves. I don't have a closet up here; I use the one downstairs in the hall.

Jake wanders tentatively, taking in one piece at a time. He moves toward a pair of my beat-up pointe shoes hanging from a nail on the wall.

"This explains a lot." He lifts one shoe to his face, examining it. "Is that blood— Holy crap, these smell worse than my hockey skates."

"And that's with more than a year to air out." I laugh at

his expression. "Ballet is brutal."

"Apparently." He shakes his head, moves to a shelf with a few framed photos. He picks up one of my dad and me at an art gallery event for my mom. In the photo, we're standing near a bronze sculpture of a naked man.

"Your hair…" He looks closer. "You got rid of the pink?"

I shrug. It was part of my transformation, part of me trying to be a regular Juniper Falls girl, satisfying my grandmother and her old-fashioned views. "Outgrew it, I guess."

"Oh, wow…is that a sculpture of—"

My face flames. "Of my dad? Yep."

"Jesus." Jake returns the photo to the shelf, shifts his attention elsewhere. "I don't even know what to say."

"You can say what my dad said, 'At least she wasn't inspired to sculpt another man naked.'" I laugh, my face still warm. "It is *the* worst part of being the child of an artist."

"I bet."

Jake browses my book collection while I pick up a few stray clothing items, drop them into the laundry basket. I hadn't planned on having company in here. He tugs a photo album from the shelf between two thick novels. I move closer, watch him study a photo of me three or four years ago, dressed in a very expensive white tutu that was strategically streaked with red paint. I'm underwater, surrounded by dangling red pointe shoes; my hair is loose, floating all around my face.

Jake's forehead wrinkles. "What am I looking at?"

"Isn't it cool?" I flip to the next page. In this series of photos, my eyes are closed and I look dead. "One of my mom's best friends back in Austin took these… She's a photographer…really famous now. She's done lots of book covers, some celebrity shoots, big-name designers."

"So you're a model, too?" He smiles at me from over his shoulder. "I'm still getting used to this conversationalist version of you, and now you're springing ballerina and model on me. Are you an actress, too?"

"I've done some voice-over work," I say automatically. Jake's mouth falls open, and I laugh again. "Just a few radio commercials and one cartoon series on Nickelodeon."

"Seriously?" he asks, closing the book and turning to face me. "Like paid work?"

I nod, then bite my lip. Maybe it seems bigger than it was. Didn't seem like a big deal to me back then. "It's not like I spent the money or anything. My parents put it in a fund for college."

One I'm about to use for my mom's treatment.

"I wasn't a child actress with stage parents taking me around to auditions," I explain, because Jake's shocked expression is still a bit off-putting. "My parents are sort of in the entertainment industry through music and art, so it was just one of those things where a friend needed someone and casting me made sense."

"So your dad's music, can I find it anywhere?" Jake asks.

I shrug. "If you look hard enough. But his own record isn't very well known. He sold a few songs at least ten years ago, and that's what really helped pay the bills. And he was a regular with a local studio for guitar and back-up vocals. That's how I ended up with the radio commercial. In one of them, all I did was scream in like fifty different ways, and they used maybe four seconds of one of those screams."

"That is so…" He returns the album to its shelf and turns to face me. "Cool."

"Cool?" I meet his gaze, but nerves hit hard and fast. My hands start to sweat despite the cold house. "It's not cool; it's weird."

Jake rests a hand on my hip, gently lures me closer until our feet are lined up toes to toes. Despite my confidence last night, today, alone in this big house, it's hard not to focus on the fact that Jake Hammond is a senior. A popular, confident, athletic senior who likely has had a lot of girlfriends—or a lot of hook-ups, at least...

He leans close, our noses nearly touching. "So...what do you have planned today? Does your grandma need you, or—"

I shake my head slowly, not sure if I want to highlight our aloneness or the length of time it would likely last should we stick around here today.

"Good." He grins, releases me, and heads toward the steps. "I have a surprise for you."

Cool air rushes into the space Jake had just occupied. I'm both relieved and disappointed by his distance, if it's even possible to feel both at once. "Do I need any specific attire for this surprise?"

This Texas girl needs advance notice if four-wheelers or snowmobiles are part of the plan.

Chapter Thirty-Two

–JAKE–

Brooke walks slowly up the 150-year-old staircase in town hall, pausing to look at each photo of past years' princes and princesses.

"Oh, wow…" she says. "It's your parents."

"Yep." I exhale, let the pressure of living with those expectations roll over me for a moment, and then I move on. "I think there are five generations of Hammonds on this wall."

"Tanley," she reads at the bottom of one photo. "Related to Tate?"

"Yeah, that's his dad and mom," I say, frowning at the photo. I know too many bad things about Keith Tanley to have any respect for the guy. "They're divorced now. His mom remarried last year. Roger Cremwell. He's one of Oz's best friends."

"They're in a band together, right?" Brooke says, moving on to newer photos. "With Tate's girlfriend, Claire, and

Haley's dad... Is that right?"

"How did you know all that?" I ask, surprised.

"Just picked up stuff here and there." She stops at the current prince and princess photo. "Someone familiar..."

She studies the photo of Haley and me from the New Year's Eve ball last year. Haley in a fancy long dress and me in a suit and tie.

"It's a nice photo," she says. "You look good together. Did you two ever date?"

"No, not beyond going to the ball together."

She turns to face me, her brows lifted. "But you've been more than friends before... Maybe hooked up or something?"

I take a step back, caught off guard by this. "How did you—"

She smiles, easing the tension. "I could hear it in your voice...just now. Almost like you wanted me to know."

"Only because I want to be honest," I admit.

Brooke leans closer, rests a hand on my face, then kisses me. I return the kiss but keep things dialed back. We are on the stairs of a very old and public building, after all.

I usher her away from Haley's picture and toward the real surprise in the upstairs town archives. I leave Brooke sitting at a long table for several minutes, and then I return with a stack of giant books all labeled UNITED STATES FEDERAL CONSENSUS: MINNESOTA, JUNIPER FALLS, DISTRICT 0082.

"You know how your grandma's house has been in your family since it was built?" I say and then backtrack in case I'm jumping ahead too fast. "Did you know that?"

"My mom has mentioned it a few times," she says, biting her thumbnail. She looks nervous, and I have no idea why. "But I wasn't sure if that meant like, a hundred years or like, fifty."

"A hundred and eighty-two to be exact," I tell her, and smile at the shock on her face. "Some of the house has been remodeled, obviously, probably had lead paint or something."

"Might still have lead paint," Brooke says cryptically.

"This town was founded after the Revolutionary War, before the Civil War," I say, more excited than I expected to be about historical facts. But it's cool because it's my history, and now I can show her how it's hers, too. How it's always been hers even if she only just got here. "You said something last night about being an outsider, and that got me thinking…your family is actually one of this town's oldest families, as old as the Juniper family."

She opens the book on top, dated 1910. "Seriously? As old as the founder of the town?"

"Yep." I flip several pages over and stop at the one that lists the Gleason farmhouse. "And we have the proof right here."

"A census report?" She studies the page in front of her. "That's the list of all the people in each household reported to the government every ten years or something?"

"Exactly," I say. "Basically some dude rode around on a horse from house to house, knocking on doors, asking the same questions, writing everything down."

"But people could lie, right?" she says, eyeing the page skeptically. "They could say whatever they wanted?"

"I don't think anybody really had a reason to lie. The questions weren't very personal. And for you and your family, it's even easier to trace your history and family tree because you don't need to know married names and all of that." I scan the left column with my index finger and pause on dwelling 013. "You just have to look for the house."

"Ward comma James," Brooke reads aloud. "Head of household. Wife Hannah… Wow, they had eight children?"

"In 1910 they had eight children," I point out. "Might be more that weren't even born yet."

"Sex—male," Brooke reads, following James Ward's line across the page. "Race—W—white, I assume?" Her head tilts downward, following the race column while her figure holds its place with the Ward household. "Looks like everyone was white in this town…"

"Um," I say, slightly uncomfortable by this fact. "That hasn't changed much."

"James Ward was thirty-seven at the time of this census," Brooke continues. "Homeowner, farmer, he didn't attend school, and wow…it says both he and his wife couldn't read but several of the kids could."

"Maybe schools were slow to open here? Or farmers didn't send their kids to school until after 1900?" I suggest. "My family looks pretty similar. My dad was the first to attend college."

Brooke slides the top book from the stack, glances at the rest of the books, then back at me. "These all have different generations of my family?"

"Or just different versions of the same generation."

"This is really cool, Jake," she says, sounding so genuine I regret not showing her this sooner. "I had no idea all of this was here. I think my mom was just so determined to put her small-town upbringing behind her that she didn't really offer many details, and it was hard to imagine her being anywhere but Austin with my dad and me, you know?"

I laugh. "No, I really don't know. My parents have actually been here their whole lives, except for college, so yeah…"

"Where did they go to college?" Brooke asks.

"University of Minnesota in Duluth, or UMD is what everyone here calls it," I say, and it occurs to me how weird it is to tell someone this. I'm so used to existing in a world where everyone already knows these types of things about me. "What about your parents?"

"My dad didn't go to college," Brooke says. "My mom went to Vanderbilt and then an art school in Paris for her MFA, but I can't remember the name of that school."

Okay, so Lauren Gleason definitely went off the beaten Juniper Falls path. And it's so strange how even my own parents made it seem like she was just some less-popular classmate of theirs in high school. They never mentioned her going to a college that Mr. Smuttley claimed, during those boring information sessions, is the "Ivy League of the South." Guess it's not all that surprising considering Claire O'Connor goes to Northwestern, an equally prestigious university, and hardly anyone talks much about that because she's studying musical theater and their hockey isn't ranked in the top ten, not even the top twenty.

"Jake...?" Brooke says, like maybe she just asked me a question and I spaced out. "Where are you going to school? Have you already applied?"

"I wrote my essays over the summer, took the ACT test last year...got my letters of rec taken care of already," I rattle off as if it's one of my mom's friends asking about my future plans. "Just waiting to submit everything until closer to the deadline."

"Submit to which schools?" Brooke presses.

"Schools with top-twenty division-one hockey teams." I flip through one of the newer, less battered census books from 1960. I scan pages looking for Hammonds or any of the other married names on my dad's side. "UMD, St. Cloud, Michigan, Ohio State..."

"Anything not in the Midwest?" Brooke asks, then after watching me for several seconds, she changes gears. "I'm sorry... This is making you uncomfortable. Is it because you aren't cleared to play yet?"

"Yeah, kind of," I admit. "It's hard to explain… It's just that I've done well in hockey the past three years. I've gotten calls from coaches since January of my sophomore year—the earliest they're allowed to contact players—but the signing period just started, and not only am I injured but I also haven't really gotten to show everything I can do, you know?"

"The schools you're applying to, I'm guessing they're going to offer you a spot? Athletic aid?"

"As long as they know I can still play after…" I stop there, not sure if I can keep going with this conversation. The truth is that I'm not 100 percent positive that I can still play, like before.

"Are you interested in college without hockey?" she asks.

I scratch the back of my head, look away from her. "I've never really thought about it."

"I'm sorry," Brooke says, worry all over her face. "I'm ruining this."

Maybe *this* is still salvageable. I turn and rest both hands on the side of her face, then I kiss her until I feel her cheeks heat beneath my hands. After a minute or so, Brooke pulls back, rests her forehead against mine, and whispers, "The old man at the front desk is watching us."

"Yeah, he's Oz's neighbor," I tell her, earning a frustrated groan. "Secret kissing—basically secret anything—doesn't really work around here."

She moves away, returns to looking at one of the census books. "Except hockey team secrets. Those seem to stay locked up in some hundred-year-old fortress."

Can't really argue with that.

We're both busy for a while, reading, researching. Pretty much any of these books that I open hold interesting facts. Nearly every page has someone I know or a family name I recognize. Thirty minutes into the 1960 census book, I land on an unfamiliar name that should be familiar. "Paulson Matthew Hammond...I don't know this person."

Brooke leans over to look, spotting the head of household before I do. "Eugene Hammond... Four children—"

"Four?" I read it closely. "That's my great uncle Eugene. He died right before I started middle school. He only had three kids. I know because they're all my dad's cousins, all within five years' age difference."

"Looks like Paulson is the oldest," Brooke says. "Maybe twenty years older than your dad?"

I frown at the book. "Big difference in age for first cousins. Kinda weird, right?"

"Think it's my turn to say that I literally have no idea," Brooke says. "Only child, my mom is an only child...I have no uncles or cousins. Pretty sure most of my relatives live in these books."

"What about your dad?" The question comes out before I can stop it. Not sure if she's cool with talking about her dad much, given the circumstances.

"He doesn't talk to his family at all." Her voice is back to the quiet, barely audible state that I remember from our early conversations. "He left home when he was fifteen, Oklahoma, I think, and he never went back."

Then maybe she's right—maybe all of her family is right here on this table, in these books.

"They used that against him," Brooke says, as quiet as before. "In court, the prosecuting lawyer. They brought up the fact that he was a runaway as testament to his character. Only in Texas with a conservative family-oriented judge and jury can you get away with holding a forty-three-year-old accountable for his poor choices at age fifteen. Juvenile records are sealed for a reason. People grown up. I can't even imagine if I had to justify stuff I did last year, at fifteen, when I'm much older."

By the end of that long explanation, she returned to the stronger, more vocal girl I've enjoyed the past twenty-four hours. I wrap an arm around her shoulders. "For a minute there, I thought you were reverting back to giving me the silent treatment. Not sure I could handle that after all of this."

She looks at me, more serious now. "I'll try, okay? At least for you."

We go back to reading for a few minutes, and then Brooke speaks again. "It made things easier for me…being in the background, a fly on the wall or whatever. I lived in the spotlight last year, everywhere I went, and I just couldn't breathe after a while. Mr. Smuttley calls it survivor's guilt. I did things I shouldn't have, and yet I still get to have a life while my dad is locked up and my mom…I can't exactly call the pill-induced zombie state she's perpetually in *living.*"

Survivor's guilt? I have some concept of what that feels like given that Elliott Pratt suffered a much worse fate than I did.

But I really hope it's never me who makes her feel like being alone and silent is better than hanging out with someone who has your back. Because I do have her back. I owe her at least that much; she's had mine ever since I jumped into that frozen pond and couldn't pull myself out.

Truth is that I couldn't have survived all the shit that happened after that night at the pond on my own, without Brooke being there for me. As much as I like talking to her like this, like last night and this morning, I'll take whatever version of her she's willing to give me.

And yeah, that scares the hell out of me. Needing someone this much.

Chapter Thirty-Three

–JAKE–

"Guess that antler crown looks better on you anyway," Red says when he sees me at the winter carnival, inside the varsity hockey tent. "And by better I mean fucking ridiculous."

I shove him, hard. Harder than I should with my still-healing collarbone in the mix.

"Leave the prince alone," Haley says. "It's not easy being the star and then watching from the bench. Give him a break."

"Awww," Red says. "Poor Jake. I'm sorry, man. I should have been more sensitive to your situation."

It might be a little bit funny if it weren't him who got me into this situation. What had he said that night at the pond? *If your captain says jump, you jump.*

I glance around, looking for Brooke. She wasn't in school today or yesterday. Her mom got moved to that special treatment center in Rochester a few days ago, and Brooke went with her grandma for some kind of family screening so she would be allowed to see her mom when the doctors okayed it. I pull out my phone and send her a quick text.

ME: everything ok in Rochester?

She replies just seconds later.

BROOKE: I'm home now. It was weird but ok. I think?
ME: winter carnival is happening, right across the street, u want to come?
BROOKE: Maybe in a bit?
ME: cool, lmk when u get here

"Uh-oh," Red says, reading over my shoulder. "The sophomore again."

"Did somebody say sophomore?" Cole asks, his mouth full of food. He's balancing a completely full plate in one hand while the other holds a giant glass of milk.

"Not you," Red says. "The girl Jake is courting."

"Courting?" I shake my head. "Seriously?"

"Oh, Brooke," Cole says, eyeing me. "She's cool. Doesn't seem like your type but…"

"Hammond doesn't have a type," Red says. "He can't pick."

"Well…" Cole chugs half his glass of milk. "Guess he does now."

Cole leaves Red and me alone and goes off to find a place to sit.

"Is it really that weird?" I ask Red. "That Brooke is a sophomore? I mean, she's sixteen; I'm seventeen. Doesn't seem like a big deal."

"Whatever." Red shrugs. "You and a sophomore isn't weird, but she's weird, you know?"

I fold my arms across my chest, glare at him. "No, I don't know. Care to enlighten me?"

He laughs, holds his hands up in surrender. "Okay, I get it. This is what you want. I'm staying out of it."

He backs away slowly and then turns around to talk to one of Haley's friends. I spot my dad talking to Tanley and head over to them in case Tate needs backup. He let a goal slip by tonight. Might be an unsolicited coaching session.

"Jake and I are looking at a trip to Notre Dame next month before the winter break," Dad tells Tate, though it's the first I've heard of this. "You should come along, talk with the coach, see what they have to offer. Eight schools. That should be your goal."

I move right into their conversation, hoping to rescue Tate if needed. "We're going to Notre Dame?"

"You still have two more official recruiting trips," Dad reminds me. "Best to take advantage of them."

"I'm just looking forward to getting my hands on a stick again." I grab a plate from the buffet and toss some random items on it.

"Maybe the extra practice time will keep you out of the town hall record books." Dad points out a table for the three of us to sit at, and we settle into chairs quickly. "Arnold is on me the second I walk into the office in the morning, telling me you owe him some books?"

Tate looks very confused. "Wait, why would you steal record books from town hall?"

"Borrow," I correct. "That's allowed, according to the sign on the door. I've been reading the census reports, looking at our family history."

"Is this for a school project?" Dad asks.

"Just curious, that's all." I shovel in a few bites of potato salad. "I didn't know Uncle Eugene had four kids—thought it was just the three. But then I saw Paulson Matthew Hammond in the 1960 report. What happened to him?"

"He died young." Dad glances over my shoulder, probably making eye contact with someone who wants his attention or wants to talk about the game tonight. "Drunk driver, I believe. Tragic. I think Eugene didn't like to talk about it."

"But he's a Hammond; why haven't I heard of him?" I point out. "Did he play hockey?"

With the exception of my uncle Oz, all the Hammond men played hockey and have some kind of recognition on the Otter Hall of Fame wall in the ice rink. I've never seen Paulson's name on the wall.

"Not sure. He was much older than me." Dad stands, waves at someone behind me. "Gotta go talk shop. See you boys later. Stay out of trouble tonight."

"Did it seem like he was dodging my question?" I ask Tate.

"It seems like you're spending too much time with the sheriff." Tate watches three guys dressed in shirts and ties enter the tent together. "Wow, this is crazy, right?"

Elliott, Connor, and Troy stand awkwardly inside the varsity tent despite the fact that none of them have ever played even one second of a varsity game.

"I don't know about crazy, but it's something." I make eye contact with Elliott, offer a nod.

"Bakowski has a method when he puts freshmen on varsity," Tate says, keeping his voice low. "He's all about the sink-or-swim philosophy. He threw you in right away, didn't he? And left you in the game longer than any other player, if I remember right."

I definitely remember. I puked for two hours straight after that game. "He did the same thing to Clooney last season."

"And yet those guys haven't gone in at all. Four games down." Tate shakes his head. "Elliott I get—he's barely out of the hospital—but the other two…"

"The tent's getting kinda full." I stand. "Want to go walk around?"

"Yep." Tate tosses both of our plates into a nearby garbage, and then we hustle out of the tent and stroll past the O'Connor's Tavern booth where Davin O'Connor and his brother-in-law are serving their famous walleye horseshoe.

"So…" Tate says. "Guess you took my advice about Brooke?"

I laugh. "Yeah, you could say that."

"Good for you, man," he says. "Has it been weird, with you coaching the girls and all that?"

"Surprisingly, no, that hasn't been weird." I glance back at the varsity tent where Red and Collins are laughing loud enough to hear them a ways away. "But hanging out with our crowd…that might get weird."

Tate offers a sympathetic nod. "Might be better to get it out of the way sooner rather than later."

"Yeah." I release a nervous breath. "Maybe."

Chapter Thirty-Four

–BROOKE–

I tug my knit hat down over my ears and curl my fingers inside my mittens, trying to keep everything warm. I get a whiff of chili and cornbread and my stomach rumbles. I stop at a booth to my right and dig for some cash in my pocket. A minute later, I'm strolling happily through the carnival, a paper cup of chili warming my hands. Main Street is blocked off tonight for this event, and a massive sculpture made of ice sits right in the middle of the road. I move to get a closer look. It's a man on a horse.

"James Juniper, town founder," a voice says from behind me.

My insides warm, and I curse myself for feeling this much. "The evil man who pushed all the natives off the land."

"Sad but true." Jake slips an arm around my waist, pulls my back against him. "Is it too cold for you?"

From the corner of my eye, I spot two of my teammates—Rosie and Samantha—watching us. My face warms. I fight the instinct to move away. Do I want people to talk about us? Do I want them to notice me with Jake before they even really know me?

Before I can make any decisions, Jake places his mouth close to my ear and whispers, "Want to go somewhere with me?"

"Yes, definitely."

Two times before, Jake has said basically the same words to me as tonight, inviting me to an adventure between the two of us, free from the rest of the town. Tonight, however, "somewhere" meant something very different—being crammed in a booth at Benny's, the local late-night hangout with Jake and all his popular senior friends, along with half the high school population.

"I'm still trying to get over the sight of Hammond stuck on the bench all night," Red says in a taunting tone.

"We needed you tonight," a guy whose name I don't know says. "Could have used a few more goals."

I glance at Jake and see that this is getting to him. Must have been hard to watch that game and not be able to play.

Jake lifts a napkin from the table, tears it into pieces. "Clooney did well."

"Yeah, but I'm getting sick of hearing about that kid," Red says. "His head is blowing up, don't you think?"

I check Jake again, wanting to see his reaction. He opens his mouth to speak but is interrupted by another guy whose name I don't know.

"Saw you and Clooney doing a little private lesson together a while back," the guy says, wiggling his eyebrows at me. "I take it you traded up?"

"Dude, what the hell?" Jake rises in his seat like he's about to punch the guy.

I tug his jacket, pull him back down beside me. I give him a look that hopefully says, *Be cool.* The last thing I want is this little bit of teasing escalating into some big rumor.

The guy seems to enjoy Jake's reaction, but at the same time, I feel the team-captain card vibrating in the air. Jake has power over these guys. The rude teammate pulls out a flask and proceeds to pour what look like water but smells like vodka into his soda. Then he passes it to Red, who does the same.

This all feels so familiar, and not in a good way. It's too much like my time hanging out with the "wrong crowd" freshman year. Except back then I wasn't rejecting offers to pour vodka into my soda. I shake my head when Red tries to tip the flask into my Dr Pepper. I bring the cup closer to me and place a hand over the lid. He takes the hint, tucks the flask away before the Benny's workers notice.

"Clooney isn't into Brooke," Red says to the rude teammate. "He's got his eye on someone else…"

I know where this is headed, and I cringe on Cole's and Rosie's behalf. It isn't fair that they aren't here to defend themselves. Rosie probably doesn't even know how Cole feels about her. I wouldn't know if Jake hadn't pointed it out.

Outside, in the parking lot, I spot Haley and Fletcher, leaning against an SUV. I whisper to Jake that I'm gonna say hi to Haley, and then I hurry off before he can stop me. It's so cold outside, but right away I'm looser, less constricted.

I need to get out of here. But I don't want to be that girl who drags the guy away from his friends—those guys will just start talking about me as soon as we leave. I debate walking home, but Haley stops me before I can make it to the road.

"Hey, what's wrong?"

"Nothing." But I accidently glance back at Jake and his table of friends. Haley's too smart to miss that slip. "I'm just…tired."

"We're heading out," she says, pointing at Fletch. "You want a ride?"

"Yes," I say, and then guilt hits hard. I can't just leave Jake here. I'll send him a text from the car.

Haley tugs me by my jacket sleeve, away from the SUV. She looks over her shoulder at Fletcher. "Excuse us for a minute…girl talk."

She angles herself so her back is to Fletcher and then whispers, "Sorry, this is weird, but…" She lifts my hands so they're out in front of us, palms up, then she dumps a bunch of hand sanitizer from a small bottle in her coat pocket right in my palms. "Fletch has a bunch of allergies… Just being cautious."

"I can go in the bathroom and—" I start.

Haley shakes her head. "It's fine, I'm sure. I'm just protective."

A minute later, we get into the car. My stomach churns with nerves, but I don't let myself look back. I pull out my phone and send Jake a quick text.

ME: sorry for leaving. Just wasn't my scene. Getting a ride with Haley

Then I shut my phone off so I don't have to feel guilty.

"Benny's isn't your scene, huh?" Haley says, startling me with her mind-reading powers.

"Not really."

"Me neither," Fletch says from the driver's seat.

Haley angles herself to face me from up front. "So what

is your scene? What did you do for fun in…"

"Austin," I supply.

"Austin." Haley nods. "I knew it was Texas but couldn't remember where. I've heard Austin is amazing. Probably have much more exciting Friday nights there."

When I don't say anything for a long beat, Fletcher speaks up. "Ballet, right? That's what you did in Austin?"

Haley gives Fletcher a bewildered look. "Ballet? Where did that come from?"

Yeah, where did that come from? Jake? Smuttley? My grandma?

"Just a hunch." Fletcher laughs at Haley's look, probably mine, too, because I catch him glance back here through the rearview mirror. "Sorry, I just— When Cole was helping you with skating, I could tell."

"You could tell?" Haley presses.

Fletch seems embarrassed. "Dancers aren't hard to spot. It's not rocket science. She turns her feet out. The posture, too…"

I start laughing, mostly because this is, like, the weirdest conversation ever. "He's right. Ballet was my thing for a while. Every day, practically, even Friday night."

"She speaks," Fletcher says. "And between us, I also have some dance experience."

A dancer-slash-hockey-player, now that's hard to believe. "Your secret is safe with me," I promise.

"Jake is being nice to you, right?" Haley presses. "Because if he's not—"

"He is," I say right away.

Fletcher pulls up to Grandma's driveway, and I'm so ready to hop out. I like Haley, but I'm not sure I want to talk about Jake anymore. He is great. His world is just so different from the one I want to be in.

"Thanks for the ride," I tell both of them. Then I head inside, lock the front door behind me, and make my way upstairs. I finally turn on my phone.

Six missed calls from Jake.

I don't know why I'm so afraid to face him at the moment, but I am. I send him another quick text.

ME: made it home. Going to bed. Call u in the morning.

I turn off my phone before he can reply.

Later on, I'm under the covers, eyes closed, halfway to falling asleep when I hear a *tap, tap, tap* at my window. I sit up, startled, and then nearly scream at the sight of a large shadow outside my window on the roof. I hold perfectly still as a face comes closer, revealing itself.

And then I release a breath, toss back the covers, and rush over to the window.

Chapter Thirty-Five

–JAKE–

Brooke opens the window with shaking hands. "What are you doing, Jake?"

"Shhh…" I glance down at the ground below. This was quite a climb up. "Can I come in?"

Instead of moving aside to let me through, Brooke practically pulls me by my jacket through her small window. We land on the floor, tangled together in a heap. I help her to her feet then close the window gently.

Brooke fumbles around in the dark, flips a switch, turning on a dim reading light beside the bed. "You gave me a heart attack."

"Sorry," I say. "You didn't answer your phone."

Now that I'm standing here, having climbed in her window, this plan seems incredibly impulsive.

She sinks back onto her bed, lifts a hand to her chest. "I told you I would call in the morning. It's not like you didn't know where I was."

"I'm sorry." My face warms, even though I will it not to. "You're right. I should have just waited. I thought you were mad or upset, that it was something I could fix."

"Such a handyman." She gives the tiniest of smiles. "I'm fine. We're fine, okay?"

I gesture to the bed, asking if I can sit. She nods.

"You were uncomfortable tonight," I say, knowing the answer already. "Was it me or my teammates?"

She brings her thumbnail to her lips, biting down on it gently, a nervous habit of hers, I've learned. "It's hard to explain. Even to myself."

"Just try," I tell her and then add, "please."

I tried to let it go, tried to wait for her to call in the morning, but I had this feeling something was really wrong, and I couldn't sit still. Then next thing I knew I was walking through the woods, climbing Judy Gleason's drainpipe.

Brooke looks me over for a long beat then rests both hands on my arms. "You look so worried. I'm fine—I swear." She leans forward, kisses me on the mouth. "And you're freezing."

Already I'm relieved; I can tell she means it. She's okay. And yet something made her leave. "You can tell me if you hate my teammates. Sometimes I hate them, too. It's not like—"

She presses a finger to my lips, stopping me. "We can talk, okay? Just take off your coat and the muddy boots you're about to put on my nice clean comforter."

I relax a little more. She really does seem fine. I unzip my jacket and hang it over her desk chair, then unlace my boots and stick them near the window.

Brooke flips a switch, turning the reading light off, and then crawls across the bed and touches a button behind her headboard. A row of tiny white lights illuminates along the edge of her ceiling. She tugs my hand until we're both lying on our backs, staring up at the ceiling where Brooke has pinned posters of dancers and abstract art with blobs of colors.

"Even if you're really, definitely super into me," Brooke starts, "I still can't picture someone like you coming over here in the middle of the night to make sure that I'm not mad at you."

"Even if I'm super into you?" I repeat, then turn on my side to face her so she can see me roll my eyes at that. "Since when does worrying about someone equal obsession?"

Okay, so I'm a little ticked off about where this is going. I thought we were talking about her leaving Benny's, not me coming here.

She rolls over, faces me, and then before I can get any more annoyed, she lays a hand on my cheek. "I keep forgetting about that night at your house, after my mom went to the hospital—you've been so cool about everything, not labeling me or even my mom, but you did overhear something, and we've never talked about it."

The cutting. Not leaving her alone. So yeah, maybe I thought about that a little while I was restless and anxious.

"I just have a feeling that if it were anyone else, you would let it go until the morning," she says. "But you thought maybe if I were upset and by myself…"

I lift her hand from my face, hold it against my chest. "Is that— I mean would that be—"

"That's not a thing for me anymore," she says. "Hasn't been for a long time."

"Promise?" I ask. I can't help it—I have to know.

"Promise." She tugs her hand free and scoots back toward the wall, as if wanting to see all of me. "When that was a thing for me…some of the stuff that happened tonight, they went hand in hand."

"Drinking? Partying?" I prompt.

She nods. "But really, I don't think that's what made me uncomfortable. It's just, when I came here, I wanted to fit in so badly. It's what made me want to join the hockey team. I thought it might make my dad proud, my mom happier. And I wanted a do-over from my first year of high school."

"Minus the parties and drinking?" I guess, still trying to grasp where she's going with this.

"Well, yeah, but I can go to a party and I don't have to drink." She shrugs. "But I thought if I did fit in, it would be as me. Not as Jake Hammond's girlfriend."

I rest my head on the pillow near my elbow, mulling that over.

"I'm sorry," Brooke says. "I sound like a judgmental snob—why are you smiling? I'm being serious."

The smile happened without my realizing it.

"Sorry." I reach over, touch her hair, her cheek. "I heard you say *Jake Hammond's girlfriend* and now I can't think about anything else except you saying that and how much I like it."

Chapter Thirty-Six

–BROOKE–

My insides warm. I feel myself returning the smile without permission. "I meant it hypothetically or how other people might just assume—"

Jake's mouth crashes against mine, and he kisses me once, twice, a third time that stretches out for several seconds. "Okay," he says, breathless. "Even hypothetically, I still like it a lot."

I watch, amused, as he extracts himself from me, scoots back until he bumps into my nightstand. "I promise this is not why I climbed into your window tonight."

"Sure it isn't."

He sits up, seems to contemplate standing, then continues to look adorably conflicted. "I should probably go."

I push up to my knees, enough to reach him and tug him back to the bed. I'm not going out into the woods tonight, chasing after Jake because I'm worried that he's mad at me. Not when I have him here right now.

"I was kidding," I assure him. "But if you want, we can be completely serious."

I sit back on my heels and wait for him to respond.

"The girlfriend thing," he says again. "I mean do you think—is that what you want?"

"In theory, yes," I say honestly. "But as a someone who goes to Juniper Falls High, being your girlfriend is a lot to take on."

"I'm sorry." He shakes his head as if clearing it. "I'm distracted again…" He touches the frayed neckline of my long-sleeve T-shirt. "What are you wearing? It's, like, full-body coverage and…why does it look so hot? I can't think about anything else now."

I laugh for several seconds, and then it's cut off by the blazing look on Jake's face. "The shirt is big because it's my dad's. And it gets really cold in my room at night. Hence the leggings and wool socks."

Jake scrubs a hand over his face then glances at the window. "What is it called when you feel something so strongly you start to see the same feelings in someone else?"

"Projecting?" I supply.

"Yes, exactly. I think that's happening now."

My heart gives a loud *thump-thump-thump*. My stomach bubbles with excitement. Something about seeing Jake Hammond flustered, insecure… A wall drops between us.

He draws in a breath. "Okay, so maybe it's not just me."

"Definitely not just you," I tell him.

I scoot closer, and Jake does the same. We meet in the middle, both of us kneeling on this squishy mattress. I lose my balance a little, and Jake sets a hand on my waist, steadying me.

"I don't feel like we figured anything out," he says. "And is this okay? I'm a senior and you're—"

"How old are you?" I ask him.

"Seventeen."

Warm fingers brush over the skin on my back. "Well, I'm sixteen."

"That seems okay, right?" Jake asks, his mouth hovering over mine.

I nod. "Pretty sure it's fine."

"Sorry, that was a weird question." He holds my face with both hands, kissing me until I'm dissolving into a puddle of T-shirt and leggings and wool socks. "Not that things are going that far."

"No?" I pull back, watch his face.

He takes a second to process this, and then slowly, he grips the hem of my shirt, lifts it up over my head. "We should probably have a line of some kind. Just so that I know where or when to stop—"

"I'll let you know," I tell him. I touch the buttons at the top of his shirt, unfasten the first one. Then the second. "And you can let me know, okay?"

He helps me lift his shirt over his head, tosses it aside. And then we're stretched out across the bed. His mouth finds mine again, and we're kissing, our bodies pressed together. I think my enthusiasm for this surprises him; maybe it surprises me a little, too.

"Do you want to…" Jake says, breathless between kisses. "I mean, do you think we should—"

"Do you?" I ask, then I lean in, kiss the side of his neck. He smells so nice, feels so nice.

"Yes." The answer escapes quickly, but then he backtracks. "I definitely do, but I don't think we should."

"No?" And I feel both disappointed and a tiny bit relieved. "Why not?"

His fingers drift up my back and then press gently,

molding us together. "I just… I really like you, and I want to figure out this thing with us; I want to make it work. But if we do *that*, I'm not sure it'll be so easy, you know?"

There's a good chance he's right, and yet I still want to. "Yeah, okay."

"I think maybe we just drew a line?" He lifts his head, looks at me for confirmation.

My eyes burn, my throat constricts. The feelings comes out of nowhere. The guy I did all this with last year—who I refuse to name even to myself in this moment—never asked me any of these questions, never cared enough to ask. I would love to erase all that, replace it with something much better. But Jake is right—it can't be too hurried. Not when there's so much we still need to figure out.

I set both hands on his face, bring his mouth closer to mine. I wonder how many people have seen *this* Jake Hammond? Maybe I overreacted tonight. There has to be a way to be myself, *with him*.

"I'm sorry about earlier," I tell him. "At Benny's."

He pauses, hands on my cheeks. "We're okay?"

"We're okay," I whisper against his lips. "We were always okay."

The two of us stretch out across the bed again. Jake leans over me, kissing my mouth, my neck. His left arm drapes across my stomach. I take his hand, place it higher, near my breast. Jake tentatively glides a hand over my chest, then lower, resting on my hip. My heart threatens to explode out of my body. It doesn't help my pulse that Jake, without his shirt, looks like a sculpture one of my mother's art students might make and title it something like, *Beautiful Male Form*.

His hand drifts from my hip to my thigh then between my legs, rubbing gently over my clothes. Instinctively, I deepen our kiss when he does this. He moves his hand, slides on top of me, balancing his weight with his arms. The pressure of him against me feels amazing. I glide my fingers over his back, the sides of his jeans, press his hips against mine until we're both breathless and weak.

Jake slides over, lays my head against his chest. But all the good feelings quickly shift to embarrassment, and I sit up suddenly, startling Jake. Feeling naked, I snatch a tank top from my bedroom floor, toss it over my head. Probably inside out.

But then I look at Jake, still stretched across my bed, his face a reflection of the insecurity I'm currently feeling. I touch his chest, slide my hand down his stomach. "How do you get abs like this? I don't think I can be shirtless around you."

He laughs, relaxing. When I return to laying my head on his chest, his arms wrap tightly around me. "Are we still okay?"

Now it's my turn to laugh. I lift my head enough to kiss his cheek before resting against him again, closing my eyes. "I wish everyone in town could see you like this. Then it wouldn't seem so strange, you and me together."

"I know what you mean," he says.

We're both quiet for several minutes, but just when I'm sure Jake has dozed off, he says, "Just to be clear…that was a mutual experience?"

My face flames, and I bury it in the crook of his neck. "Yes."

"Wow." His fingers touch my cheek. They feel cold against my heated skin. "Your face is awfully hot. We should talk about this some more… The pros and cons of clothes-on sex."

I laugh, my face growing hotter by the second. But I pull myself together, raise my head. "Sure. Let's talk about it. We can talk all night if you want."

"Nice." He smiles up at me, smooths my hair behind my ears. "Well played."

I kiss him again, rest my forehead against his, and inhale this memory in a long, slow breath. I've gotten used to being on my own, to handling everything with my mom and dad without having anyone to talk about it with, and I know that I can cope solo. But having someone here, holding on to me, at least for a little while, is not something I want to forget.

"Can you stay here for a while?" I ask, resting my head on his arm again.

He kisses my forehead, runs a hand over my back slowly, using just his fingertips. "Yeah, I can stay."

"Next time we're out together and I want to leave," I mumble, feeling sleepy, "I'll let you take me home."

"Good," he says. And then he adds, "Let's try again tomorrow night. I have practice until five."

"Practice," I repeat with interest. "Tomorrow's the day you get to play full out again, right?"

"Yep," he says, "according to the trainer, I'll be off the bench the first game after New Year's. If everything goes well in practice this week."

"It will," I tell him. "I know it will."

"If you want…" he says tentatively, "you can watch practice."

I kiss him again, rest my ear against his chest. "I'll be there."

Chapter Thirty-Seven

–JAKE–

I fly past Red, maneuver around an East Duluth player who's coming at me, and head straight for the goal. This goalie is ready for me; his glove is fast. I spin around the backside of the goal and then send the puck straight to Clooney, who's in position right in front of the goal. Clooney fakes a shot, hooks the puck on the end of his stick, tosses it to me. I slap it into the net before the goalie even has a chance to reach a glove out.

The sirens in our home arena blare, everyone on their feet. We're winning 6-0. I've scored five of those goals.

"Jake Hammond is back!" the announcer says like I wasn't back the last six games. "Setting a new personal record for goals scored in one game!"

While the announcer is yapping, I skate to the other side of the rink where Tate is tending goal. "Number twenty-eight is the one with that funky spinning slap shot. Watch out for that."

"Thanks, man." Tate nods. "Pretty calm down at my end."

"Calm before the storm," I remind him. But unfortunately, remembering might not be enough for Tate. A calm goal means a cold goalie. Not much we can do about that.

I head over for the face-off, passing Red and Fletcher on the way. "Keep up the defense—let's make this a shutout."

I skate up behind Cole and whisper, "If you're in position, set up that other thing we practiced."

Not sure if the pucks will land in the right spot for another play we've been working, but if it does, it would be nice to run at least once before Sections.

The ref blows the whistle, and already I can feel desperate hunger. East Duluth wants a goal, at least one, before the game ends in five minutes. I go after the puck and get checked at least three times. One hit causes the rink to go dark for a split second. Then I'm back on my feet shaking it off, but these guys are all over me. I look around, see who they've left open.

Fletcher.

He's going head-to-head with East Duluth's best forward. I get around them, jam my stick between them, and send the puck flying in the other direction. Fletcher plays mostly defense, but he's one of our fastest skaters. Two guys slam into me, trying to keep me from breaking away toward the puck. But in the meantime, Fletcher's up there in my spot. The goalie's distracted, yelling for his teammates to get their asses down there to help him. Fletcher spots an opening and takes it, a fast shot to the bottom left pocket.

The sirens blare. Cheers get louder.

"Nice one, Scott!" I yell from the other end.

"Goal for number eighteen, Fletcher Scott!" the announcer says. "First career goal for the Otters from Scott."

Fletch skates toward me, takes off his helmet for a

second. "What the hell was that?"

"They were all over me, left you wide open," I tell him as we're passing each other.

He shakes his head, looking confused or shocked, either from the fact that he just scored a goal or that I set him up to do it, I'm not sure. But Fletch is focused. Hopefully he'll get over the shock quickly and maybe even repeat that play, because these guys are never going to let up on covering me.

But East Duluth turns it up a notch. They're fighting down at our end; Tate is throwing himself in front of shot after shot.

"Get your damn head out of your ass, Collins," Bakowski says. "You clear that puck to the outside!"

I try to get in there and help my teammates, but these big guys keep slamming into me. Finally East Duluth takes a shot at the top corner pocket, Tate snatches it up with his glove, hangs on for several seconds while the crowd counts down. The buzzer sounds, signaling the end of the game. I'm still keyed up, ready to play another three periods, ready to make up for the missed games early in the season.

After the game, when I come out of the locker room, the lobby of the rink is still full. I'm hoping to sneak out the front without anyone stopping to talk—Brooke should be home from visiting her mom in Rochester. I make it out the doors and halfway to my truck, but then I hear my name.

"Jake!" Dad shouts. "Come over here. I want you to meet someone."

I mutter a few choice words under my breath before turning around and heading over to my dad. "I was just heading out to meet—"

"Ignore his rudeness. He's just in a hurry to see his girlfriend," Dad says to the older man beside him. Then he gives me a look. "How does Judy Gleason feel about you ringing her doorbell after ten o'clock?"

"That's why I'm planning to use the window." Shit. Definitely didn't mean to say that out loud. "Kidding."

The man beside Dad laughs at my "joke," and then he sticks his hand out to shake mine. "Ralph Cameron. I coach the Duluth Falcons—"

"Yeah, I know who you are," I say. "I mean, your name anyway. I'm a big Falcons fan."

"You dad mentioned that," he says. "I really enjoyed watching you play tonight. If your dad hadn't mentioned it, I never would have known you're coming off an injury."

"Thanks, I'm glad to be playing again."

"Obviously you have an impressive number of goals scored this season," he says. "But I wasn't expecting such great teamwork. Plus your defense is strong, one of the fastest skaters on your team... Your dad says you're thinking about Boston University?"

"I applied," I tell him. "But I haven't done my official visit yet with the coach."

"Have you considered playing junior hockey next year? Make it a gap year or possibly two?" he asks.

"Well..." I glance at my dad, who gives a little nod. I take that to mean I can speak freely. "My mom really wants me to go to college right away."

"I get that," he says. "Education is important. But I have two guys this year, one admitted to Boston U and one to Ohio State. Both were allowed a gap year, no problem. Not telling you what to do. Your parents will do enough of that. But just something to think about. I would love to have you on my team."

He hands me a business card and invites me to a team practice. Dad points him in the direction of O'Connor's for a post-game drink.

"I'll meet you over there in five," Dad says to Ralph. "Tell Davin, the owner, that you're with me. He'll hook you up with all the local favorites."

Ralph leaves us, and Dad fishes in his briefcase for a folder. "Before you go crawling through windows, mind dropping this off at the station? Oz needs it for traffic court in the morning."

"Yeah, sure." I glance at the folder and then back at my dad. "What does Mom think about junior hockey?"

"Let me work on that," he says suspiciously. "I was making a wild guess earlier about the girlfriend bit. Was I right?"

I roll my shoe over the parking lot gravel. "Yeah, I think so."

"Okay, well, guess I was supposed to just wait for the neighbors to tell me," he jokes, then turns serious again. "How is she doing? After her mom and everything, I've been worried."

"She's fine," I say automatically. Then, when it's clear that Dad isn't taking off right away, I add, "It must be hard for her with her mom away and her dad... Do you know about her dad?"

He scratches the side of his face, nods. "Do you think it might be a bit much for you right now? A girl who's been through all that is bound to have struggles, you know? Might be a lot for a seventeen-year-old to take on."

"Dad, she's got her shit together much better than I do," I say, not hiding the annoyance from my voice.

"Okay, okay." He holds up his hands. "And that's the other side of the argument. She's got some maturity from everything she's dealt with. I'm glad to hear that."

My anger fizzles out. "I'm gonna go drop this off at the station."

"Stay out of trouble," Dad says, teasing.

Even though I was ready to head over to see Brooke, now I'm stuck on something my dad said. She's been through a lot. And then she got here to Juniper Falls and had to watch not one but two classmates fall into a frozen pond and nearly die. If I have nightmares about Elliott's blue face, his body lying by the pond like a murder victim in a thriller movie, does Brooke? Does she have anyone besides me to talk to about it?

O z tosses the folder onto his desk. "Been looking all over for this."

"Hey! Hey, you! Can I borrow your cell phone?"

I lean around Oz's desk to see the man occupying one of two cells. "Sorry, dude, against the rules."

"What are you in for, my friend?" he asks me, obviously too drunk or whatever to notice that I'm not actually behind any bars, unlike him.

The Juniper Falls police station is pretty much what you might expect from a small-town police station. You can see almost everything from the front entrance. Including anyone who's been arrested. That works out great for the town gossip mill.

"Just breaking and entering," I tell him.

Oz shakes his head. "Don't engage."

We move away from the sheriff's cubicle and closer to the help desk, out of earshot of the prisoner. The wall beside the area features a large framed photo of Oz, with a plaque sitting below that reads: SHERIFF OSWALD HAMMOND. Above Oz's photo is a row of smaller pictures...the last ten sheriffs.

"So whenever you're not sheriff anymore, you'll get

demoted to a smaller picture?"

"Don't be an ass." Oz digs through the help desk drawers and then triumphantly holds up a bag of pork rinds. "Heard you broke some records tonight."

"You weren't at the game?"

Oz nods toward the prisoner. "Been busy."

"The Falcons coach talked to me tonight about playing for them." I scan the dates of each sheriff. Jack Rhodes came before Oz. Served nineteen years as sheriff. He and Oz cover the entire span of my life. And then some.

"Yeah, is that something you want to do?" He offers me the pork rinds, but I shake my head. "Thought college was your plan?"

I explain a bit about the gap-year thing the coach explained. Then I move on to the next sheriff photo. Eugene Hammond. My great uncle.

"Hey, Oz," I say, because he's wandered over to the safe across the room. "Do you know anything about Eugene's oldest son? Mathew Paulson, I think?"

"Paulson Mathew," Oz corrects. "And why do you ask?"

"I saw his name in the 1960 census report, thought Eugene only had three kids." Eugene has a bushy mustache, makes it hard to tell if he resembles any other Hammonds. "He must not have been a hockey player because he doesn't have anything up on the Otter wall."

When Oz doesn't say anything, I turn around to make sure he heard me. He's staring at me, deliberating something.

"He played hockey." Oz takes a set of keys from the safe, unlocks a dusty cabinet and then walks back over and drops a thick folder on top of the help desk. "Ask anyone around here, anyone older, what happened to Paulson, and they'll tell you the same thing. He was a great hockey player for the Otters, recruited by Minnesota State, hit by a drunk driver and killed at twenty years old."

"Well, this took a dark turn," I say, but of course I'm already moving away from the wall toward the mysterious folder. This isn't the first time Oz has enticed me with a juicy case file. But this one happens to be a cousin of mine. Even better. "So he died young... That's why Eugene didn't ever talk about him?"

"That's certainly one reason." Oz opens the folder, revealing a police report on top. "This is an ongoing investigation. One I'm personally handling. So we keep this between us, understood?"

"Yeah, okay."

"When Paulson was a senior in high school," Oz says, "he was being recruited. Not like you, but close. A report was filed that September from a classmate. The girl claimed Paulson forced himself on her."

"Dark turn" was an understatement. The hot dog I ate right after the game churns in my stomach.

"Two months later, another report was filed, this one from a sophomore boy, said Paulson shot him in the leg with a BB gun. Several times. Harassed him daily. The reports are here but no record of any charges made, no interview hearing Paulson's side of the story in order to clear him. Just copies of two checks for five thousand dollars each, one made out to the girl and one to the BB-gun kid. The man who wrote the check was the hockey team booster club treasurer at the time." Oz flips through papers and laughs darkly. "The thing that throws me the most is the fact that no one shredded anything. They literally kept all of it. That's how confident they were that future sheriff's would support their methods. I don't have to have been there to hear that conversation... 'The boy's being recruited by colleges; he's the best goalie we've had in decades; this stuff gets out and it'll get in the way of all of that.'"

Cold dread washes over me, running through my veins. I can hear that conversation, too. In fact, it sounds pretty familiar. "I mean, that was a long time ago…" I prompt, hoping to get Oz to agree with me.

"You're right," he says. "If *I* took those reports, you can bet your ass I wouldn't hide them away and pay off the victims."

That's true, he wouldn't. Knowing that, I feel a tiny bit less sick. But if he doesn't know exactly what happened, if it isn't reported to him directly by a victim…

"So was it true about the drunk driver? Is that how he died?"

"*He* was the drunk driver," Oz says. "Ran into a tree out in the middle of nowhere. Eugene knew the sheriff where it happened, kept a tight seal on the accident file."

"Wow, so Paulson was a nightmare." Questions sit at the tip of my tongue, but this is already a hell of a lot more than I wanted to know.

"Not just Paulson." Oz points a finger at the old file cabinet he pulled Paulson's folder from. "I got a whole cabinet full of stuff like this. The sheriff before me, he was even worse than Eugene at covering stuff up for hockey players. You know in the late eighties, a hockey player robbed the hardware store… That was before Artie owned the place. But he showed up with a pellet gun and took the money out of the register."

"Wait…seriously?"

"I got a laugh out of that one, actually," Oz admits. "Dumbass kid put a ski mask on and thought no one would recognize him. In this town? Right."

I glance at the door, rub the back of my neck, and then look at that cabinet again. "What else is in there?"

Chapter Thirty-Eight

–BROOKE–

"So how did your uncle get these files?" I scoop up the puck with my stick and then try to snap it toward the goal. It moves a lousy six inches.

"Cradle, slide," Jake says, demonstrating the movement with his own stick and puck, "and snap."

The puck soars perfectly into the net. I look down at my puck and sigh. Clearly we aren't communicating well.

"It's just sheriff stuff, I guess," Jake says. "Access that comes with the badge. But he's only been sheriff for a couple of years."

I screw up another attempt at this wrist shot Jake is trying to teach me. He drops his stick, skates behind me, places his hands over mine. I crack up laughing. "Really? This is your teaching method? Can you be any more cliché?"

"Maybe if you had done it right…" He shifts my hand so it's lower on the stick, then he cradles the puck at the end of it. "Feet a little wider. You want to be able to shift your weight easily."

It's not easy to concentrate with Jake Hammond literally whispering in my ear.

"Cradle, slide…" he recites. "And snap."

The whole routine is so much smoother in Jake's demonstration. I have a much better sense of the gradual pressure to put on the stick. I try again without him doing most of the work, and this time I remember the slide, and the puck stops right in front of the goal.

"Not bad, Parker," Jake says.

The rink is empty, which is unusual for early on a Saturday morning.

I retrieve the puck to go again, but Jake stops me. "Only one hour until game warm-ups. No more of this."

"Fine, now you can finish telling me what your uncle said last night about Paulson."

We head over to the bench, and Jake pulls one of my skates onto his lap to dry off the blade. "So apparently he was a hockey player…"

He proceeds to tell me all the details Sheriff Hammond shared last night. The muffin I had brought for breakfast sits untouched on my lap while this story unfolds. By the end, I'm too sick to eat any of it.

"How did the sheriff just hear that stuff from those kids he hurt and not do anything?" I ask. It seems impossible.

"That's the thing," Jake says, "his dad was the sheriff when all this went down."

"That's messed up."

Worry creases his forehead. "I know."

"Doesn't it feel so familiar?" I set my muffin aside and scoot closer to Jake. "Like Coach Bakowski writing that list for you to name people who weren't even there."

The look on Jake's face, it's like I punched him in the

stomach. "I would never do anything like what Paulson did. Why would you—"

"I'm not saying that you would," I tell him, setting a hand on top of his. He pulls it away immediately. "I'm talking about the way that you were *told* to handle it. It really is about what's best for the team. That saying takes on completely new meaning here."

I hold my breath for a long moment, waiting for Jake to say something, like he liked me better when I hardly talked. But behind that flare of anger, it's clear he's afraid. Afraid of being the one to hold this information.

He scrubs a hand over his face. "It's not like I can do anything. I mean, if the town sheriff is still holding on to a file that no one cares about, there's no way I'll have any more success telling the real story."

"There is a real story you can tell that your uncle can't," I remind him. "If it comes from Sheriff Hammond or even if it came from me, it doesn't hold the same power as if you—one of the best on the team—tell the truth."

"Okay, but what will that accomplish? I have two more months of being on the team, and then I'm done. Why rock the boat now? It doesn't make sense."

The more I learn about this hockey program, the more it reminds me of a big cavity, the kind that you have to drill into just to know how deep the rot is.

"I haven't forgotten what you looked like after your uncle told you what Elliott said in his statement," I remind him. "It was a massive burden on you. It's not going away."

Jake stands, leans against the half wall, his head down like he's trying not to yell at me. "You know I never meant for him or anyone else to step on that ice, right? That was never the plan."

I nod.

"It kind of feels like you don't know that," he says. "This is my fourth year on this team, and I've never once done anything to hurt anyone, definitely nothing like what happened in these stories Oz told me."

Jake steps one skate onto the ice, and I can tell this conversation is over. "You should suit up. Warm-ups are in ten."

He takes off, snatching his stick from the ice. I watch for a minute or two while he absorbs himself in skating drills, maneuvering the puck, taking shots at the goal.

I leave him to think things over and head to the locker room. But when I come back dressed and ready, he's still in a funk, avoiding me. I turn my attention to the game against Homewood and leave the Jake stuff for later. I start off with an assist to Sam, who scores an easy goal. But then Homewood comes back and scores three goals in the next fifteen minutes.

About thirty people are here in the stands watching this game. The place was likely full to the brim last night when the guys played. I channel some of the tension from this morning into my playing—I'm dying to test out the wrist shot. During the second period, I get the perfect opportunity. Kendra sends the puck straight to the end of my stick, making it easy to cradle it. The goalie leaves a small opening in the bottom corner pocket. I slide the puck just how Jake showed me, but before I can do the snap part, someone slams into me from behind.

My skates come out from underneath me; my body rotates, hips going over my head. I reach out a hand to break the fall, but then I remember not to do that and instead, I duck my head, roll on the hard ice, landing on my back with a *thud* that echoes.

The lights above my head flicker, and then the room goes dark.

Chapter Thirty-Nine

–JAKE–

A Homewood girl skates right at Brooke as she's preparing to take a shot. She slams into her hard from behind, sending her up in the air. She rotates over and lands on her back, her head smacking the ice.

My heart jumps out of my throat, and I'm already swinging a leg over the wall.

"Oh shit," Oz says from behind me.

The ref has stopped the play, but still, I have to shove players out of the way to get to her. She's not moving. Holy fuck, she's not moving. Frantically, I work on getting her helmet off her head. Rosie unbuckles the chinstrap, and I manage to wiggle it off her head.

Oz appears beside me. "Careful, don't move her."

"Brooke!" I will her eyes to open.

And they do. In a freaky way. She looks up at us, utterly confused, and then she shoots upright and is on her feet before anyone can stop her.

"Whoa…hold up," Brian, our team trainer, says. He's just made it out here and is probably going crazy seeing her jump up like that after falling on her back. "Stay right there."

"I'm fine," Brooke says, and then she looks around, seems to take in all the eyes on her. "I'm completely fine."

I wrap an arm around her waist, guide her off the ice and toward the training room.

"Jake, I'm fine," she insists. "I'm the only extra player. I can't just—"

"You blacked out," I tell her. "League rules: You can't go back in until you've been cleared by a doctor."

She climbs onto the training table, and Brian instructs her to lay all the way back. "I blacked out? Seriously?"

"Look straight ahead," Brian says, then he shines a light in each of her eyes.

"I waited way too long to take that shot," Brooke complains. "Am I good to go now?"

"I'm a trainer, not a doctor." Brain feels around the back of her head. "Only a doctor can send you back out there."

"You mean like at a hospital? I'm not really big on Western medicine," she says. "Ow…"

"Quite a bump on your head," Brian tells her. "And I'm sorry, I left my acupuncture needles at home today."

I reach under her head, feel it for myself. "Wow, that's bad."

"Where is your grandma?" Brian asks her while filling a large bag of ice.

"She's in Rochester."

Brooke accepts the ice but leaves it on her lap. I lift her head, place the ice behind it.

"Well…" Brian says. "So either my boring self can take you to the emergency room or this beautiful specimen beside me…which would you like?"

She pulls herself upright, releases a sigh, and then points unenthusiastically at me. "Can I watch the rest of the game first?"

Brian shakes his head. "Sorry, not with that bump."

"Can I at least change first?" she tries.

"Yes, but quickly."

"If you know you haven't had major issues with any of your vital organs, I can say no to like, twenty-five of these questions."

"My organs are good." Brooke keeps her eyes closed and relaxes against the exam table. "It's a bad sign that the light is hurting my head, isn't it?"

"Probably not," I lie.

It's definitely a bad sign.

I answer no to all the organ-related diseases and then skip the "are you pregnant?" and "date of your last period" questions. She can write those down herself. "Last tetanus shot?"

"No idea."

I set the clipboard down. The medical history can wait. I pick up her hand, bring it to my lips. "You gave me a heart attack. Seriously. I'm gonna ask if they can check me out with one of those monitor things because I think mine stopped for a second."

"God." She covers her face with one hand. "This is so embarrassing. Everyone's probably making up stories about my back being broken."

"It kind of seems like it should be broken. You fell right on it," I remind her.

"I'll live." She turns toward me, hanging her legs off the

side of the exam table. "It's a concussion, isn't it?"

I debate lying again but then instead say, "Probably. Brian thinks so, too. But he's not a real doctor."

"When do I get to learn how to knock people over? Seems kind of important, don't you think?"

"You mean checking?" I say, and then scoot my chair closer until we're at eye level. "I'm sorry about what I said earlier. I shouldn't have snapped at you. I just—"

"Oh my God, are you saying this because I'm dying?" she asks. "I really do feel fine; there's no way I'm dying."

I lean forward and kiss her. "Nothing to do with your mishap, I promise. I just think maybe…maybe you're right. Maybe I should tell the truth."

That weird cold dread feeling sweeps over me again.

She rests a hand on my cheek. "It'll be okay. You're gonna get a couple of allies—you won't have to do it alone."

"Allies?"

"A teammate who is feeling like you are at least enough to be convinced after you tell them what you know," she explains.

Tate. He's the only one who might be feeling even a little like I am about the team.

The door to the exam room opens, and a tall blond older woman enters. I scoot away from the exam table when I see her. "Hi, Dr. Westmont."

"Jake," she says, "good to see you, especially in a healthy capacity." She picks up the clipboard, reading it. "Brooklynn Parker, injured hockey player. That's new."

"Should I be worried that you know the emergency room doctor?" Brooke asks me.

"No ER docs here," Dr. Westmont answers. "Small town, they call me when someone comes in under eighteen. Looks like you missed a few questions on the forms…"

Brooke sinks back against the exam table, closes her eyes. "No, there's no chance and fourteen days ago."

"Fantastic," Dr. Westmont says. "Let's get some X-rays, then. And blood work."

Two hours later, Dr. Westmont returns with a scary stack of paperwork and a Popsicle for Brooke. "X-rays look okay: definitely signs of a mild concussion. Blood sugar was low."

Brooke removes a banana from her gym bag and hands me the Popsicle. "How long before I can play again?"

"If no other symptoms come up, then probably a week or two."

"That's not so bad," I point out when we're outside again, heading toward my truck.

"I guess." She glances at her phone and shows me a text from Rosie that says, *We lost. Final score 0-8.*

Ouch. That's worse than our goals against Northwood last night. I take the phone from her and open the passenger door. "You did your best."

"Who are you going to talk to first?" she asks.

"Tate." I walk around to my side, hop in. "Then maybe Fletcher."

Chapter Forty

–JAKE–

"So are we gonna tell him about the list Bakowski made?"

I keep my eyes on the road, avoid looking at Tate. It's the question I've been stuck on since I told Brooke I'd talk to Tate and Fletcher first.

When I don't answer, Tate adds, "It might help get him on board."

But on board with what? That's what we haven't figured out yet. And until I know the exact plan of action...

"We're not telling him unless we absolutely have to." I turn the truck onto a dirt road on the outskirts of town. "I want to see if he's with us even without knowing that."

Tate nods. "Got it."

Both of us are silent for a few minutes, just the sound of the truck tires grinding over rocks on the road. When a farmhouse is finally in sight, I glance at Tate for a split second. "This is crazy, right?"

He laughs darkly. "Oh yeah. Definitely."

Fletch shifts in his chair at the Scotts' dining room table. He hasn't said a word in nearly fifteen minutes.

My palms are sweaty, my stomach a mess. It isn't the anticipation of Fletch's response that's got me all wound tight, it's the finality of telling someone else that I'm going to do something about this hockey shit and promising to be in charge. There's no going back now.

"What exactly do you plan to do?" Fletch asks. "And why would I be of any help?"

Tate tosses me a wary look. It's clear Fletch is on the defense. He doesn't need to back up with his hands in the air for me to know this. Honestly, it probably started when I texted him to ask if Tate and I could come over to talk. We've never really hung out before, and the message sounded cryptic in that context.

"We haven't figured out the exact plan," I tell him. "It depends a lot on who is with us and what everyone is comfortable with."

Fletch scrubs a hand over his face. "Honestly, I'm not comfortable with any of this."

"Right… Okay." I sink back against the chair and try to hide my disappointment. "I get that. It's easier to just keep on playing, not think about all the bad shit."

"Exactly," he agrees. "I'm just finishing the season, then I've got junior hockey lined up. I don't have control over whether or not Bakowski gives me decent playing time, but I've always felt like I had control over everything else. Not like I had a ton riding on this season's outcome. I'm not the star. Kinda hard for him or the program to ruin things for me."

And there is my cue. Fletch just led me right to it. I

glance at Tate, and he seems to understand my silent question because he offers a small nod.

I take a breath and then say, "That isn't completely true."

"Which part?" Fletch's forehead wrinkles in confusion.

"That things couldn't be ruined for you." Looking at Fletch, knowing what I'm about to tell him, that list is more real and concrete than it's ever been before. "There's something you need to know."

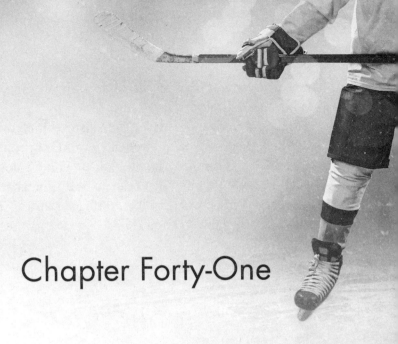

Chapter Forty-One

–BROOKE–

"You did the right thing," I say, and then watch Jake's face for any flicker of regret. I feel responsible—I pushed him to take this leap. I don't want him to have regrets. *To resent me for it*, I think silently.

The floors creak downstairs, below my attic room. Both Jake and I freeze in place, staring at each other. I press a finger to my lips, stand, and then walk carefully across the room. The attic staircase is open to the floor below. I check for any light shining from downstairs. It's almost midnight, so everything is dark, usual for this time.

"False alarm." I return to my spot on the floor across from Jake. "So what did Fletcher say after you told him about the list?"

"Not much. But I could see it in his face—it killed him. He's worked so hard, and to be completely disposable to the person he's trying to impress…" He shakes his head. "But it did the job, that's for sure. His grandpa overheard some of it. He and Fletch's dad aren't going to let Fletch play hockey at JFH anymore. But they did agree to give him time to quit his own way."

"And you've found a few more guys ready to join your revolt?" I ask, already thinking, trying to find the most effective angle.

Jake laughs, breaking the tension. "Revolt? Seriously? You make it sound like we're overthrowing a communist government or something."

Hard to disagree with that comparison. But I decide to keep that comment to myself. "Okay, so the plan…it needs to be something big. You need leverage, and the biggest leverage is probably—"

"The scoreboard," Jake finishes, and I can see the wheels spinning in his head. "We have to do something that threatens the team's season at State or Sections."

"But something that isn't permanent," I add. "Like if it's all lost already, then there's no leverage."

"Sections is double elimination." Jake stands, starts pacing my room. I touch his leg, quieting his feet. The last thing I need is Grandma waking up and finding Jake in my room. "Meaning we can lose one game and still qualify for State."

"Okay…" I say, catching his train of thought. "So you boycott a game, make a big statement—what if you boycott, and then the team still wins?"

Jake nods, agreeing. "It'll only work if we get the right combination of guys joining us. I'm not the only one who can score goals, and it can take just one goal to win a game, assuming the other team doesn't score…"

"Well, good thing the goalie is joining your boycott."

"You're right. Thank God for Tate." A grin spreads across Jake's face. "I think this might actually work."

He sits down again, closer this time, then he leans forward, rests his hands on my face, and kisses me. "What are your feelings about sneaking out?"

I pull back, give him a look. "You know I've done it before. Why?"

"Let's get out of here." He kisses me again and then stands, reaching a hand out to pull me up. "Bring your skates."

I spin the possible bad outcomes around in my head, making Jake wait with his hand still outstretched. In those long seconds, I replay each time I snuck out while Grandma slept. I'd felt like an emotional bomb ready to explode. Those times, I couldn't stand to be in this house for even one more second. It was like that in Austin, too, last year. The tension around my dad's trial and what it was doing to both of them had been hard to witness. But the crowd I hung with late at night was the real mistake. Running had been a healthier outlet for my emotions and stress.

Tonight, though, it's completely different. Sneaking out for fun, for the thrill of it. To spend more time with Jake, who I'm completely falling for. Slowly I lift my hand, place it in Jake's. He tugs me to my feet and, after a bit of preparation, we're climbing out the window together, following a path down that's easier to maneuver than I originally thought. Grandma likely assumed she'd keep me in at night, putting me in a room up this high.

Guess she's never tried climbing out.

Chapter Forty-Two

–JAKE–

"It's safe," I tell Brooke again when she hesitates to put a skate on the pond. I don't blame her for being scared, considering she saw two people fall through the ice. Part of the reason I wanted to do this. I point a finger at the grassy spot nearby where I parked my truck. "I could drive over this ice now and it would hold."

She nods, her face serious. "I know."

"I'll go first." I step onto the ice and hold out a gloved hand to her. She joins me, gripping my fingers tight. "Maybe we should have put a helmet on you, just in case you decide to try another of those front flips to your back."

"Funny." She sticks her tongue out at me and then skates away, easily covering the large square someone had already cleared of snow before we got here. She returns to me, stopping with such sharpness that she sprays snow all over my jeans. "This ice is a bit rough compared to the rink."

"Yep, no Zamboni," I say. "Pond hockey is a completely different game."

She glances out at the water, turning her back to me. "No boards... That is different."

"It's pretty fun, though." I move closer until I'm right behind her, looking out at the pond. The clouds tonight left the sky well lit for this hour, and it isn't difficult to see even without lights. "We'll play sometime."

She moves away and attempts a spin in a circle, looking more like a figure skater than a hockey player. "If someone had told me, a year ago, that I would be living in mounds of snow, playing hockey nearly every day, I never would have believed it."

If someone had told me a year ago, I'd be sneaking through a girl's window in the middle of the night, not necessarily to hook up but just to be with her, I never would have believed it. Haley was right when she said I was married to hockey. But that definitely isn't true anymore.

I watch Brooke twirl herself in circles, her skates tracing a large circle around her, and a wave of fear hits me, hard and fast. My heart picks up speed; a rock tumbles around inside my stomach.

"This is probably easier in figure skates. Maybe I should get some?" Her face goes in and out of focus in front of me, the ends of her hair flying out all around her. "I need a job. Know anyone who's hiring?"

I'm too busy listening to the roar of my heart in my head to answer her.

Finally, she stops, adjusts her knit cap, tugging it over her ears. She looks at me, and her fingers pause on the edges of her hat. "What's wrong?"

"Nothing." I shake my head, attempt to fake calm. "It's

cold out here; we should probably call it a night."

She ducks her head, and hair falls forward, covering her eyes. She digs the toe of her skate into the ice. "Yeah, sure. If that's what you want."

It isn't. Or maybe it is? God, I don't fucking know. I just—

"I don't have any leverage," I say, spitting out the words too loudly and with too much force.

She lifts her head, her eyes wide. "With what? The team? I thought we already decided—"

"No, not that." I scrub a hand over my face. "I mean with you."

Shit. I shouldn't have said that out loud.

"With me?" she repeats. "You don't have any leverage with me? What the hell does that mean?"

"Nothing." I attempt to move toward her, but she skates backward, heading for the edge of the pond. "Just forget it. I don't know what I'm talking about."

"Yeah, sure," she says, this time the words dripping with sarcasm.

The idea of her leaving right now, like this, without any more from me, scares me more than being honest with her. "Don't go...please."

I reach for the sleeve of her jacket, then when she doesn't resist, I close the gap between us and rest my hands on her arms. She looks so pretty, her cheeks pink from the cold, her hair long and spread out over her shoulders.

"I think...maybe..." I tug my gloves off, stuff them in my pockets, then I rest my hand on her cheek, needing to touch some part of her skin with my skin. "I think if you wanted to, you could really mess me up." I squeeze my eyes shut for a second. I really suck at this. "What I mean is..." *Just say it, idiot.* "I love you."

After a long beat of silence, I brave looking at her.

"Wow…" she says, staring at me as if trying to see inside my head. "That went in a completely different direction than I imagined."

Already I feel lighter, the rock inside my stomach rolling to a stop. Those words are easier to deal with outside my head than inside it. Relieved, I pull her against me, rest my chin on top of her head. "I'm sorry. That was really messed up."

She leans into me, lets me hang onto her a little too tightly. Then she steps out of my grip, takes my hand, and leads me off the ice. "Let's go to the tree house."

The tree house. Together. Maybe I haven't managed to ruin everything.

But there's something about the way she's looking at me now, the serious tone she used moments ago that has me nervous again, but for different reasons.

Chapter Forty-Three

–BROOKE–

After Jake closes the door to the tree house, shutting out the icy wind, I glance around. It looks different. There's a small roll-out mattress covering half the floor now, and the dirty blanket Jake's mom had taken from me a while back is cleaner and covering the mattress. A stack of books sits beside the mattress—those definitely weren't there before. I scan the titles…all history biographies.

Jake catches me staring at the books and laughs. There's a hint of nerves in the sound. "Haley told me I was married to hockey. Apparently I am capable of loving other things…"

His voice trails off, and even in the dark space, even knowing we've been in the cold air, I can see heat flare up on his face.

I slide over to a space heater placed beside the mattress. This wasn't here before, either. I remove my gloves before fiddling with the knobs, trying to turn it on. Jake reaches around me, pushes the correct button, igniting a low hum from the machine and the scent of burned dust. Kneeling on the tree-house floor, I feel the warmth hit my thighs almost immediately. I unzip my coat, toss it toward the empty wall with the window.

The tree-house ceiling is too low for either of us to stand, so after ditching my thick jacket, I end up right in front of Jake, both of us kneeling. I rest a hand on his face like he'd done to me by the pond a few minutes ago. Slowly, with my other hand, I pull the zipper of his coat down. It's still very cold in here, probably reaching forty degrees thanks to the space heater, but there are way too many pieces of clothing between us.

Wordlessly, he removes his gloves and coat, pushes them off to the side. He tugs my hat off, tucks my hair behind my ears. "You are so pretty."

Heat rushes to my face. "Even with my hair sticking up all over the place."

"Especially like that," he confirms.

We stare at each other, and I want to say so many things… like telling him that he's pretty, too, even if he might hate that. If I were an artist like my mom, I'd want to sketch, paint, and sculpt Jake all day long. I'd never need a new subject. And if I were brave enough, as brave as him, I'd tell him that I think I might love him back. Maybe. Probably.

But instead, I kiss him, putting all the unsaid words into moving my lips against his. He responds with devoted enthusiasm, his lips taking control of mine, teasing them open until our tongues touch. It's such a shift from emotion to physical—feeling, touching—that I have to remind myself that he loves me. *He loves me*. And all the touching and feelings take on a whole new meaning.

Two sweaters join the coats. Then a T-shirt and tank top. The cold air chills my bare shoulders and back. When I shudder, Jake stretches out on the floor, pulls me on top of him. He's warm…warmer than should be physically possible, given the still very low room temperature. He wraps his arms around me, warming my back with his hands, and I dip my head, kiss any bare skin on his neck that my lips can find. I tangle my fingers in his hair and shift my attention to kissing his mouth. His heart thuds against my chest, picks up speed. Soon he's rolling me over, stretching out beside me. The heater works hard at warming the small space, and when Jake's fingers trail down my stomach, causing me to shudder again, it isn't because of the cold this time.

He unbuttons my jeans, gently tugs the zipper and then slips a hand inside. His fingertips move gently over the top of my underwear. I fumble around, reaching for the snap on his jeans. His breath catches when I finally get his zipper down, but he stops me from touching him. Instead, he works on removing my snow boots, then his boots. I wiggle out of my own jeans, and before long, we're lying beside each other, me in only underwear and a bra, Jake in just a pair of dark-gray boxer briefs that are tight enough to hide nothing.

I've imagined this a dozen times, or maybe more, but never once did the imagined version move from one stage to another so smoothly without a word. It's almost alarming, how easy it is to be like this with him. How much I want more than this.

"Are you cold?" he asks.

I shake my head. "Are you?"

"No." He slips one of my bra straps from my shoulder, lets it fall down my arm.

My heart thuds, anticipation and nerves sending extra adrenaline through my veins. I trail my fingers down his stomach, pause at the waistband of his boxer briefs, and then I move lower, touching over his underwear like he'd done to me. His breath catches again; his eyes close briefly. And for a moment, I can enjoy watching him enjoy this.

"Do you—" he starts, but can't seem to complete the sentence.

"Yes," I say, whispering the word, and then I turn my head, pressing my face against his shoulder. "I mean, if you want to, and if—"

I stop talking when I hear the crinkle of foil. I lift my head, and he's holding a shiny packet in one hand. Must have come from his wallet.

My heart thuds even faster while he puts on the condom. After, he gives me this look, almost panicked, as if to say, *Now what?* And before I can stop myself, I start laughing. I can't help it.

"I'm sorry." I scoot closer, kiss him quickly. "That look you just gave me... It was..."

"It was what?" he asks warily, not sharing my amusement.

"I don't know... But now I'm definitely sure that I love you back. Just for that." I kiss him again, meaning for it to be quick again, but his mouth captures my bottom lip, and then fingers brush the back of my neck, holding our lips together. And there's a shift in the air, in Jake's movements. Something that tells me he needed to hear that before things went further. My panties join his underwear, and then he's on top of me.

I don't know if subconsciously I'd guessed this about Jake or if maybe I just wanted it to be true, but I'm not surprised when he says, "I haven't done this before... Just thought you should know in case it's—"

I touch two fingers to his lips. "It's okay."

He kisses my fingers then my palm and wrist. Then he buries his face against my neck, and moments later I feel pressure between my legs. Instinctively, I tense. Jake's lips brush against my ear and he whispers, "It's okay. Just relax," in such a sexy, soft voice that I have no choice but to relax without question.

I try not to think about the other time I did this. I wasn't ready to understand, to feel all these feelings. For me, the experience had been more triumphant than anything else. More about being in control, proving I could make my decisions. It certainly wasn't about that boy. He's faceless in my memory.

But now, here, it's definitely about this boy.

Jake kisses me, long and slow, giving me time to marvel at the fact that we are literally connected in every single way possible.

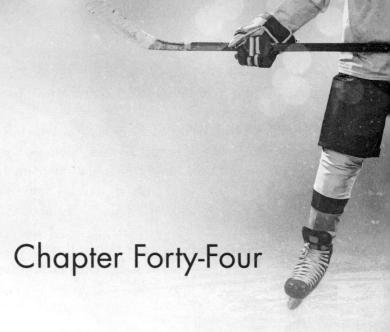

Chapter Forty-Four

–JAKE–

It was Brooke's idea to race back, so I don't feel guilty at all when I catch up to her in a matter of seconds. I hook an arm around her waist, step in front of her, then scoop her off the ground. My head is still back in that tree house, and I kiss her as if we were still there, no clothes between us.

Breathless, she pulls away long enough to say, "At this rate, the sun will be up before I even get home."

It's three thirty in the morning. The sun won't be up for a few more hours. But just to satisfy her, when I kiss her again, this time I walk forward a few steps, in the direction of her house. She laughs at that, tries to wiggle out of my arms. Finally I set her down and take off running.

"Hurry up before the sunrise happens," I call over my shoulder.

She manages to catch me and jumps on my back, trying to slow me down.

I hold her legs behind her knee and continue to walk

forward. "That works, too."

This time Brooke doesn't fight me, instead loops her arms around my neck and rests her chin on my shoulder. And I'm warm again. As warm as I was in the tree house with the heater and her body wrapped around me.

Both of us are quiet, comfortable, the rest of the way to her house, and soon we're climbing through the window again, landing safely on her soft carpet.

I'm about to leave out the window but catch Brooke wiggling out of her jeans. My hand is on the window lever, preparing to open it, but now I can't move. So it isn't just that we've reached a point in our relationship where we've had sex—now changing in front of each other is normal. Only it doesn't feel normal. It feels like a reason to not go out the window.

She plucks a pair of pajama pants from her dresser drawer but pauses when she catches me staring. "What?"

"You're not wearing any pants," I say, pointing at her bare and incredibly sexy legs.

She laughs. "A little while ago, I wasn't wearing under-wear, either."

"Good point. But none of this is helping me leave," I say, and my feet seem to think on their own, crossing the room quickly.

The folded fleece pajama pants fall from her hand to the floor right before our mouths collide. I walk backward, dragging her with me until I'm seated at the edge of the bed. Brooke climbs onto my lap, one leg on either side of me.

She kisses me while unzipping my coat and ruffling my hair. A talented multitasker. I'll have to find a comb before I go home. One look at my hair and my mom will know exactly where I've been all night and what I've been doing.

"I should go," I say between kisses. I slip my hand under

her tank top, move my fingers up and down her back. "Your grandma might wake up."

"Yeah, probably." She sinks her hips lower, pressing more weight against me in all the best ways.

"Maybe just five more minutes…"

"Or ten," she mumbles against my lips.

Insecurity invades all the blissful feelings, and suddenly I'm analyzing this moment, maybe overanalyzing it, and wondering if her enthusiasm right now is because her experience earlier was less complete than mine.

I lean back enough to remove my coat. I toss it over Brooke's head, and it lands on the floor. She pauses to smile at me, and I'm instantly relieved—I couldn't have messed everything up.

"Fifty minutes, right?" I say, kissing her again.

She laughs. "Right."

The sun is beginning to rise by the time I'm landing on the snow behind the Gleason farmhouse and heading toward my truck. I'm too keyed up to go home, and also it's too early, considering I told my parents I was crashing at Tate's.

I glance across the street at O'Connor's Tavern. Tate is there, in the apartment above the bar, with his girlfriend, Claire, who's home from college for a few days. The plan Brooke and I concocted earlier comes back to me. I tug my phone from my pocket and head across the street. Maybe he's awake. I send him a quick text.

ME: r u up? I'm walking ur way

By the time I reach the parking lot of the bar, the door to the apartment above it opens, and Tate clambers down the steps.

"A little early for a hangout, man."

"Yeah." I laugh. "I was in the neighborhood."

He's holding a giant ring of keys. He searches for one and then opens the door to the bar kitchen. "Let's go in. It's fucking cold out here."

"Does Davin know you have the keys to his bar?" I joke, already knowing the answer.

Tate shrugs. "I promised to look at the stove. It's dying a slow death. I've been keeping it alive for a year now."

We enter the warm space, and Tate turns on the lights.

"Plus, I can make my girlfriend breakfast." He flashes me a grin before opening the door to the walk-in fridge.

Maybe I should have offered to get Brooke breakfast. I hadn't even thought of that. We could have gone to Benny's. It would have been a lot less crowded than the last time.

While Tate makes eggs and bacon on the large grill, I relay the plan and discussion from the night before.

Tate looks as nervous about it as I feel, but he nods. "That's what it's gotta be. Nothing else will be enough."

"If we can get the right guys on board."

He hands me a plate of eggs and bacon that look surprisingly edible. I'm starving, so I scarf them down.

"So that's what I was covering for you for?" Tate says, still busy over the grill. "All business, no fun?"

I set my plate down on the counter I'm leaning against. "Actually...."

"So there was some fun." He nods to himself. "That's good."

"We had sex." I scratch the back of my head, wishing it hadn't come out like that. Tate leaves a sizzling egg on the fryer and looks over at me.

I wait for laughter or a *good job, man* to follow, but Tate is quiet for several seconds before saying, "New thing for you guys?"

"Yeah."

"Was it her first time?"

I shake my head. "Not hers but…mine."

"Yeah?" he asks, and I nod. "That's cool."

And just like that, he goes back to the sizzling egg and I go back to my breakfast. A few seconds later, I notice Claire standing in the doorway that leads out to right behind the bar. She's wearing fuzzy pink pajama pants and a giant purple and gray Northwestern sweatshirt.

Tate grins when he sees her. "Just in time."

He slides two eggs onto a plate that already has several slices of bacon and hands it to Claire. Tate exits into the storeroom to fetch tools for the stove, and Claire leans against the counter beside me.

She takes a bite of bacon, her eyes on her plate when she says, "You know, that conversation, for girls, lasts hours."

My neck warms and heat travels up toward my face. "What conversation?"

Claire looks at me, one brow lifted. "The 'I had sex for the first time' conversation."

I know my face must be red based on how hot it feels, but there isn't anything I can do about it. I shovel eggs into my mouth and avoid looking at her.

"Okay, okay, I get it. We're not there yet," she says. "But we could be. My two best friends are Jodi and Haley—sister and ex-girlfriend of Tate. I have to edit so much with them."

"I prefer the edited versions, too," I tell her.

"Fine." She sighs, looking disappointed but only for a few seconds. She goes back to eating her breakfast and shifts topics. "It's pretty amazing what you guys are doing. I'm all for it. So if you need me to make posters or whatever, I make a mean poster."

And even though I know Claire isn't part of the hockey program—she's away at school most of the time—it still feels good to hear one more person is in our corner.

"I'll let you know if your services are needed," I tell her.

"How is Brooke doing?" she asks me after a beat of silence. When I give her a look, she backtracks. "Not about *that*. I mean in general... It can't be easy being new in town, and I know her mom is struggling. I've been there. My dad was caught walking down the middle of the road in his underwear."

Claire's dad survived a rare brain cancer last year but caught an infection after surgery, and somehow the fever led to him being outside in zero-degree weather in his underwear. It makes sense that Claire would worry, and for a second I'm worried, too, but then I remember Brooke, that night her mom was taken away in an ambulance, crying in my tree house. She bounced back so quickly, and she's held it together since.

"Brooke is tough," I tell Claire. "Like you."

Tate returns to the kitchen with a tool belt and grease already on his shirt. He removes large parts of the stove, surprising me not only by how he looks like he knows what he's doing but also by the fact that Claire's family trusts him to take apart their shit. Kind of a big deal.

I haven't met Brooke's dad, haven't formally met her mom. I don't know if they'll like me, let alone trust me the way Tate is obviously trusted by the O'Connors. Months ago, that wouldn't have mattered to me, but now it feels important.

My phone buzzes in my pocket. I glance at it and see a

text from Brooke pop up on the screen.

BROOKE: why is ur truck still here?
ME: I'm across the street w/Tate and Claire. Why r u still up?
BROOKE: couldn't sleep

The eggs sit like a rock in my stomach. I glance at Tate—he's busy with the stove, and Claire is now cleaning up the breakfast mess.

ME: everything ok?

I wait, unable to move, until her reply comes through.

BROOKE: yeah, just thinking about you :)

Relief hits me, and a grin spreads across my face.

ME: me too :)

"Tell her to come over," Claire says, breaking me out of my bubble.

I look up from my phone, and Claire is right beside me, reading over my shoulder. I glare at her. She offers a sweet smile in return. "I'm making French toast. To go with the eggs I already ate. Invite her over."

Instead of arguing with Claire, I send another text.

ME: Are you hungry? Claire's making French toast.

She replies seconds later.

BROOKE: Give me twenty minutes

I glance over at Claire. She's cracking eggs into a bowl.

"Do you need help?" I ask then add, "I should probably help."

Claire laughs. "Yeah, you should. But wash up and put on an apron in case my dad comes in early."

I grab an apron from a hook on the wall, roll up my sleeves, and jump in to help Claire with this post-sex breakfast. Feels like something a good boyfriend would do.

Chapter Forty-Five

–BROOKE–

A tall, gorgeous redhead opens the door to the kitchen. Warm air hits me like a well-placed welcome sign. My hair is wet from the quick shower I took. I thought a hat would help me survive the short walk, but I was wrong.

"Come in; come in," Claire says, tugging me by the jacket. "I'm Claire, and you're Brooke. Nice to meet you."

I laugh and gladly step into the warm air then wait for the door to shut behind me. Tate is sprawled out on the floor taking the stove apart. Jake is wearing an apron and standing in front of the grill. It hasn't been very long since he climbed out my window, but it feels impossible to jump right back into that level of openness and ease we had.

He drops two thick slices of French toast onto a plate and hands it to me. He nods toward an open door to my right. "Take it in the dining room. I'll be right there."

Claire hands me a fork and a bottle of syrup. I wander into the dining room, choose a booth in the corner near

where a keyboard, guitar, and microphone are set up. I'm
starving, so I devour the food and have nearly finished by
the time Jake joins me, holding a glass of orange juice in
one hand and milk in the other.

I take the juice from him and drink half of it in one
long gulp. "I thought this was a hockey bar. What's with the
music equipment?"

"I know, right?" Jake says. "Claire told me they're offering music gigs to people, probably to get more revenue in
the off season."

My stomach is full from breakfast, so I abandon the
plate and wander over to the keyboard. I turn it on, play
a few notes. Jake walks up behind me, plants a kiss on my
cheek. Reaching around me, he places his right hand on
the piano keys.

"You play?" I ask him, surprised.

He laughs, and it tickles my ear and makes goose bumps
form all over my neck. "Only a little. My mom made me take
lessons in elementary school."

Both of his arms envelop me as he reaches around and
plays a bit of a classical piece I recognize from my beginning
piano books.

When he stops, one hand shifts to my waist, and his lips
are right on my ear. "How are you? I mean, how are we…?"

My face warms, but I turn to look at him from over my
shoulder. "I'm good. Really good."

He turns me around, and his face is far more serious
than I feel at the moment. One hand lifts and rests on my
cheek. "No regrets or anything?"

"Just one," I say, dead serious. Worry creases his forehead.
"Not drying my hair before I left the house."

He laughs a short laugh, relieved. "That was evil."

I know. I kiss him quickly on the mouth and then duck

under his arm. I pick up the guitar, toss the strap around my neck. "I'll play you a song to make up for it."

It takes a bit to tune the guitar, but when I finish, I fulfill my promise and start playing a song. It's one that starts out slowly, builds, and has such a great upbeat hook. Claire enters the dining room, and she's already nodding along to the music. She sings a line of the chorus. Her voice is amazing.

"What's the next part? I can't remember," she says.

I repeat the opening line to the second verse. "Hand me your heart…"

She picks up from there, singing the rest while placing salt- and pepper shakers on each table. Jake just looks back and forth between the two of us like we're weird aliens. When I finish playing the final note, Claire grins at me. "I love that song."

I lift the guitar strap from my neck and set it carefully in the stand beside the keyboard.

"Do you make a habit of learning indie country songs?" Claire asks.

The question hits me in the gut. I pretend to fiddle with the guitar knobs. "It's my dad's song."

"Wait…" Claire spins around, ending up three feet in front of me. "Your dad is Jason Maze?"

"No." I smile at that. Jason Maze isn't even thirty years old. "He wrote the song for Jason."

"That is seriously so cool," Claire says.

A loud *clank* in the kitchen stops me from responding. Claire looks alarmed, but Jake jumps up from his seat in the booth.

He jogs across the dining room. "I'll see if he needs help."

"You need help?" I ask Claire, pointing at the dozen or so salt- and pepper shakers on the bar counter. She nods, and I'm happy to have something to do. It makes the conversation feel less intimidating.

"So, you and Jake?" she says after a bit. "It's good?"

"Yeah." I can't help smiling when I say that, and it seems to give away much more than my answer. "He's great. Much different than I thought."

"Much different than I thought, too, if I'm being honest," Claire says. "Without hockey comes new hobbies, apparently."

"Yeah, I guess so," I agree.

Claire looks at me for a long moment, as if leaving an opening for me to add more. When I don't, she says, "I should check on Tate."

Jake returns, passing Claire on the way. He stands in front of me, holding his phone up for me to see. I take it from him and give it a closer look. There's a photo of a large envelope lying on what looks like Jake's family's kitchen table.

"Does that say Boston University?" I ask.

He nods. "My mom just texted, asking if she can open it, but I'm not sure she needs to."

"It's big," I say. "That means you got in, right?"

"I think so," he says slowly. Despite the hint of unease in his voice, I can tell he's thrilled. "I completely forgot to check the online portal thing yesterday when decisions came out."

Guess he was busy planning a war to overthrow a hundred-year-old hockey program.

I push aside my own concerns. Next fall is so far away. "That's a great school, Jake. Will you be able to play hockey?"

"Yeah." He tucks the phone away and holds my face with both hands. "The coach was pretty stoked about me applying; he liked my game highlights video. And my mom is really on board with the Boston plan. She's all about the academics."

He leans down and kisses me. It's so sweet and honest that tears prickle at the corners of my eyes. I force them back and focus on returning this kiss. Jake lifts me onto the table behind me and stands between my legs. Our mouths collide again, and then a minute later we part, both of us breathless.

"I should hate guys who act like me right now," Jake says, laughing. "Eventually we'll get tired of it, right?"

"I'm tired of it already," I lie, and then I hook my arms around his neck, bring his mouth close. "Yep, definitely bored with this."

"Jake!" Tate says, walking in on us. "Good news."

We separate quickly, before Tate looks up from his phone and sees us.

"Fletch says that Clooney is in," Tate tells us. "Collins wants to meet up in an hour or so; are you good with that?"

Jake nods. "Definitely."

"And Steller says we can come over anytime," Tate tells him, and he looks up from his phone. "I think we've got everyone we need."

"If all goes well today," Jake says, playing devil's advocate, but he does look excited. "I can't believe we're doing this."

"Me either," Tate says, shaking his head. "But I sure as hell can't wait to start imagining the look on Bakowski's face when his players don't show up for the first game of Sections."

"Mike first?" Jake says, and Tate nods. "My truck's across the street. I can drive."

He turns to me, probably realizing that he invited me here and is now going to take off. I shake my head. "It's fine. Go get your big players."

Claire appears in the dining room again. She looks at me and nods at the music equipment in the corner. "Another jam session?"

I smile. "Sure."

Jake hesitates before leaving, gives me a second quick kiss. "I'll call you later?"

I wrap my arms around his neck and whisper as quietly as possible in his ear. "I love you."

His cheek heats up against mine, but he squeezes me tighter before letting go. "Kinda feels like the calm before the storm, doesn't it?"

"Maybe, but it'll be okay," I tell him, and as he leaves, I silently wish to whoever or whatever that I'm right. Boston University is waiting for Jake, and maybe some other schools, too. If he comes out of this act of rebellion looking bad somehow, I wouldn't be able to help feeling responsible.

"Know any Broadway tunes?" Claire asks, distracting me. Then she gets a look at my face and adds, "They are definitely doing the right thing. It'll be okay."

I nod, feeling about 10 percent better. *Please let it be okay.*

Chapter Forty-Six

–BROOKE–

"Remind me why we're hiding out during warm-ups?" Cole says, rubbing his hands together nervously. "And why not just ask for the meeting without risking our state qualifications?"

Jake gives Fletcher a pointed look. "I thought you filled him in?"

I brush the snow off the picnic table by Juniper Falls Pond and take a seat a short distance away from the guys. I'm here to support their endeavor, but I don't want to interfere with whatever Jake and Tate told everyone.

"If you want to play, Cole, we're not going to judge you," Tate says.

The have eight guys here, but according to Jake, only four or five really valuable players in terms of compromising their chances of winning this first game of Sections. Must be nice to have so many extras. But Tate is the goalie for the varsity team, and Jake is the leading scorer. Two juniors are really strong defenders, Jake says, and that might mean Centennial High could score more easily.

Tate whispers something to Jake, and then he nods. "Clooney, you should go suit up. Tell a few people where we are... Let's get the ball rolling."

"Yeah?" Cole says, already standing. This is too much for him. "You sure?"

Everyone watches Cole cross the railroad tracks then Main Street, until he's entering the rink.

"Really starting to feel nauseous," a junior defender named Jimmy says.

The guy beside him chimes in. "How do we know Bakowski won't come out here himself and drag us over to the game?"

"He's going to drag all seven of us?" Collins, a sophomore, points out. "Dude, you're way stronger than he is."

Jake glances at his phone. "Don't worry about Bakowski. It's game time; he'll send someone else out here. Plus, I called for backup."

"Who do you think is playing goalie?" Jimmy says.

"Wait...don't you guys have a backup?"

"Yeah, Collins." Tate points a finger at the guy standing beside him.

Even though the tone here is clearly tense and serious, I can't help laughing. "That's pretty brilliant."

"We thought so, too," Jake says.

"They do have Gunner on the bench," Tate says.

This gets all of them laughing. Obviously a joke I don't quite get, but I know Gunner is one of the freshmen who Jake thinks was bribed by Coach Bakowski.

Tate's laughter dies, and his expression turns grim. "Now I kind of feel bad. I know what it's like to go in after someone leaves. I was freaked out."

Jake slides onto the bench beside me, starts to say

something, but then he looks out across the street, and his eyes widen. "Here they come."

I turn around to see the high school principal, the athletic director, and Coach Ty, the JV team coach, all walking quickly this way. The sheriff car pulls up along Main Street, and Sheriff Hammond gets out and makes his way more slowly than the others.

I snap around to face Jake. "I feel like I should go. It's weird if I'm here."

"Yeah, okay." He looks as nervous now as Cole had a few minutes ago. He kisses my cheek quickly. "Thanks."

"Good luck," I whisper right before scurrying off to my grandma's house.

I won't be able to hear anything, but I can at least watch from my bedroom window.

Chapter Forty-Seven

–JAKE–

I know this whole thing was my idea, but now it really feels like it. Like I'm the one who is gonna have to speak in a matter of seconds. Our athletic director, Mr. Toalson, reaches us first. His gaze bounces between me, Tate, Fletcher, the other guys. He's trying to figure out if someone is bleeding or having a breakdown or something.

"What's wrong?" he asks. "The game is about to start."

The principal walked over in his suit and dress shoes, so his feet are now covered in snow. Ty looks more frantic than we do. I feel bad because he's a cool guy, but right now he is part of a system that is definitely not cool.

"Several of us," I say, looking at the guys here, "have decided that we aren't going to play until we can have a repeat of that school board hearing from last November. The one where I told everyone it was my fault Elliott Pratt nearly died right here."

Ty scratches his head, looks at each of us one by one, and

I can tell he knows we're serious. "So I should let Bakowski know we're gonna need another goalie?"

"Definitely," Tate and Collins say together.

"Okay…" Ty shakes his head. "This should go over real well."

He turns around, jogs away from us.

"Boys," the principal says. "Whatever is on your mind, I promise you playing tonight is okay. We'll all get together first thing tomorrow, invite the school board if that's what you want… But right now, we've our first Sections game, and all you boys are important to this team. We've got a full house tonight, all there to see you qualify to State."

I doubt I'm the only one who hears the waver in our principal's voice, the hint of fear. I look at the guys, and silently we all sit down at the table, indicating our feelings about his plan. "We've already decided: We're not playing tonight. But if you can set up this meeting or hearing or whatever before Saturday, there's a chance we'll be at that game and win our bid to State."

The principal turns to Toalson. "You reason with them; I'll make some calls."

He walks off toward the Gleason farmhouse, his phone already at his ear.

"Need I remind you boys," Toalson says, "that each of you signed an athlete responsibility contract at the start of the season. You agreed to be at every practice and game. None you look like you've got a serious illness, and I haven't heard about any deaths in any of your families, which means you're in violation of that contract—"

"We're minors," Fletcher says. "Except me, but everyone else is under eighteen. Those agreements are internal; they don't hold up anywhere."

"There isn't anything you can do to get us to play today,"

Tate tells him. "You're wasting your time. Saturday is a different story. You might be able to do something about that game. Maybe help our fearless principal with those phone calls."

Toalson looks at a loss for words. He glares at us for several seconds, and then he heads over to where the principal is talking on the phone.

"Nice move with the underage contracts," I tell Fletcher. "But what about you? Does that mean you're violating the contract?"

Fletch shrugs. "Don't care. After what you told me Bakowski did, I'm not sure I can play for this team again even *if* things change."

We all sit on that for a long moment. I can't disagree with Fletcher's choice, especially if he does have the option of joining the junior team early.

"I turned eighteen months ago," Tate says.

"Just don't tell Toalson that," Collins says.

Toalson and the principal return about ten minutes later. Toalson still looks so pissed, but he holds it together when he says, "Tomorrow, one o'clock. Town hall courthouse. The school board members would like at least one parent for each minor present." He zooms in on Fletch when he says that part.

After they leave us alone again, we're all fucking cold; we've been out here for an hour. Oz joins us. "I've got pizzas coming to the station and the radio all set if anyone wants to listen to the game."

All seven of us jump up and follow Oz.

"This flu couldn't have come at a worse time for the Otters," the announcer says. "It's catastrophic for the team."

Collins sets down his slice of pizza, and Jimmy looks like he's about to barf.

"Another goal for Centennial... That makes eleven so far at the end of the second period. Clooney managed to get two goals on the score board for the Otters tonight, but it would take a miracle to come back from this deficit."

"Dammit, Clooney," Jimmy says. "That would have been a shutout."

"And something is happening..." the announcer says. "Looks like the coaches are discussing something. I wonder if Coach Bakowski has decided—yes, I've just received official word that the Otter coach has decided to call the game at the end of the second period. According to Coach Bakowski, his team needs time to recuperate from this terrible flu."

"The flu?" Collins says, throwing his pizza crust at the radio. Oz gives him a look, and he jumps up to retrieve it. "Sorry."

I'm about to talk strategy for tomorrow's meeting and hopefully getting some more of the guys to speak up, but the door to the station opens, a bell chiming above it, and my dad walks in. He doesn't speak, just nods at the door, and I quickly follow him back outside. My stomach is in knots.

"What the hell are you doing, Jake?" He's wearing that same look of panic Toalson had on earlier.

I kick a loose piece of parking lot gravel. "I don't know exactly, but I'm doing something. I have to do something."

"No you don't." He inhales a sharp breath. "The Boston U coach is coming to watch you play on Saturday. This is serious, Jake. You open this box and instead of a hero, a team captain, you're gonna be under a microscope, all your

actions twisted into something malicious. I'm a lawyer—I
know exactly how these things happen. Ask your girlfriend,
she'll tell you how this could play out."

"I can't play for that team, Dad," I say. "Not when I know
everything I know now."

"Then don't play," he says. "If that's what you really want,
we'll pull you for the rest of the season, say your injury is
flaring up and you want to take the time off to make sure
you're healthy for college or junior hockey… You've more
than proven yourself in the handful of games you've played
this season."

"Dad—" I start, but he doesn't let me talk.

"If you're fed up with Bakowski," he says, "I'll support
you being done."

"What about the rest of the guys?" I say. "What about
the kids who are years from being on the team?"

"My priority is you," he says simply. "It always has been.
It isn't your fault if the other players don't have someone
looking out for them at home."

I glance back at the guys inside the station. I don't
know if all of them, or any of them for that matter, will
have someone to help them figure out their hockey shit,
and maybe that's reason enough for me. But there's also
Oz's file of unsolved mysteries, one of those being the bad
behavior of my own relative. And then there are kids like
Elliott and Gunner, who would do literally anything to win
Bakowski's approval. Their judgment, their reasoning skills
are being shaped by a system that ignores laws, ignores the
lines between right and wrong.

But the thing that really has me rooted to this position
demanding change is what Bakowski tried to force me to
do to Fletcher Scott. That situation likely represents one of
many. Who knows how many lives were ruined as a result

of this "for the good of the team, to uphold standards and traditions of a more than one-hundred-year-old program" mentality. No matter what kind of deal Dad can swing for me, I can't just move on and forget what I already know. Maybe last year or the year before that, I could have just looked the other way, but things have changed. I've changed.

"Jake…?" Dad prompts.

I look at my dad again and wish he could see what I see, feel what I feel. "This fight isn't only about me. Most of it isn't about me at all. But I am the one who has to speak up, or no one else will."

He gives me this long look, one filled with disappointment and desperation but also resignation. He knows I'm not changing my mind.

When neither of us speaks for a lengthy moment, he finally turns around, walks toward his car, and just leaves. Oz joins me outside as Dad is turning onto the main drag and speeding away.

"He'll come around," Oz says.

I shake my head. "Not sure he will. He's too scared."

"Yeah," Oz agrees with a nod. "Too scared he can't save you this time."

"Maybe he can't." What Dad said is definitely true. I might be ruining more than just my senior year season.

And I still want to do it.

Chapter Forty-Eight

–BROOKE–

I twist my hands in my lap and try to take slow, deep breaths. Beside me, I'm sure Jake is dealing with nerves of his own, and I don't want to make things worse by looking petrified. But if someone had told me back in the middle of October, when I watched Elliott Pratt and Jake fall through the ice, that I would have to stand in front of the school board, athletic director, Mr. Smuttley, and the principal, I may have just left Jake in the pond. I draw in another slow breath, shunning that image from my brain. I wouldn't have left him in any scenario.

Tate turns around in his chair to face Jake and me. "Why do we have to have this meeting in an actual courtroom? Do you think they're trying to intimidate us?"

I had been wondering the same thing. I don't exactly have fond memories of courtrooms.

But Jake shakes his head. "This is where they meet monthly. Same day and time, too."

"We'll hear from Miss Parker first," a woman on the school board says.

"I'm sorry," Jake whispers, giving my hand a squeeze. "I didn't know you would have to go first."

Okay, so I guess I'm not retelling my version of the story; I'm telling the story for the first time. That's just great. I walk with shaking legs to the front of this small-town courtroom. There is a spot for me to sit, facing every single person in this room, including the long table of important adults. Several of the men on the school board narrow their eyes at me as if I'm already a threat to the Otter hockey dynasty. Mr. Smuttley watches me take my seat with a look of concern on his face. He knows my history, knows this is a tough place for me to be. I take another slow, deep breath. This is the right thing to do. I just hadn't realized it would be my story to tell.

"Can you start by explaining to everyone on this committee why you've only just now come forward with new information regarding what happened to Elliott Pratt last October?" one of the men asks, clearly trying to remain impartial.

I scan the room, take in all the faces staring at me. My heart thunders in my ears and my palms are sticky. I will myself to speak, but my jaw tightens, refusing to open.

"Miss Parker?" the man prompts.

My gaze lands on Jake. Worry creases his forehead. He needs me. All these guys made a huge sacrifice, and they're counting on me to do my part. I clear my throat, force out the words I need to say. "I just… I was afraid to say anything. I'm new here; I didn't want to be involved in something—Well, I didn't really know what it was, not for a while."

I know I'm being too vague. The man who asked me the question looks annoyed, even rolls his eyes. But then

Mr. Smuttley whispers something to the man, and soon my guidance counselor is leaning into the microphone.

"Did you see Elliott Pratt or Jake Hammond fall through the ice at Juniper Falls Pond last October?" he asks me.

"Yes," I say, nodding, grateful for the direct, simple question. "I saw Elliott fall through the ice and Jake jump in after him."

"Did you see anything else before that?"

"Yes." I exhale. "I came out of the woods and heard voices, then I saw a large group of teenage boys. There was a truck parked nearby, the headlights shining on several of the boys. About fifteen or so of them were standing in a row wearing nothing but underwear."

"None of them was clothed?"

"No," I say, then realize my mistake. "I mean yes, some of them were clothed, shoes and jackets and everything. The ones with clothes on put handcuffs on the other boys, told them to lay on the ground facedown. And then they stepped on their backs…"

One of the men on the school board uses a handkerchief to wipe sweat from his brow while another man loosens his tie.

"What did you see next?" Smuttley prompts.

He goes through each and every aspect of that night, pushing me to re-create it in painful detail. Then, using a recent game program, he names each player on the hockey team. The ones who chose to be here today, he tells them to stand up one at a time and asks me to say yes, no, or not sure for each one as to who was there that night. With the players not here, the athletic director walks over to me each time, showing their photo in the game program. I try my best to use only my own memory, not any detail Jake has told me. This means that with a couple of freshmen and seniors, I have no choice but to say that I'm not sure. However, when Fletcher Scott is named and stands up, I shake my head. "No, he wasn't there."

"At what point during all this did you make the 9-1-1 call?"

I look across the room at Jake. This is something we haven't talked about before. "When I saw the boys being handcuffed."

There is a hum of chatter following my answer, but then the room goes quiet again.

"One last question," Mr. Smuttley says, looking right at me, no longer reading from the paper in front of him. "In your opinion, based only on what you saw that night, what do you believe was happening?"

The man on the school board seated beside Smuttley tugs the microphone closer to himself. "Don't answer that."

Another male school board member chimes in. "Given that she's just identified several players being there that night, not all of whom are part of the group requesting this committee meeting, it hardly seems fair to let her hypothesize on why those boys were there."

A woman jumps in, taking over a nearby microphone. "Larry, she saw the whole thing. She heard it, too. She'll answer this question."

Everyone goes quiet, and I swallow back a new wave of nerves. "I believe it was some kind of initiation for the high school hockey team between the freshmen and seniors. I heard someone say that it was more than a hundred-year-old ritual."

I'm excused after that question, after I assure Smuttley that I don't have anything else I want to say. Tate takes a turn. He begins by confirming his presence at the pond the night Elliott and Jake were hurt. As a group, they decided it was best to start with that so as not to seem like they only want to be viewed as victims. Then he talks about a practice where Bakowski made him take off his protective goalie pads and told everyone to take shots at him. He was left with some bad bruises. He shows the entire school board a scar on his chest from freshman year when he was forced to lie on the cold ground at the pond wearing nothing but underwear. He moves on to discussing the Otter alumni group, who know about his dad's drinking problem and his illegal recruiting practices but continue to cover them up and to bring him back into town for hockey-related events, showing him off as a role model.

Cole Clooney goes next. He's shaking nearly as bad as I was. Unlike Tate, who had maintained eye contact with the school board members, even staring right at some of the alumni, Cole keeps his head down, his voice so low he's asked to repeat his answer a couple of times. Cole confirms the ritual by the pond, explains his experience as a freshman last year. But then it's clear he's ready to be done talking. After Cole, a few players ask to be added to the list. They speak on behalf of the team, program, and their coach. I can literally feel tension building in Jake beside me and Tate in front of me. Obviously some of the passionate, inspirational stories are either lies or half-truths.

A senior named Lance, someone Tate and Jake hadn't even counted on speaking today, talks about how last year, he bullied a younger player into quitting the team. All of us sit there, watching in horror as the guy completely breaks down. Obviously there was potential for someone to hit an emotional tipping point, but Lance is, like, the biggest, toughest-looking player on the team. And from what he's saying, he did some horrible stuff to a teammate. When he pulls himself together, he admits that he only bullied the player because a group of the alumni guys told him it was his job to "wean out the weak."

After Lance, the school board calls for a break—it's been two hours already—and most of the information being given is heavy and difficult to hear. The room clears out halfway, and Jake leans forward, rests his head in his hands.

"God, Lance…" he mutters. "Where the hell did that come from? How could he—"

"You wouldn't have done that, right? Bullied someone into quitting?" I ask because I know that's what's going through his head right now. He looks up at me, almost mad that I would even ask that. "Don't you think the alumni who told him to do that knew who they could manipulate? And who they couldn't."

"I guess." He sighs. "But still… If I were the school board, after hearing all this shit, I wouldn't let any of us play hockey. I'd put an end to the whole program."

Unless you're both a school board member and devoted Otter hockey alumnus. But still I see his point; it's hard to imagine any responsible adults hearing all this and choosing to let it continue. Then again, that is exactly what's been happening for years and years.

"I knew we were risking losing everything, ruining hockey for the younger guys," Jake says. "But seeing things head in that direction…"

"Just wait and see, okay? That's a worry for Future You." I rub a hand over his back, hoping to offer some comfort.

The room is nearly full again, all of the school board back in their seats. They ask to hear from Mike Steller next. Jake and Tate both straighten up in their seats. Mike is the wild card. He didn't want to do this.

Jake and I are both too busy watching Mike work his way up to the front that neither of us notices someone new enter the back of the room and slide into an empty chair across the aisle.

But after Mike takes the seat up front, where all eyes are on him, I glance to my left and then turn quickly back to Jake. I tug his sleeve, and when he looks at me, I nod across the aisle.

Jake's dad is here.

Chapter Forty-Nine

–JAKE–

My dad is here. Wearing his work suit, holding a yellow pad of paper and a pen. What the hell is he doing? I mean, yeah, I wanted him here but to support me, not to spy for Bakowski or anything else he may be up to.

"…I've been on both the freshman and the senior side of the pond initiation ritual," Mike says. "My experience was pretty much how Brooke Parker explained it, minus anyone falling through the ice. Oh, and Clooney was the freshman underneath my foot last year." He looks right at Cole. "Sorry, man. You know I love you."

That gets a few laughs from the group. Not exactly what we needed from Mike, but I have to trust him. He didn't want to do this, didn't have to. If he's here, I have to hope it's to tell more than a cute story.

"Freshman year was amazing for me," Mike says. "Once I got over the whole pond ritual. Things weren't great at home, but at practice, at the JV games, I could relax, be with my friends. Coach Ty is tough, but he's there for us, you know? Maybe if I could have stayed at JV another year, things would have been different for me."

"What was different about being on the varsity team?" Smuttley asks him.

"It counted for something," Mike says. "Whether we won or lost, it mattered to everyone in town; it mattered to my dad a whole lot. Coach Bakowski picked up on this early on. He saw what would happen to me if things didn't go well at the game, probably saw that I came back the next day and played harder, better. He would tell my dad if I had an off practice, and I don't mean that I slacked off or played like crap, but if I let one goal in during a scrimmage or couldn't stop one of Hammond's five dozen trick shots…"

I straighten up in my chair, stare at Mike, wishing I hadn't tried so hard to score on him.

Mike takes a breath, a hard look in his eyes. "One tiny misstep and Bakowski called my dad or cornered him in the rink lobby. And then a little while later, Dad was beating the shit out of me. Usually in the privacy of our home but not always. Sometimes he'd hit me with my own hockey stick. The failure stick, he'd call it."

I sink back in my chair, feeling like I've been punched in the gut myself. I knew his dad was an angry bastard, obsessed with the hockey scoreboard, but I didn't know there was an entire system built around Mike's playing. This program, it's like a giant hundred-year-old onion, and we're all sitting here peeling back layer after layer.

For a second, when I look over at my dad again, even though I'm pissed as hell at him for not supporting me, I have the urge to hug him, to tell him thanks for not being like Mike's dad. I have it so much better than a lot of these guys. Especially before this season happened.

Mr. Smuttley clears his throat before leaning toward the microphone. He's somber now. A program he loved as a fan and outsider is now tainted in his eyes. "Mike, we all appreciate your honesty. I know this must be very difficult for you to talk about. But just for the sake of clarity, Coach Bakowski wasn't aware of how your father responded to his feedback, correct?"

Mike nods. "That's what I thought for a while. That's what I made myself believe for a long time, actually. But junior year, after we lost to Longmeadow by three goals, my dad was so pissed at me, he didn't even wait until we got home that time. Just started wailing on me right in the parking lot. There I was, crying, my nose fucking bleeding all over the place, and Bakowski walked by; he looked right at me. And then he just left."

A massive lump sits in my throat. I stare down at the floor, take a few deep breaths. I don't know how much more of this I can listen to. Beside me, Brooke is frantically drying her face with her sleeve. I reach over and take her hand, lace our fingers together.

"I'm sure if you ask Bakowski if he knew, he'll deny it," Mike continues. "Probably give a convincing retort like, 'Since when is communicating with the family of my player a crime? This is a family sport…' It's why I never bothered to tell anyone. But he saw me that night in the parking lot, and I bet he saw something way before that night. So yeah, he knew what he was doing. And you know what? I don't think Bakowski sits around planning how to torture us. That's not what I'm saying here; that isn't what any of us are saying. He gets pressure from everyone to win—he wants to coach a winning team. That's what he thinks about—what can I do to get this team to win? But the problem with that is that no one was looking out for me. No one is looking out for these kids, not as hockey players but as human beings. And it doesn't have to be like that... We've got a helluva lot of talent in this town. That first year I played, for the JV team, there's no reason why it couldn't be like that all the way through." He pauses, exhales. "Okay, I think that's all I've got."

He starts to rise in his seat but returns when Smuttley crosses the room, puts a hand over the microphone, and whispers something to Mike. Mike listens and then nods. "Yeah, that's fine. You can use that if it helps."

Mike walks toward the back of the room and then keeps on walking until he's out the door. I fight the urge to go after him. I haven't done my part yet. But later, I have to say something, anything that will help him feel better about digging up those memories.

"Mike just gave me permission to share something I have on file," Smuttley says, addressing the school board. "He referenced an incident with his father after a game, two years ago last November. One of Mike's teachers reported concerns about Mike having a black eye and possibly a broken nose. When I brought Mike into the office, he said he was hit with a puck at practice. I followed up with Coach Bakowski, and he confirmed the story."

Larry Jones, who had been sweating bullets earlier while Brooke spilled one of Otter hockey's oldest secrets, addressing Smuttley. "Do you have any reports or notes taken at the time of the complaint from Mike's teacher?"

"Yes, I have a report stating that the injury occurred during hockey practice. Coach Bakowski signed it, as well as Mike's father."

I glance across the aisle at my dad—I can't help it. I know the lawyer in him will give something away. But he's just sitting there, frozen, the yellow notepad hanging halfway off his lap.

Several of the school board members are carrying on side conversations or asking Smuttley further questions regarding the mentioned reports on file. But the woman who had been so hard on me during my hearing interrupts and calls my name. I brush past Brooke, look at my dad for a second to try and read him, but he's wearing a blank expression.

I knew I would be interrogated today, probably the only one questioned like that, but I hadn't expected the mean lady to jump right to it.

"Jake, I think I can speak for all my colleagues when I say that we're a little confused about your statement back in November," the woman says. "Why did you lie back then and now you're leading this brigade? That part is a bit concerning to me, at the very least."

"Yeah, I get that," I tell her. "I could go on about the pressure to keep the team out of it or to allow a very bad and dangerous tradition to continue for the sake of tradition, but really, I didn't lie to you last November. Not completely." I glance at Brooke, let her unwavering support fuel me, and then I turn my attention back to the woman. "I'm the one who gave the command for those guys to run on the ice; I'm the one who said jump. I had power over them, and I abused it. That part of the story hasn't changed throughout all of this. But believe me when I say this: I didn't want to be there that night. It was the last fuc— The last place I wanted to be."

I search all the seats for Red until I'm looking right at him. He was in this seat just a little while ago, singing Otter hockey's praises. There's a fracture between us that I'm not sure either of us can repair. But I know he knows the truth. He knows I didn't want to be there. He can vouch for that.

But he probably won't.

"I think we can all agree, based on what we've heard today from these boys, that outside forces may have influenced some of their decisions," Smuttley says. "Might be best to move on from this line of questioning. We aren't here to discuss any accusations against Jake. We're here to listen to what these boys have clearly been afraid to say in the past."

I toss Smuttley a grateful look. Then I go on to explain the list that Bakowski made for me. I explain how Fletcher's name was on the list even though he wasn't there that night. I also make sure to add that my dad hadn't known that. Still, he doesn't come out looking great in this.

"So the other names on this list," someone says, "these are players who Coach Bakowski was willing to sacrifice for the greater good of the team, as you put it?"

"Yes, sir," I say, leaning forward toward the microphone. "Because they didn't have a future in hockey beyond high school. His words, not mine. I don't agree with his assessment."

"Can you tell us the other names on that list?" Smuttley asks.

I wring my hands together. "Casey Overstreet, Lance Ellis…" Even though I try not to look at him, I catch Lance's reaction. He looks like he's about to break down again. "And Paul Redman."

I do look at Red when I say his name. He needs to know what he defended today. Red actually leans back like someone just slapped him.

"Since you've been the most vocal, Jake, the one demanding today's meeting," one of the board members says, "can you tell us exactly what you're hoping to accomplish? Are you looking for legal action? Change in coaching staff? More supervision for team players? What is the endgame?"

This guy played hockey with my dad. He's saying all the right things, but there's sarcasm behind the words. It's likely what any player or parent heard when trying to challenge the system. If you're complaining, it's because you're jealous of the talent of others, because you wish you were better. If you don't like it, walk away. Doesn't matter to us; we've got five players ready to take your spot. Those are the words nobody ever says but everyone somehow hears in the air at every practice, every game…and right now in this room that's supposed to be a safe space for us to tell the truth.

And that really pisses me off.

"What am I hoping to accomplish?" I repeat, not hiding the disdain from my voice. "What's my endgame? That's the thing; it shouldn't be up to me. The only reason any of us is here today is because the adults in charge of our hockey program failed us. They don't have our best interests in mind when they make decisions, and I think we've all shown that the consequences aren't small, insignificant problems that you can sweep under the rug. Elliott Pratt nearly died last October. And Mike Steller…" I gesture toward the door where Mike exited. "He needed a safe place to play the sport he loved, but because everyone wanted more wins, his safe place turned into a nightmare. And some of my friends, my very talented teammates, don't have a future in junior hockey or college because Coach Bakowski decided they weren't good enough, didn't send their tapes to college coaches, didn't back them when anyone asked, told their families it wasn't realistic.

"Maybe it sounds like no big deal to some of you, but what if Mr. Smuttley refused to fill out a recommendation form for my college applications but completed forms for other students? We all know that wouldn't fly. Our varsity team deserves to have an impartial third-party person educating them and their families about the recruiting process. We deserve a coach who cares more about the players than the scoreboard. And even though many of us don't want this, we deserve to be held responsible for our mistakes, our failures. If half of what Sheriff Hammond said is true, and same goes for Lance…by failing to discipline players for violating school rules, academic cheating, and crimes in the same way we would non-players, our town is condoning sexual assault, bullying, and lack of adequate education."

I stop, take a breath, let that sink in deep. "So what I want, what all the guys who forfeited the game the other night want, is a plan, from all of you, that says, *you're safe here. We know that you're a team but also individuals, and we're not going to let anyone on our side screw you over.*" I point a finger in Fletcher's direction. "Fletcher Scott worked hard all summer, earned a spot on varsity, never even heard of the pond ritual, definitely wasn't there that night, and as a result of his hard work, he nearly got pinned with criminal charges. He's number one in our class, the best student our school has had in decades. His life was almost ruined. Because Bakowski was more attached to my future than Fletcher's."

Fletch is going to be ticked at me for bringing him so far into that closing argument, but I couldn't help it. For just one second, I want those people to think about a future that isn't all about hockey. I head for my seat beside Brooke without being dismissed. I can't say anything more without yelling or throwing something.

A lady at the very end of the long table—she looks as exhausted as I feel right now—addresses the entire room. "Is there anyone else who would like to speak to this committee before we call it a day?"

A long pause follows. Everyone on the list Tate and I

made has already been up there. Oz turned in his statement via written report because it contained confidential police files on a need-to-know basis. The board is about to call it quits for the day, but my dad stands up, lifts a hand to acknowledge his desire to speak. I suck in a breath and hold it while he walks up to the front of the room. He doesn't take the seat up front like the rest of us had done. Instead, he stands, his presence large and powerful.

"What's he doing?" Brooke whispers to me.

I shake my head. I have no idea, but it can't be good. Not after the conversation he and I had.

"I would just like to say," he announces, his voice projecting perfectly without a microphone, "that I'm sorry to hear all the struggles you boys have had to endure while playing for your school team. I'd like to offer my legal services to any of you who feel that legal action is necessary—"

"What are you doing, Rhett?" the board member who asked my game plan earlier says to Dad. "This is neither the time nor place for you to go fishing for clients."

Oh shit. Even I know this dude went way too far.

"Excuse me," Dad says, glaring at the school board member and then addressing the room again. "To be clear, I was offering my services free of charge. Because these boys deserve to get any help they need. My law practice is doing just fine, Larry; I haven't advertised my services since…" He pretends to think. "Never, actually."

I release a long breath of relief before I even allow myself to process what just happened. Dad heads right over to Red and Lance, and I swear I hear him say something that sounds like an apology.

The exhausted woman who spoke just a minute ago stands again, turning to face all of us. "The committee made up of school board members here today, the guidance counselor, principal, and athletic director will meet to discuss everything we've heard. Per your request, tomorrow at noon we'll gather here again and announce any plans or changes that will be implemented to the hockey program and potentially all athletic programs at the high school. All are welcome to hear those announcements, but I will warn you, we aren't planning an open forum tomorrow. Thank you, everyone, for your time."

I'm nearly to the exit, Brooke a few steps ahead of me, when a pair of hands lands on my shoulders, gripping them tight. My dad leans down, speaks low enough for only me to hear. "I'm proud of you. Took a lot of balls to do that."

I start to respond, but he stops me. I guess he doesn't need any validation.

"Let's go home," he says. "Your mom's making enchiladas."

"Sounds good," I tell him, not knowing what else to say.

He releases me, catches up to Brooke, and slings an arm around her shoulders like they're old pals. "How do you feel about dinner at our house? Mrs. Hammond would love to see you again."

Brooke glances over her shoulder at me, looking for approval. At my small grin she says, "Sure…that sounds great."

"Fantastic," Dad replies. He releases her, heads for the front doors. "Give me a minute to warm up the car, then I'll pull up. Gotta keep the Texan from freezing, right?"

When he's outside, I stand behind Brooke, wrap my arms around her shoulders, halfway leaning on her for support. "I think I'm ready for months of silence…"

"Me too." She grips my arms, pulls them tighter around her. "And you were amazing, Jake. Amazing."

I kiss her cheek. She's probably my toughest critic, so if I've impressed Brooke, this is a very promising sign.

Chapter Fifty

–BROOKE–

I refuse Jake's offer of the front seat and climb into the back of his family's large SUV. Jake buckles his seat belt, and then while his dad is putting the car in reverse, he says, "Thanks…for what you said to everyone."

"What you said was better," Mr. Hammond tells him.

"I meant it." Jake glances at me for a beat and then faces forward again. "But not so much for me, more for the other guys. After hearing all that…I get it now. You've always had my back, made it easy for me to just play."

Mr. Hammond sighs, pulls the car forward, and turns onto Main Street. "But I screwed up. Back in October… I panicked, and then suddenly I was doing something I promised myself I'd never do…selling out to Bakowski." He looks away from the road at Jake. "I'm sorry. It won't happen again."

I hear Jake draw in a breath, and then he nods slowly. "Okay."

Both men seem to relax a bit, and a little while later, we're all sitting around Jake's dining room table, waiting for his mom to finish making dinner. Jake's sister, Maddie, is at a sleepover tonight, so we're able to speak freely about everything that went down today.

"I wanted you to tell the truth at first," Mr. Hammond says. "That day in your room, with Oz and Bakowski, I hated the idea of you going down for the whole team. But then when you refused to name names, I got sucked into Bakowski's compromise plan. He really made it sound like Fletcher had been there that night. Like I said, never again. But I get how it happens, being sucked into Bakowski's world."

Jake's mom joins us, bringing a giant casserole dish and plate of fresh fruit. I don't realize how hungry I am until I smell the food. It was a long afternoon, and I'd been too nervous to eat lunch. Nobody fills her in on the recent events, and yet when Jake's dad brings up Mike Steller, she shakes her head and says, "He was very brave to speak up like that."

Jake and Mr. Hammond don't look surprised about her knowledge. Town gossip works fast, I guess.

"I used to get so excited when Jake would get a goal past Steller during practice," Mr. Hammond says. "But if I had known…"

"Isn't the school a mandated reporter?" I ask. "Shouldn't they have called DCFS or whatever it is in Minnesota?"

Mr. Hammond stares at me, one brow lifted. "Smart girl."

Mrs. Hammond piles my plate with three enchiladas. Cheese oozes out the end. "Just like her mother."

"Top of our class, if I remember correctly. Where did she end up going to school?" Mr. Hammond asks.

I feel myself beaming. I love hearing about my mom, in the same place where I am now. "Vanderbilt."

"What's a mandated reporter?" Jake asks.

I take a sip of the glass of water in front of me. "It means they're required by law to report any signs of abuse or neglect to police or Child Protective Services."

Jake's dad passes me the plate of fruit. "Any interest in law?"

"Besides following it?" I pick up my fork and select a ripe strawberry from the plate.

"Another good answer," Mr. Hammond says. "And you are correct. The school would be required to report suspected abuse, and it sounds like Mr. Smuttley looked into it—"

"But he was told it happened during practice, an accident," Jake finishes.

We eat in silence for a long minute, then I finally have to ask. "What do you think is going to happen?"

"Not sure," Mr. Hammond says. "It was a good idea to do this thing today, let everyone tell their story. But we're dealing with people who don't like change and have a whole lot of pride weighing in on their decisions. The thing is, laws were broken, and none of those committee members are law enforcement or judges of any kind. They can pretend to be all-powerful, but their decision is nowhere near the end of this."

Jake looks worried. "But legal action takes time… The Sections game is on Saturday."

"Jake, honey, we can't let you play for Coach Bakowski after all this is out in the open," his mom says gently. "You know he's heard everything by now. It would be an even more toxic environment."

"Yeah, I know." Jake ducks his head, picks at the food in front of him. "I get it. Just not how I wanted to end my high school hockey career."

"Maybe this doesn't have to be an all-or-nothing thing," I say. "I think you should get everyone together and all of you decide what're the minimum changes you'll accept to play on Saturday."

Jake looks up at me, and I see a glimmer of hope. It's clear now how these things have gone on so long. Guys like Jake, they just want to play so badly that it's easier not to fight the program.

"Whoa, be careful with that fire!"

I yank my roasting stick back away from the bonfire, and Jake quickly blows out the flame. My marshmallow is charred. "Just how I like it."

"Seriously?" Jake looks at the marshmallow, disgusted. "I'm not sure we can be together."

I make a big show of stuffing the blackened marshmallow into my mouth in one bite. I'm about to go in search of the bag to make another, but Jake hooks an arm around my waist and spins me to face him. "You have something right here…" He brushes my top lip with his thumb, then leans in closer, kissing me.

"Hey, Hammond, check this out!" someone shouts from the other side of the fire.

Jake's version of getting the guys together has turned into more of a party than a meeting. About twenty of us are here in Fletcher Scott's backyard. His grandpa and dad run a farm on this land, and he even has his own lake.

Jake leans in, kisses me once more on the mouth, and then we both turn around and watch Cole, skating on the pond. He's determined to learn one of Jake's most famous trick shots. Cole bounces the puck from the crossbar to sidebar then back to the corner before it drops into the goal.

"It's a great shot," Tate says from just a few feet away from us. "Assuming you don't have a goalie."

Jake laughs. "I made that one up years ago just to show off."

"Right, back when you were all flash," Tate says, and even in the dark we can see him roll his eyes. "'Cause you're not like that anymore."

Jake takes my hands, holds them between his. "Are you cold?"

"Why does everyone ask me that?" I laugh. "All of you are out here. You act like being from Texas is a disability or something. Besides, don't you have something to accomplish tonight?" I prompt.

"Oh, right." Jake turns around, facing the frozen lake, and raises his voice. "What's our minimum to play on Saturday?"

"No Bakowski!" Lance shouts.

"I can live with that," Tate agrees. "For now."

"Everyone cool with that?" Jake asks.

A chorus of *yes*, *I guess*, *sure whatever* follows. And Jake turns back to me. "Okay, that's done."

"I feel like the committee is going to try and force Bakowski to apologize," Tate says, moving closer to us. "Or offer us honorary varsity spots or whatever crap he fed Pratt's family. And they'll call it done."

Jake nods. "My dad is expecting something like that. Think everyone will stick to the plan and not play Saturday?"

"Don't know." Tate shakes his head. "But you got me, at the very least."

Jake's phone makes a loud noise, startling the three of us. He pulls it out of his pocket, turns the volume down, but then pauses to read a text from his dad.

DAD: from my buddy at the Minneapolis Times

There's a link to an article posted only minutes ago. The headline reads: *High School Hockey Team Sacrifices Season to Protest Corrupt Program.*

"Holy shit," Tate mutters.

Jake just stands there staring at the headline, shocked.

"That's gotta send a message, right?" I say.

Jake tucks the phone away, not even reading the article, but that glimmer of hope is there again in his eyes. "Guess we'll find out tomorrow."

Chapter Fifty-One

–JAKE–

The courtroom is so full today that people are standing up in the back. If I thought I was nervous yesterday, it's nothing compared to today. I don't know if the guys are really gonna stick with the plan. I know Tate will, probably Fletch. Maybe Lance and Collins, but it's hard to say. Today, at least, both my parents are here sitting on the other side of me.

"*New York Times* picked up the story." Dad tilts his cell phone screen toward me, showing a new article.

"Is that good or bad for us?" I ask, not sure what this media attention means for the change we're asking for.

"Kinda hard to ignore a problem that the whole world is looking at," Dad says.

I really thought this would put a splinter between us. But Oz was right. My dad has always been involved in hockey here in town but not like the other alumni, not because he doesn't have anything else. He just wasn't as willing to turn everything upside down for the truth. Sometimes being passive is just as dangerous as fueling a toxic environment. But it seems like he's moved on from that role; hopefully he'll keep it up,

I try to catch Mike Steller's attention from his spot near the front, but he hasn't turned around even a little. I tried three times to call him last night, but he didn't return the calls. He's got a baby to take care of, so I'm not too worried, but still, yesterday must have been tough for him.

"We're going to get right to this," the school board lady says, standing in front of the group. She's got a wireless microphone in one hand and a sheet of paper in the other. "First order of business… The committee has asked for Coach Bakowski's resignation…"

She says something right after that, but I can't hear or process over the ringing sounds in my ears, the thudding of my heart and the words "Coach Bakowski's resignation."

"…through some generous overnight donations, we've gathered enough funds to bring in an experienced Junior Olympics coach and consultant to help create training plans, rewrite team bylaws, and be a neutral party looking out for the individual athletes." She looks at me when she says that last part. "For those of you who spoke up yesterday, we were all humbled by your bravery and realize your actions have not gone without consequence. However, in light of forthcoming changes, players who wish to continue as a member of the team, please know that any hazing or bullying from this point on will not be tolerated. You will be held responsible for your own actions regardless of outside influences. Make your choices wisely."

She allows a pause, allows all that to sink in for a moment before continuing. "Many of you spoke positively about Coach Ty… We've offered him the head coach position effective immediately. For the freshman and junior varsity teams, we've decided to bring in Mike Steller. The committee feels his talent, experience, and understanding of athlete needs will be of value to the high school program. Are there any questions at this point?"

I look over at Mike, shocked. He grins, gives me a thumbs-up. A year ago, practically the entire town hated Mike Steller. But maybe they just needed to hear his side of the story.

Tate turns around in his seat, holds his fist out to me. "Saturday..."

"We're qualifying to State this season; I'm gonna make sure of that. Win Saturday, win the next game, win Sections. Then State. No second place this year." I bump his fist.

"I'm feeling much better about having my jersey hanging on the Otter wall."

I laugh. "Me too."

Chapter Fifty-Two

–BROOKE–

Sweat trickles down my face. I follow the puck as best I can, but it's hard not to look up at the stands. We've never played in a full arena. And this was supposed to be our courtesy spot, just a shot at Sections simply for having a team this year. But the score is 1-1. And ten minutes are left. We weren't supposed to win. The team is ranked pretty high; they have twenty players on the roster. We're up to ten players now. Sheriff Hammond found a loophole in the rules that allows us to use eighth graders on a high school team and then snagged three girls who were just finishing their club hockey season.

I move from side to side, attempting to escape this Northwood player who's right on top of me. Her teammate has the puck but quickly loses control of it. I lunge forward, swipe it right out from under her. I head toward the goal, looking around for Rosie or Sam to pass to. But someone hits me hard from the side. I smack into the boards but manage to stay upright. I'm chasing after her when the whistle blows, Northwood calls a timeout.

Jake has the door open, and all of us rush to the bench, grab water and Gatorade. I look up in the stands, scanning until I spot my mom and Grandma. I wave, earning a smile from my mom. She's spent most of the game looking utterly confused. Probably not so much by the hockey—she is from Juniper Falls—but more because it's me playing hockey. Hearing about it was one thing, but I imagine seeing it is a whole different thing. Regardless, I'm thrilled to have her home now and seeming more like her old self every day. This morning when I woke up, she was in the sunroom painting. Other than my bedroom walls, I haven't seen my mom do anything artistic since before the end of Dad's trial.

"Are you okay?" Jake sets his hands on my shoulders and looks me over. "Got hit pretty hard."

"I'm okay." I give him a light shove backward. He lacks professionalism when it comes to his assistant coaching duties. But he is really nice to look at.

Sheriff Hammond sets his clipboard down, leans in to talk to all of us. "Who thought we were going to lose today?"

Slowly, everyone lifts a hand in the air.

"Me too," he says. "This team is ranked top ten. They came in overconfident; we're using that to our advantage. Whatever happens, I want all of you to remember how our little team sent them calling a timeout ten minutes before to come up with a strategy to beat us. That's something to brag about."

The game resumes, but I'm on the bench for a few minutes. Jake and I practically hang over the edge, moving along with the girls on the ice. Northwood takes three shots at goal, and we stop them all, but then when it's our turn, both Rosie and Sam miss scoring.

"Look at Northwood's goalie," Jake says to me. "See how she follows the puck? She's way too far forward. The goal is wide open on her left side."

It takes me a minute, but I start to understand what Jake is saying. With four minutes still on the clock, Sheriff Hammond sends me back out on the ice. I put all my attention into keeping the puck on our scoring end, but Northwood keeps getting close to the goal.

With less than two minutes left, what Jake pointed out happens again. The goalie comes too far forward—she's following the puck. From my spot to the left of the goal, while I'm staring at the goalie's back, I make eye contact with Kendra, who has the puck. She doesn't hesitate, just slides it right around the goalie until it's cradled in my stick. I lunge forward, tap the puck right into the abandoned net.

Another player hits me right from behind, a few seconds too late, and I slide across the ice and end up on my back staring at the arena lights. I can't see the crowd, but I hear the roar. A second later, Rosie and Kendra pull me to my feet, and we're all screaming and cheering. But then it stops; we still have a minute left and need to reset. I'm shaking all over, my muscles tense and ready to pounce like I've had too much caffeine. I follow the puck, plow into any player who gets a hold of it, all while reciting, *Don't let them score; don't let them score.*

In what feels like milliseconds, the buzzer sounds.

Game over.

Final score: Juniper Falls, 2. Northwood, 1.

The Northwood girls are in tears. A few toss their sticks or helmets.

The six of us on the ice all skate toward one another. Rosie is the first to take off her helmet. She's wide-eyed, shocked. "Oh my freakin' God. We won."

Everyone on the bench joins us and the host arena brings us a trophy. It isn't huge like the ones earned by the boys' team from many state championships. But it lands in my hands first, and I hold it out to examine it. It's the most beautiful trophy I've ever seen. I pass it off to someone else right before Jake reaches me and lifts me off the ground in a very unprofessional hug.

"You looked so shocked," he says, laughing at my face. "Game-winning goal will do that to you."

He's speaking from experience. He scored the game-winner last Saturday, launching the boys' team into the State tournament.

"I just didn't know it would be like that," I tell him. "That rush when you know you've figured something out that someone else hasn't. Makes me want to win every game."

He sets me down, laughing. "Uh-oh. Turned you into a monster already. Next season should be fun."

I try not to show anything on my face, but I can't help but think…*next season Jake won't be here. I'll be alone at JFH.*

Rosie plows into me, and even though we're the same height, she succeeds in lifting me up. "Dad, this is our MVP. Anyone disagrees, I might have to punch you!"

"Rosie…" Sheriff Hammond warns.

"Or engage in a civil argument."

"Killer assist, Kendra," I tell her, and she beams. "I just looked at you, and you read my mind."

The Northwood coach comes onto the ice, offers her polite congratulations, and then adds, "You girls are the beginning of something—don't forget that. Enjoy it. Every new girls' team in the state adds to the competition, makes us all better. Hopefully we'll see you next year."

Oz shakes her hand, thanks her for the words of encouragement. Then she looks right at Jake. "You're the start of something, too. Be proud of that."

He nods but doesn't say anything. Jake and some of the other guys (though mostly Jake) have made national news several times over the past couple of weeks. I think he's ready to just focus on State now.

"Team celebration at O'Connor's," Oz tells us, and we head for the locker rooms to change.

I walk out of the O'Connor's restroom, still drying my hands with a paper towel, when someone tugs me by the waist into a hidden corner. Jake's mouth is on mine before I can even toss the paper towel. I dive into kissing him and then remember where we are and who's around.

I press a hand to his chest, forcing him back a few inches. "Someone is going to come back here."

He starts to turn away from me, but I pull him back again, bring his face close to mine. "Five more seconds…"

We're there for at least two minutes, my back pressed against the wall and Jake's body pressed against me. But then a large hand reaches around the corner, grabs the back of Jake's shirt, and yanks him away from me. My face flames, but I head out into the open. Just in time to see Sheriff Hammond give Jake a shove toward the well-lit part of the bar where some of the girls are playing darts.

"None of that here," Sheriff says. "Stay where I can see you."

Jake and I engage in a pretty competitive game of darts. Most of the girls abandon the game when the baskets of chicken fingers arrive at our tables, but Jake and I keep going.

"Something else you're good at," Jake mutters, then he

stares at the two darts in one hand. "Maybe I should use these as decision makers. If the green one gets on the board, I'll go to Boston U, and if the red one lands where I want it to, then I'll play for the Falcons for at least next year."

The Falcons are a junior hockey team located about an hour from here. If Jake goes that route, then he'll take a gap year from college.

"Boston U is a really good school," I say, because I'm too afraid to tell him what I really want. I still have two years of high school after this year. It isn't fair for me to weigh in on this decision.

"How about this?" he says, sounding very serious. "Whichever is closest to the bull's-eye, that's what I'll do. Green for Boston U, red for Falcons… What do you think?"

"Jake…" I shake my head. "You can't just—"

"Okay, watch closely. I need a witness." His back is to me. I tug on his shirt, but he doesn't stop. "My future is in… Well, it's in my hands, but you know what I mean."

"Come on—"

"Red is up first." He aims and tosses the red dart. It hits the board firmly but still a little ways from the bull's-eye. He lifts the green dart, glances back at me. "You look nervous."

"I'm just concerned about your sanity at the moment," I say.

"All the great Otter hockey players made big decisions on this very dartboard."

I give him a look. "Seriously?"

He shrugs. "No, but it sounded cool. Oh, guess I can be first. That's cool, too. Ready…?"

"No, definitely not."

This is so stupid, but still I hold my breath while he reels back and tosses the green dart. It misses the board completely, landing on the wall right beside a giant moose head.

He turns to me, sets a hand on my arm. "Guess I'm sticking around here for a while longer."

I look at the red dart on the board then back at Jake. I open my mouth to speak but then close it quickly. His face breaks into a grin. "It's okay. I was just being cool. I already requested a gap year with admissions at Boston U, and yesterday I accepted the junior team spot."

"What?" I shake my head. "Seriously?"

"Yes, seriously." He laughs then holds my face with both hands, plants a kiss on my forehead. "Both my parents think it's a good idea, and so do I. I was hoping you would, too…"

"Yeah, definitely," I whisper.

"Good." He glances sideways, where his uncle has a good view of us. "I would kiss you right now, but I'm not allowed to."

I take a second longer to process this, then I drag Jake by the arm out of the bar, outside in the cold, and around the corner. "What about college?"

"I'll go," he says, sounding sure. "After I play a season of junior hockey."

"Okay…" I don't know what else to say. I'm too happy and in shock. I wrap my arms around his neck, press my mouth to his, and kiss him. He lifts me off the ground, my feet dangling in the air. And it occurs to me how many girls probably shared an amazing kiss right next to the high school, in the dark with the bite of cold air and the smell of fresh snow. It feels warm despite the cold, familiar. Like home.

STAR-CROSSED
by Pintip Dunn

Princess Vela's people are starving. She makes the ultimate sacrifice and accepts a genetic modification that takes sixty years off her life, allowing her to feed her colony via nutrition pills. But now the king is dying, too. When the boy she's had a crush on since childhood volunteers to give his life for her father's, secrets and sabotage begin to threaten the future of the colony itself. Unless Vela is brave enough to save them all...

PAPER GIRL
by Cindy Wilson

I haven't left my house in over a year. The doctors say it's social anxiety. All I know is that when I'm inside, I feel safe. Then my mom hires a tutor. This boy...he makes me want to be brave again. I can almost taste the outside world. But so many things could go wrong, and it would only take one spark for my world made of paper to burst into flames.

VALIANT
by Merrie Destefano

Earth is in shambles. Everyone, even the poorest among us, invested in the *Valiant*'s space mining mission in the hopes we'd be saved. But the second the ship leaves Earth's atmosphere, the alien invasion begins. They pour into cities, possessing humans, forcing us to kill one another. And for whatever reason, my brother is their number one target. Maybe if Justin and I can save my brother, we can save us all…

ILLUSIONS
by Madeline Reynolds

1898, London. Saverio, a magician's apprentice, is tasked with stealing another magician's secret behind his newest illusion. He befriends the man's apprentice, Thomas, with one goal. Get close. Learn the trick. Get out.

Then Sav discovers that Thomas performs *real* magic and is responsible for his master's "illusions." And worse, Sav has unexpectedly fallen for Thomas.

Their forbidden romance sets off a domino effect of dangerous consequences that could destroy their love—and their lives.

entangled teen

an imprint of Entangled Publishing LLC